PRINCESS
THE VOO... ...DILLAC

Fred Willard

PRINCESS NAUGHTY AND THE VOODOO CADILLAC

NO EXIT PRESS

First published in Great Britain in 2000 by
No Exit Press,
18 Coleswood Road, Harpenden, Herts, AL5 1EQ
http://www.noexit.co.uk

Copyright © 2000 Fred Willard

A CIP catalogue record for this book is available from
the British Library.

ISBN 1–901982–87–4

2 4 6 8 10 9 7 5 3 1

Typeset by Palimpsest Book Production Limited,
Polmont, Stirlingshire
Printed by Omnia Books Limited, Glasgow

Acknowledgements

I'D LIKE TO thank the following people for their help.

First, a big thanks to Ion Mills for having the exquisite taste and judgement to buy the book for No Exit Press.

Thanks to my wife, Brianne, and daughter, Rainbow, for being my wife and daughter.

My agent, Frances M. Kuffel of the Jean V. Naggar Literary Agency, provided phone therapy and support above and beyond the call of duty. Thanks Frances.

Eric Haney, Command Sergeant Major, USA ret., was a source of information, insight and great conversation. Tim Hardeman helped me remember Atlanta lore. I'd like to thank them both and add that any factual errors are mine and due to the demands of fiction.

Once again I'd like to thank the members of the Intown Atlanta Writers Group: Diane Thomas, Bill Osher, Anne Lovett, Anne Webster, Skip Connett, Nora Harlow, Devaun Kite, Linda Clopton, Jim Taylor, Gene Wright, and Karla Jennings.

Thanks to Aurora Coffee for the use of the table.

And another secret handshake for the crew at the corner at Los Angeles and North Highland.

Thanks folks.

For William Diehl

Panama

SOMEWHERE IN THE wetlands up country a jaguar stalked a fat capybara. Bill Schiller knew this because it was the rainy season and he was losing his mind.

At two-thirty the air had been thick and claustrophobic so he drank and waited for the rain to build in the thick of the Darien jungle, and he thought about things that would have been better left alone.

By three, dark clouds swept across the jumbled semi-arid hills to Rio Hato. The air cooled, and the rain fell. It pecked at the dry roof of the pole and thatch cabana like a hungry bird.

He lit a joint, and the automatic weapons' fire died for a moment, then started again. Schiller enjoyed watching the rain, hearing it sound the syncopated rhythm of the tropics, but it didn't lessen the loneliness that ached from his heart to his hands. He imagined his tombstone: here is a man who lied himself to loneliness and drank himself to death.

Billy had been the first liar's pay day. He was old enough that they had begun calling him Bill Jr. He was Schiller's only child.

He thought he had him safely tucked away in a fastidiously liberal university where for years everyone had known the Vietnam war was a lost cause.

And so, when he visited Billy on campus and his son asked about the war he had taken it as curiosity about his father's involvement.

He should have said, "Son, I'm a man of conscience who is paid not to have one for his country," or maybe, "I'm an intelligence operative and as a result have to lie when the U.S. makes mistakes."

Instead, he had given the Company line about falling dominoes and democracy and he had spiced it with a few Viet Cong horror stories.

A month later when Billy called to say he had dropped out of college and enlisted and was volunteering for Vietnam, Schiller tried to sound like he was proud of him and he was such an accomplished liar that he could tell Billy believed him.

Jesus, America would have been out of the war in three months, and Billy was barely in country when he was killed.

His wife hung the basic training photograph with the earnest smile on the wall next to his decorations and pretended for a while that being the mother of a hero was some compensation for the death of a child.

Schiller found himself talking in phrases that sounded more like propaganda than comfort.

He didn't blame her when she left him.

He held a lock-blade pocket knife in his fingers like a dart and threw it into the top of the table that held the scotch. It stuck straight up, and the rain stopped. The sun was low and the brown grass sparkled like rhinestones had been sown across it.

A flock of a hundred parakeets attacked a tall palmera near the beach like a threshing machine. They weren't the familiar birds you saw in pet stores in the states. More like small green parrots that screamed and cackled as they ate the fruit hanging in bushel-size clusters.

His mind was stumbling now, like a drunk trying an unfamiliar dance.

He'd been a damn fraud all his life. Even before he met his wife. His trademark rumpled linen suit implied generations of secure and comfortable wealth.

The impression was bullshit, of course. He should burn all those damn suits and put on some blue bib overalls. Honor what he really was – a hungry cracker from Cedartown, Georgia.

The time had come to feed that hunger. Let the big dog eat, as they said back home.

The goal was simple to understand, but its execution would

require all of his skill and more than a little luck. A fortune in cash would attract attention. It would invite betrayal. It would excuse the worst sort of violence. Hell, it could unleash every crazy son of a bitch in Atlanta, Georgia and that included some of the strangest most demented people in the known world.

The most he could hope for was that the trajectory of the operation would be like a ball tossed high in the air. Many might scramble for it, but the advantage would go to the one who knew where and when it would land.

After all, anyone can steal six million dollars, but very few could steal it and get away with it. And at the end of the day, they may be very good at their work, but they were still thieves.

The real gift lay in stealing that much money and being asked to join the country club afterwards. That was the difference between a thief and a player.

The air crackled again with the percussive melody of a fire fight several hundred yards in the distance. It was a comfortable touch. It meant something vital was about to happen.

While Plank and the cadre kept sharp by hosing plywood targets with black-market ordinance bought on the cheap, Schiller sat and drank. The best division of labor he could imagine.

A cooling breeze blew from the Pacific. A half mile up the beach was a home of Manuel Noriega, former Panamanian strong man and current inmate at the Federal Prison in Marion, Illinois.

Now there was an object lesson. Noriega had forgotten the two basic rules of dealing with the American intelligence bureaucracy:

1. Always make sure it costs more careers to shut you down than it does to allow you to remain at large and
2. If you fuck the United States Government, never laugh about it in public.

When you got down to grits and groceries this whole mess

was the government's fault anyway. The only reason it started was that one fine day, the Central Intelligence Agency decided to purge its ranks of anyone who knew what they were doing, resulting in Schiller's forced retirement at age sixty-two.

A saner man would have gladly taken the generous pension and served out his days as a security advisor to people rich enough to worry about being secure.

But Schiller heard another tune being played for the last waltz of his sunset years. It was the rude zip gun and switchblade serenade of gangsterism – a song as American as Jesse James and apple pie.

He thought it would be a lot more fun than saying, "Yes sir" to morons, and it was the only other profession he was actually qualified for.

Anyway . . . losing his job had caught him at a bad time. He was having the sort of identity crisis many people have in their mid-teens. No, he wasn't ready to be an old fart quite yet. He was pissed, and he wanted to kick the world's ass.

He wanted to be the jaguar hanging on Johnny McLendon's throat. He wanted to draw blood. He longed for the chaos, the fear, the smell of burning flesh. He needed to feel that excitement one more time.

Fuck the rocker on the front porch, he wanted to burn down the house.

Frog Boy

IF YOU WANT to get the drift on Johnny McLendon, to see past the bags of money and the nerd glasses, picture this.

One day Johnny McLendon wandered into the Varsity, a chrome and plastic multiplex dog and burger heaven up the street from Georgia Tech on North Avenue.

It's a place with a history and a culture of its own. It even has its own language.

To be cool at the Varsity, you want to use the patois like it's your native tongue, so he practiced in advance.

"Two heavy weights sideways, a bag of rags, and an F.O.," he repeated over and over.

But when the big moment came and the counter man said, "What'll you have?" McLendon became tongue tied.

"Sideways bag, O.O.O., two," he barked like quarterback calling a play.

What a fuck up. Why did he say that? Why did he always fuck up every God awful thing that he did?

"Wait a minute." The order man looked at him like he was crazy. "I don't understand what you want, mister."

"Why don't you order some frog legs?" a man standing behind him in line quipped.

McLendon turned the shade called humiliation crimson because he looked enough like a frog to have suffered taunts all his life and it made him crazy.

After that, he made his chauffeur, Gordon, handle all the contacts with the general public . . . especially ordering at the Varsity.

McLendon and Gordon

GORDON BALANCED THE tray of chili dogs and drinks and shuffled toward the table like his legs were chained together, like he was still in prison.

"Here's your lunch, Boss."

"Thank you, Gordon."

Johnny liked to preserve some formality, although he didn't care to beat it to death. The chauffeur was the only person he felt really comfortable with – perhaps the only person who took him seriously and didn't think he was a joke stuffed into frog-like person skin.

"I've been waiting until we could sit down together to pass along the good news."

Gordon glanced around the room at the few people scattered around the plastic-topped tables.

"What's that boss?"

"We've just had a promotion."

"In the side business?"

"Yes. You ready for an adventure?" McLendon asked.

"I don't know. I had my adventure stepped on real bad doing my last stretch," Gordon said.

"You won't have to worry about that."

"About doing time?"

"No chance of that. We'll be the good guys."

"Good guys, huh? I always wanted to be one of the good guys, but I ended up with the shitty lawyers."

"What's that got to do with it?"

"If I'd walked, I wouldn't have no record, and I'd be a good guy, and then society and all the women wouldn't have turned on me."

"People turn against me too. I hate it," McLendon agreed.

"It sucks. So, you going to tell me about the deal, or I got to beg?"

McLendon loved it when Gordon talked like a hard case criminal. It made his life seem dangerous, like he was living on the edge.

"Most of our secret operations so far have been milk runs. I mean, how hard is it to bribe a foreign dictator? Is there a chance they are going to say, 'Hell no, I don't want the money. It wouldn't be honest.'?

"Same thing for the congressmen we're laying all this cash on. Where's the damn challenge? These guys would fuck your pet goat for five thousand dollars."

"You joking?" Gordon interrupted. "They'd fuck a goat. I'd like to see that."

"It was just a figure of speech. I don't know that all of them would do it, but I can think of a couple that might."

"That would be funny. How would you go about setting something like that up, boss?"

McLendon thought it over for a minute.

"We'd have to get him drunk first . . . and I'd have the money in small bills so it made a bigger pile."

"I'd like to see some fancy ass congressman drunk and fucking a goat. You up for financing it?"

"Sure, once we got this other thing over . . . damn, stop interrupting."

"Okay, boss."

"I got a call from Bill Schiller. He wants us to get involved in an operation – a real one."

"So we would be like spies?"

"Yes."

"I hear that spies get a lot of pussy," Gordon said.

"I don't have any of the details yet, so I don't know about that."

"You need to check on the pussy situation. I'd do it right away, if I was you."

"Can't. We need to drop by the office, then go to the Foundation to set up a secure signals channel. I meet with Schiller later."

"That's a good idea, Boss." He clearly had no idea what McLendon was talking about.

"I get to drop the bomb on that smug jerk, Dunbarton Oakes, and tell him his non-profit spy front is out of business."

"He thinks his farts are perfume," Gordon said. "Hurt him bad. Make him cry and beg, laugh at him and then really fuck him up."

"I've been looking forward to this day," McLendon said.

"Hey, I got an idea. Why not pay him to fuck a goat?"

"I don't think it would cost much."

"Maybe we could have a two-fer, him and a congressman . . . Maybe throw in a couple judges and lawyers and shit like that."

"Like a variety show. I like that," McLendon said.

"And don't forget to ask about that other thing. All right? That's real important."

"How could I forget?"

"There's something I ain't too clear on . . ."

"Yes?" McLendon asked.

"Who is Bill Schiller?"

Ray Justus

PEANUT HAD BEEN hard to find for almost a week so Ray was relieved when he called.

"Where you been, man?" he said.

"I found us a sucker," Peanut said.

"Yeah?"

"I'm at the store. Come and pick me up. We need to talk."

"Give me forty minutes," Ray said.

"Ginger and me are shooting the breeze. Take your time."

Ray took a little extra care to clean up and put on a sharp suit. This was because of Ginger. He knew that, but he figured it didn't make any damn difference as long as he kept it between him and himself. That was as far as it was going to go.

Ginger was Peanut's girlfriend, and she was beautiful. Peanut could be an irritating little pissant at times, but he was Ray's partner, and Ray couldn't field much enthusiasm for watching his back with the people who were supposed to be covering his ass.

He put Ginger out of his mind as he walked to the parking lot. He was good at making his brain work on a practical level. Whenever something troubling or frightening jumped into his mind he would think about the altogether different until his cool returned.

This morning he thought about his ride. It was a Voodoo Cadillac – a four-year-old Eldo he had gotten cheap because it was rumored to carry a curse of death.

Ray liked to tell people that the car was a lot like him. Its bullet holes had been repaired, people were afraid of it, and it was responsible for a number of unnecessary deaths.

The story on the Voodoo Cadillac was its previous owner had been cruising along Ralph McGill, minding his own business when a notorious member of the gangsta-American community placed six rounds from a nine millimeter pistol through the driver's door.

The victim died instantly, and the car veered across the road coming to a gentle stop against a phone pole. Unfortunately, it led a church bus of religious pilgrims from Snellville bound for the Atlanta Passion Play to swerve and roll three times.

The gunman expressed no remorse when caught.

"He shouldn't have messed with my old lady," he said.

This caused a great deal of confusion when it was learned the victim was an openly gay businessman. Later, when the gangsta-wife admitted that at the time of the shooting she had been doing the hokey-pokey in the back seat of Eldorado number two at Lake Lanier, it became evident that the entire slaughter had sprung from a horrible mistake of identity.

Actually, Ray didn't believe that truth in advertising applied to a career criminal like him. He told people he was like the Eldo, but it wasn't true. He was always thoughtful about what he did, had never killed anyone that didn't need it, and his bullet wounds hadn't been repaired nearly as well as he would have liked. Some mornings they hurt.

But, what the hell, if you are going to spend your life being Ray Justus, you better have a sense of humor about it, and if your legend scares some pathetic street punks, so much the better.

The Deal

THIS WAS THE deal. Ray and Peanut would pretend to be dope dealers, and they would find wealthy people like dentists who were under the impression they would make good gangsters.

They would offer to sell them a franchise. "You can be The Man in Lowest Buckhead" – that sort of thing.

Of course, it took a lot of money to be The Man in Lowest Buckhead, and when the poor innocents arrived with piles of cash, Peanut and Ray would take it away from them and give them nothing in return.

Under ordinary circumstances, the underlying unfairness of this transaction would provoke bitter protest, but in this special case the citizens would happily give Ray their money and be grateful to be allowed to return to the comfort of their homes.

This was due to the special talent Peanut and Ray had for terrifying people by imitating men with marginal IQs, permanent facial twitches, and a fondness for senseless violence.

Ray thought this was socially useful work, because it returned promising professionals to the straight and narrow path.

In many ways it was like counseling. True, it cost much more, but unlike counseling, it always worked.

The Store

RAY ROLLED TO his store on Cheshire Bridge. It was three small rooms marked only with a hand-painted sign, "Collectors' Books," in the back of an old brick building that housed a redneck lesbian bar called the Cheshire Beach.

Most of the inventory was pornography that would have been considered lame fifty years ago. The titles included: *Bad Conduct School Girls, Backseat Bongo,* and *The Island of Housewives.*

From the pictures, Ray concluded that Housewife Island was a place where women tested industrial underwear under beach conditions.

And then there was *Sweethearts of the Rodeo.* Ray didn't have a clue about the meaning of this one. Mostly it was black-and-white photos of young Japanese women fully dressed in cowgirl outfits, walking steers around what appeared to be an auction ring.

Ray had placed technical nursing texts next to The Happy Nurses section, old Carrier air conditioning service manuals by a series called Hot Dates, and generally had a fine old time with both the sublime and ridiculous.

He had told Ginger to only say two things to folks who asked about the bizarre collection of titles: "I guess there's no accounting for taste," or, "We get people looking for things like that all the time. We're the only ones who carry it anymore."

Aside from that, she was told to be rude to the customers and, whenever possible, drive them from the store. Screw all of them anyway. If they bought books, he'd just have to buy more. The whole point of the place was to wash some money through the cash register so Ray would have a visible means of support, not to give degenerates something to look at while they polished their Johnson.

He pulled across the gravel parking lot and tooted his horn. He'd decided not to go in because he didn't want to get the Ginger thing started in his head again. She came out anyway.

"I love you," she mouthed and blew him a kiss.

He wished she wouldn't do that. She had no idea what it did to him.

"He'll be out in a minute," she said as Peanut stumbled from the door behind her.

He's wasted, Ray thought.

Peanut Shoke

PEANUT OPENED THE car door and slid in the front seat.

"I like this Voodoo shit." Peanut was fingering a pair of chicken feet hanging from the rear view mirror as he surveyed the collection of impaled fetish dolls on the dashboard.

"It keeps away the car thieves," Ray said. "Are you stoned?"

"Hell yes, but you're the one who's driving."

"You're shaping up to be a responsible citizen," Ray said. "You may get high in the morning, but you got yourself a designated driver."

"I do my best work when I'm stoned," Peanut said.

"Can't see your mistakes is more like it," Ray said.

"Just watch me."

Peanut tried to change the subject.

"Head over to Lenox Square. I'm going to see if we can pick this guy up so you can get a look at him."

"What have you got so far?"

"Not much. I got a call from a buddy back home. He said this guy has been blowing smoke about how he got himself into some operation and is moving the cash around. I figured he was just drunk and talking, till I checked it out."

"That's it?"

"So far, yes. I want you to see it yourself. You're the man with the plan."

One thing that made working with Peanut easy was he knew his limitations. He was good on the street, but he couldn't put the big picture together worth a damn. Ray knew that he honestly looked up to him, and, while it made working with him easier, it made everything else complicated.

Peanut was a good ten years younger than Ray, Ginger was

ten years younger than Peanut, and those numbers didn't add up to good news.

They were driving under I-85 where Cheshire Bridge turns to Lenox, making good time.

"Turn left when we get to Peachtree. I'm going to show you a building south of Lenox Square, then we can pick a good place to watch it from."

Peanut was quiet for a while which was unusual, and Ray wondered what was going through his head or if was he was so messed up he had skipped a track. Finally, he spoke.

"I watched this movie last night," Peanut said. "These people got cat heads and ran around killing people."

"You mean they cut the heads off cats, and killed people with them?" Ray asked, "A cat head doesn't seem like much of a weapon. I'd rather use a gun."

"No, man. These people were like the gods of ancient Egypt. They had human bodies with cat heads."

"I see."

"At the end of the movie, their house was surrounded by a herd of cats who attacked and killed them."

"You sure you feel like working?" Ray asked. "Maybe we should take you down to Fulton Detox."

"I'm good," Peanut said. "The movie just reminded me of the day they took my old man off to the crazy place. Did I ever tell you about that?"

"You told me he went mental. You never told me about the big day."

"We was up at this diner, and they served us some cat head biscuits. You know what they look like?"

"Big as a cat's head . . ."

"Right. My old man looked at them and started screaming, 'Why are the cats looking at me? Why are the cats looking at me?' Then he knocked over the table and started punching everybody out."

"That's sad," Ray said.

"Yeah, my mother and all us kids were crying. The police came and took him to the crazy house."

"Must have been tough."

"Shoot, yes. They took him to the mental place and he just sat in a chair like a rock and didn't say nothing. You know what they call that?"

Ray knew he was being set up. With Peanut, you never knew if he was buck dancing or crying or maybe both at the same time.

"They call it catatonic," Ray said.

"That's right. Only when I was a kid I thought it meant something about not eating the cat head biscuits. As a result, I developed a taste for them which I have to this day. A cat head biscuit every day keeps the psycho doctors away."

"The way you've been acting lately, you should try a mental health program based on scientific principles instead of biscuit eating."

Peanut leaned his head against the door post and closed his eyes. He was more trashed than Ray had realized.

"A point I need to make," Ray said. "You can't get messed up on drugs like this or your mind won't work right even when you're clean."

Peanut opened his eyes.

"No problem, man. I got you covered."

The Shitass Ronnie Gordon

THEY WERE A couple blocks south of Lenox Square.

"Slow down and look on the left. See that brick building."

Ray saw a five-story office building sitting back from the road. It was a modern place built in the fifties – white brick and big glass windows.

"Never noticed that before," Ray said.

"See the black limo out front?"

"Yeah."

It was parked in a drive that curved past the front door – a black stretch Lincoln.

"We want to set up so we can follow him when it leaves," Peanut said.

"I saw some parking places back there. I'll go around the block."

Ray turned right, then right again and began working his way back north for a few blocks. He didn't like to use his car for jobs like this.

He'd lay back. If they lost him, Peanut would know how to find him. Next time they'd use the old Honda or the van at the shop.

"Who are we following?"

"The chauffeur."

"I know that. Who is he?"

"Guy from back home."

"You told me that. I mean what's his name?" Ray said. Peanut was being evasive, and Ray wondered why.

"The Shitass Ronnie Gordon."

"That's his name, the Shitass Ronnie Gordon?"

"Yeah, sure."

"The whole bit?"

"You mean 'the Shitass' part?"

"Yes."

"That's always been what people called him as long as I can remember," Peanut said.

"Why's that?"

"Because he's a shitass."

"I could have guessed that. I mean, was it because of one thing he did?"

"No. Lots of things for a long time."

"I get the picture," Ray said.

Ray was looking for a parking place when he saw a man in a dark suit and driver's cap walk from the building, stand at parade rest by the back door, then make a big to-do over opening the door for an oddly proportioned man with a short body but long legs, wearing a tan summer suit and glasses with thick black frames.

"You can't see him too good from here, but that's him in the uniform," Peanut said. "That guy he's driving looks sort of like a frog."

"I see him."

"Don't lose him."

Ray reached in the back seat, grabbed a straw snap brim hat and handed it to Peanut. Then he pulled into the traffic following the limo.

"Put that on so he won't recognize you."

Peanut adjusted the hat to look cool.

"You got some shades?" Ray asked.

"No, uh uh . . ."

"Look in the glove compartment."

There wasn't much traffic on Peachtree so Ray hung back four or five blocks. They passed the Arts Center, and ahead the limo slowed and signaled a right turn.

"You know where he's going?" Ray asked.

"No, I never seen him stop here before."

"Let's park and walk."

"Let's park close up and walk," Peanut said.

They parked on a side street and walked a block and a half to a mansion converted to office space, a three-story stone castle surrounded by an ornate wrought-iron fence. The limo was parked in a horseshoe-shaped drive.

"We can stand at the MARTA stop so it doesn't look like we're gawking," Ray said.

"How's this?" Peanut asked. Peanut struck a pose and became a different person, maybe a Mormon missionary or a Jehovah's Witness. He sure as hell didn't look like an outlaw. Ray was impressed. When Peanut applied himself he was damned good.

A man with a lightweight tweed coat and steel-gray hair was walking from the front steps of the building to the limousine.

"Check out the guy in the sports coat," Peanut said.

"Looks like money."

"FFA?" he said. "Future Farmers of America? What the fuck? It was never like this back home."

Peanut was looking at a large bronze plaque near the gate.

"Look at the little writing under it," Ray said.

"Foundation for Freedom in the Americas. What's that?"

"I don't know," Ray said. "But it sounds like money."

The chauffeur was climbing out of the car.

"Wait. Look at that there. That's the Shitass Ronnie Gordon." Peanut spoke with an intensity that made Ray wonder if there was something going on he didn't know about. "He looks sort of like a rat, don't he?"

"Too round for a rat," Ray said. "More like a guinea pig."

Johnny McLendon and Dunbarton Oakes

THE CHAUFFEUR OPENED the limo door as Bart Oakes walked down the Foundation's front steps to meet them.

McLendon intentionally took a long time getting out of the car, pushing his black plastic glasses back to the bridge of his nose, ignoring Oakes, letting him feel like a pathetic lap-dog waiting for attention.

"Thank you, Gordon."

Oakes was twisting in the wind.

"Oh, hello Oakes." He pretended to have just seen him for the first time.

"How are you doing, Johnny?" Oakes offered a hail fellow well met handshake.

McLendon knew it was a lot of crap, that Oakes secretly looked down on him for his lack of education and despised him for his wealth. He could see why. Supposedly, Oakes had been red hot in the academic field until he pulled some phony bullshit for the CIA, something to do with a study about Vietnam, and he had been found out and fired.

His wife had run off with a crazy artist, almost a carnie from what McLendon had been able to dig up. Now Oakes was an Ivy League bagman in a threadbare tweed coat.

McLendon had been mysterious on the phone and now Oakes had ants in his pants.

"Okay Johnny, what's so God awful important that you had to drive down here in all this traffic and make me cancel all of my appointments?"

McLendon glanced around dramatically to check if anyone might be listening, then shook his head.

"Let's save it till we get inside."

"Sure, Johnny," Oakes said.

McLendon tried to suppress his smile. He had won round one.

The Foundation for Freedom in the Americas

THE FOUNDATION WAS a legacy of the Reagan era, a CIA front established to channel government and private money to friendly politicos in Latin America. Those had been crazy years, like the wild west. McLendon had got in the rodeo early, rode this pony hard, and it had been very good to him.

The money had allowed him to live like everyone thought he should without having to beg money from his fucked-up family or live under a bridge.

When people say money is the mother's milk of politics, McLendon thought, they were only telling half the story, the other half being that politics is the mother's milk of money, and he wasn't talking milk money.

These days people were calling their Latin friends "death squads," but McLendon knew that was a pant load. They were good capitalists, more like a posse that got together to clean out scum. If a few nuns got in the way, well that's the way it goes. As far as McLendon could see, there wasn't exactly a shortage of Roman Catholics in Central America.

Oakes led him past the security guard, a man he had taken as the typical drunk Irish ex-cop until he learned his name was Frippo and he was a retired army lifer. Then they walked through Oakes's secretary's domain.

She nodded a hello, then went back to typing on a computer. She barely noticed him.

Maggie was in her late thirties or early forties and with her dark hair and fine features bore a striking resemblance to Scarlet O'Hara, or at least to the actress who played Scarlet. Who was it? He remembered now . . . Vivien Leigh.

Maggie's husband was an agency man who'd been blown up

in Lebanon. He heard she had gone to one of the fancy girls' colleges, Sarah Lawrence maybe.

He enjoyed getting a blow job from a woman with a first class education. So much the better if she looked like Scarlet O'Hara. Maybe he'd tell Bart to talk her into putting out for him tonight. She was looking damned good.

In the office, Bart led him over to the prissy corner with the wing chairs and the butler's table where he made such a production over teatime. He thought it probably meant Oakes was a homo and didn't know it yet.

McLendon sat and let the silence linger for effect.

"Well?" Oakes asked finally.

"I got a call from Schiller," McLendon said.

"You got a call from Schiller . . ." Oakes was trying to absorb the implication.

"Yes. He's got an operation going."

"An operation . . ." Oakes repeated, buying time to think. "Why didn't he contact me?"

"That is the big question, isn't it?" McLendon said. "There's no easy way to say this. I'm afraid he's cutting you loose."

He had decided to pretend to be sympathetic while he let Oakes squirm.

"I see."

"You must have seen this coming."

"Yes, of course."

"Nothing for you to worry about," McLendon said. "You've done yeoman service for your country, and you'll be taken care of. I imagine I will be funding the Foundation, although there will be some deep cut-backs. I can't afford the level of luxury you've been enjoying on the government tit."

"Certainly, I understand," Oakes said.

Oakes wasn't a particularly good liar, and Johnny saw his fear. He enjoyed mentioning the cut-backs. Oakes was probably already eating one meal a day of bread and water.

"We will be using the Foundation for a secure communications channel."

"Glad to hear it." Oakes leapt for the particle of hope.

"Until we get something else set up," McLendon added. "I know shifting your loyalty from the Agency to me will take some adjustment, Bart, but you'll rise to the occasion."

He stood to leave, then, almost as a second thought said, "Tell Maggie I want a date. She can come over at nine. Talk her into putting out. Okay, Bart?"

Oakes was stunned.

"Sure Johnny, I'll tell her."

As he walked from the building to the limousine McLendon wondered how he had managed to snatch defeat so easily from the jaws of victory. The meeting was going so well, he had browbeaten Oakes into submission, and then he had blurted out the crazy request for a date with Maggie.

If Oakes actually delivered the message, she would probably throw something at him the next time she saw him. Shitfire, why did he screw up every single thing he did?

Dunbarton Oakes and Maggie Donald

OAKES WAS DUMBSTRUCK. How could Schiller have used Johnny McLendon as the messenger of his demise? He must have known how it would sting.

Standing back from the window so he couldn't be seen, Oakes watched the chauffeur help McLendon into the limousine, sliding awkwardly into the back seat holding a finger to his nose to keep his stupid looking black plastic glasses from falling off.

The combination of arrogance and ignorance could be both funny and frightening.

He had heard it said of people that they were born on third base and thought they hit a triple. In Johnny McLendon's case, it was more like being born a foot from home plate, falling down, and thinking he slid-in for a run.

McLendon's father, J. T., had been just as rough and rapacious as the son, but there was no question he had made his money by being smart and single-minded. Johnny had inherited all of his flaws and none of his strengths. All he knew how to do was use his millions for a club.

Schiller was a piece of work. He had stood beside Oakes and held his hand through most of the traumas of his life, helped him with money when he was short, let him stay with his family as he absorbed the reality that his wife had run away with the so-called performance artist, but still Oakes had to admit he was afraid of him.

It was a colleague of Schiller's who in the Vietnamese War era had whispered in Oakes's ear, appealing to his patriotism, even offering him money to help his government by conducting a phony study of the Vietnam pacification program. He had never figured out how the press discovered the CIA involvement, but Schiller had been there damned fast afterwards, offering to help him out of the mess with a job and votes of confidence from other compromised intellectuals.

After all this time, in the back of his mind, he had a horrible suspicion that Schiller was behind it all, that he had been set up. Schiller was behind the offer, Schiller had leaked to the press, Schiller had destroyed his career, his marriage, his life, just to have a slave dressed in Ivy tweeds.

Jesus, what a mess I've made of my life, Oakes thought. He sat at his desk and tried to see a way out. Screw the citizenship awards, he needed to cover his ass before he ended up sleeping under a bridge.

Desperate times call for desperate measures. Damn, why didn't he just steal some money and disappear? That was an idea . . .

Actually, it wasn't a bad idea. It wasn't a plan yet, but it was the start of one.

"Maggie, could you come in for a minute?" Oakes asked.

Take This Frog and Shove It

THE OFFICE DOOR was open. Maggie stood at the doorway with a look on her face like there was a large rock in her high heel. He suspected she knew what was coming.

He led her over to his tea alcove.

"Have a seat. We need to talk."

"About McLendon?"

"I'm afraid so."

"The way he was looking at me on the way out, I knew it meant something."

"He wanted me to tell you to go to his apartment tonight and, to use his phrase, talk you into putting out."

"Oh shit. I can tell you right now, that's going to take more talking than you can do."

"He may not be the worst of our problems."

"I'm sitting down. If I faint, I won't hit the floor. You might as well tell me."

"We're being cut loose from the Agency. McLendon has said he'll continue to support us at a reduced level."

"That's not good news."

"I suspect that neither of us can afford it," Oakes said. "My financial position is precarious."

"Mine is probably even worse. Is there anything we can do about it?" Maggie asked.

"I think so. Schiller had contacted McLendon about an operation. That can only mean one thing. He needs a lot of money."

"I'm not sure I understand," she said.

"I think we should steal it."

"That's crazy," she answered automatically.

"Think about it a minute. We've both given the best part of our lives to this country. Your husband was a contract employee.

His death benefits barely covered his debts. Don't you think it's time we got something back?"

"I don't know anything about stealing," she said.

He noted with satisfaction that her main objection was practical rather than moral. He imagined the organized corruption inherent in their work had chipped away at her sense of what was allowable, just as it had for him.

"That wouldn't be your part of the job. We need someone close to him," he said. "McLendon is an imbecile. He thinks he has other people's ideas. In his everyday life, he has an army of advisors hired to protect him from himself. They won't be there to help him with this."

She didn't say anything, but he could tell she was thinking it over. Her thoughts were probably a lot like his had been when the idea had first come to him. Disorganized, conflicting emotions had yielded much faster than he expected to one clear understanding: in all his years of loyalty, he had forgotten to be loyal to himself.

"You want to watch or play?" Oakes finally asked.

As Maggie sat quietly, Oakes imagined her turning contrasting fantasies over in her mind, of sharing a bed with the cretin McLendon and of a life of dire poverty.

If it came to that, he would probably go to bed with McLendon before he gave up his easy lifestyle, but there was no telling what Maggie would do.

Finally, she answered in a firm voice, "I want to play."

"McLendon?"

"I could do that."

"With a little work, I think you could pull him around by the nose. I need to know where the money is. I'll take it from there."

"God, this is nuts," she said.

"He wants you at nine."

Oakes watched her as she left his office. He hated to admit it, but tonight he would envy Johnny McLendon.

Madness and Vivien Leigh

MAGGIE WENT NUMB when her husband was killed in Beruit.

She watched the honor guard carry the government casket to the beat of muffled drums, knowing there was nothing in the casket that even grief could make her want to hold.

"I want to see him," she had told the Agency man who brought the news.

"I'm afraid that isn't possible."

"Possible? I'm his wife for God's sake."

"It was a car bomb. I'm afraid there isn't much left . . . just a portion of the trunk."

He hadn't wanted to say that. She could tell.

"The trunk of the car?"

"No . . . your husband's trunk."

So as she had looked at her husband's casket, she had seen through its sides with the x-ray vision of her imagination and seen the broken ribs piercing burnt skin, and she had felt ashamed of herself because she didn't want to hold the pathetic meat of her husband's corpse and rock it in her arms.

"You'll be taken care of," she was assured. Then the Agency had patted her on the head and sent her on her way with the hope that she would honor the memory of her husband by not falling into an abyss of alcohol and inappropriate men.

"You may be approached by the KGB," they warned her. "Be careful."

She understood it was a warning from a man who was confused about who she was. This happened. She looked so much like Vivien Leigh that people of a certain age always confused her with that actress's film roles.

He was saying, "Don't be Myra in *Waterloo Bridge*. Don't let grief lead you to promiscuity."

It seemed a joke to her because, even then, she knew grief would lead her to nothingness.

A life insurance settlement paid for a small town house. Then there was a pathetic pension and the job at the Foundation which didn't pay well, but didn't make any demands, until now.

First the agency had made her a widow, then a secretary and now she was about to become a whore. She wanted to be outraged, but she couldn't summon any emotion, not even boredom.

She lay on her bed and stared at the ceiling, a hard cover copy of *Barchester Towers* open on her chest, and worried about Vivien Leigh and madness. Once, she had looked like a young Vivien Leigh, then she had looked like Vivien Leigh and soon, she suspected, she would look like a middle-aged Vivien Leigh. Vivien Leigh was filling her mind until there was nothing in it but Vivien Leigh.

Scarlet O'Hara used sex as a weapon, so did Emma Lady Hamilton, but neither of them had gotten what they wanted.

Maggie didn't even know what she wanted. Not in the big way: a house by the sea perhaps . . . but she couldn't see what she would do in that house, or even who she would be.

In the small way, she would just be happy to have a mind that was quiet enough to read Trollope and enjoy his thoughtful parsing of the human condition.

She couldn't admit to herself that she knew only too well what it was she wanted from life, both big and small: to feel something again, anything at all.

Maggie Donald and Johnny McLendon

SHE LAY ASLEEP on her stomach, half-covered by the sheets. McLendon pulled a comfortable chair next to the bed, folded the covers back so she was exposed, then sat on the chair, lit a Cuban cigar and contemplated her naked body.

He had been amazed when she had showed up at his condominium. Even more so when with a minimum of conversation she had led him to the bedroom. His meeting with Oakes had gone better than he thought. He must be shit-scared if he talked her into this.

He wondered what the health and hygiene classes had been like in that fancy girls' college because Maggie Donald sure knew something about dishing out the poontang. She had fucked his brains out. It was just what he needed, something to give him a little distance from the deal with Schiller.

He knew his government would never call on him to negotiate a treaty or mediate a crisis or carry a secret message to the President of Russia. He had too many rough edges, and honestly he had never cared much for the diplomatic types. The whole lot of them were tight asses. Schiller was a different matter.

He had gathered enough hints to piece together the legend: college grad at nineteen, running agents in Cuba when he was barely twenty-one, running secret ops in Vietnam, Guatemala, El Salvador, Lebanon, Iran, Iraq, God knows where else. His only child killed in the Vietnam war. His marriage crashed and burned after that. His life became the Agency.

McLendon didn't have any idea how to play him. He took a puff of cigar smoke and let it roll across his tongue and looked at Maggie's beautiful ass. She might be the answer to that problem. She had worked with these people, she knew how their minds work, hell she had been married to one of them.

Since she was doing the wild thing for him maybe he could get some advice from her, maybe some inside information, maybe even use her as a spy. All he had to do was keep her close and keep her happy.

He put the cigar down in an oversized ash tray and placed his knee on the bed. She rolled and stirred slightly as he pushed his weight on the mattress.

"Wake up darlin', it's time to go again."

"What do you want?" she asked with the slur of the half awake.

"You know what I want," Johnny said.

Maggie on the Balcony

THE CYCLE BEGAN with a low rumble and ended with a sharp rat-tat-tat. McLendon was snoring like an industrial machine – the one where you feed the works of Michelangelo, Monet and Matisse in one end, and the other end spits out parts for the interiors of fast food restaurants.

She pulled the covers down, as he had done with her as she had pretended to be asleep, and looked at his nude body sprawled on the bed like the victim of a random shooting. He was one strange-looking person, the squat body and long legs, no neck, big eyes and thin lips made him look like a frog. The facts that he was ugly and stupid and had a jerk for a father were probably at the root of most of his problems.

She slipped on a silk robe, picked up a lighter and one of the Cuban cigars that he had bragged cost fifty dollars each, and walked to the balcony. The apartment was the penthouse of an eighteen-story building nestled among the lights and glass of the midtown Atlanta high-rises. She guessed it was four-thirty in the morning, the total darkness before the first blush of dawn. The city lights were strangely bright for a place so deserted. She walked to the hip-high railing and looked down at the street. Not a soul was on it.

It was pleasantly cool out. She arranged a butterfly chair next to a small table, shrugged off the robe and sat in the chair naked, bit the end off the cigar, lit it, curled up and blew smoke rings past her rounded lips.

Freud had said that sometimes a cigar is just a cigar, but tonight, as she slipped it in her mouth, it seemed a lot like a dick.

Jesus, she was slow on the uptake. At forty-three she had finally figured out what most girls learned at puberty. Men had an amazing powerlessness when encountering a naked woman's body.

They had frowned on this strategy in her undergraduate days at Sarah Lawrence. Women were supposed to make it on their merits. She was determined to succeed that way. She had been smarter, worked harder than the men, and it still didn't make any difference.

Johnny McLendon was an odd one. He seemed to have some sort of fixation on being a dog. The sex hadn't been anything like she expected. She had actually found herself enjoying it, at least enjoying the feeling of power it gave her. It reminded her of the sport fucking she had done in college – fast food to satisfy a hunger but not a meal to linger over.

There was a force wakening inside of her, and it wasn't familiar. She didn't think it was the sex that had woken it as much as the death knell for the Foundation. Being screwed by a man who thought of himself as a dog had been a bizarre experience all right, but the thought that had really finally gotten through her emotional deep freeze was the realization that she could be a player just like McLendon, Oakes and even Schiller.

Perhaps she was changing to the Vivien Leigh of *Caesar and Cleopatra*. It wasn't a Seven Sisters Maggie, or a Mrs. Rick Donald, or even Widow/Secretary Maggie, but some strange, cruel, angry goddess of many arms, each one extended demanding blood sacrifice.

She waited for the second thoughts and recriminations, the argument with herself in which she would talk herself back to the comfort of her bed and the wish for a quiet mind, but the argument never came, and she realized her mind was already quiet with the calm she imagined preceded a battle.

To borrow a phrase from her late husband, she was ready to tear a new asshole in the universe.

She smoked till the first light of day, then walked back into the bedroom. McLendon's pants were crumpled on the floor. She found the belt, pulled it through the loops, folded it in half, and hit him with a vicious swing to the buttocks. If he was going to be a hound, he would learn to love the lash.

Maggie Does Dunbarton

BART PRETENDED TO be surprised as he looked up, but she had seen him watching through the window when she arrived, then scurrying for his desk.

"Let's talk," he said.

He led her over to the prissy chairs by the butler's table, but leaned forward and put his arms around her.

"I know it must have been hard," he said.

"I don't mind making the sacrifice," she said. "I know we all make sacrifices."

"You're being very brave," he said.

She acted as if she brushed her hand against his zipper by accident. She could feel his excitement.

"The hardest part was realizing it was you I should have been with," she said.

"I had no idea you felt that way," Bart said.

Their lips met, and he began fumbling with her blouse.

She could tell that Bart was quite pleased with himself that afternoon. The poor thing seemed to think he had made a major conquest. He had no idea that both Johnny and he were being led around by a protruding part of their anatomy, and it wasn't their noses.

Then the coded message from Schiller arrived and it was time for the games to begin in earnest.

Mistress Maggie To Go

AS MAGGIE DONALD entered McLendon's apartment she held a newspaper rolled around a steel rule and slapped it against her palm.

Thwap!

"Here Johnny," she called. "Where's my bad dog?"

McLendon crawled from the bedroom on his hands and knees wearing red silk boxer shorts with a print of slobbering dog heads on it. She slapped the paper on her palm, and McLendon stopped directly in front of her.

"Spike's a big dog," He said. "Spike's a mean dog."

"Then Spike is going to need to be trained. Stay, Spike," she said. "Then you can have your instructions from Schiller."

"Schiller?"

Thwap!

"Do what you're told."

"Arf," he said.

She pushed him aside and crossed the room to her purse, retrieved a plain white envelope and tossed it to him.

"He wants you in Panama," she said.

He greedily ripped the envelope open and read the single page of typescript.

"Did you see this?"

"No," she lied. Actually, she had retyped the message and added some of the more ridiculous embellishments herself.

"It's crazy."

"You're a spy now, Johnny. It's called trade craft," she said.

"Trade craft? I guess I am a spy now, aren't I?"

"Yes you are," she reassured him. "Now go to Panama and be a spy."

Breakfast and a Goddess in Distress

RAY MET PEANUT for a late breakfast at the Majestic. He had a stack of pancakes, and Peanut ordered two eggs and a breakfast steak. They didn't serve cat head biscuits.

"What's your plan to make us richer today?" Ray asked.

"Going to follow the Shitass Ronnie Gordon some more."

"Yeah? I don't know if I'm as impressed with this as you are. He doesn't really fit the profile."

"I think this could be a big one."

"Maybe so, but we don't have any idea who he's working for," Ray said. "Could be some Colombian or Sicilian gentlemen."

"That's what I'm going to find out."

"Other thing is, we got to know when he's holding the money, or if there is any."

"Yeah, that too."

"We can't exactly hit him, and if he doesn't have anything, go back later when he does."

"I know all that, Ray, but I got a feeling on this one. It's major, and I'll find out that stuff."

"Give it a week," Ray said.

"I'll tell you if I need more," Peanut said.

As he drove back to his apartment, Ray thought about Peanut's evident obsession with the Shitass. It bothered him, and he figured Ginger could probably shed some light on it.

As it turned out, he didn't have to call her. The phone was ringing when Ray opened his front door.

"We got a problem."

It was Ginger speaking.

"Some pervo acting up?"

"No, we got a demonstration outside."

"A demonstration?" Ray couldn't figure out what she meant.

"Against porno. It's a bunch of college students with signs and shit."

Ray was amazed.

"Why us? Did you show them some of our books?" he asked.

"I tried to, but they weren't interested. They said it was degrading to women. At that point I got rude."

"Probably the best plan," Ray said. "I'll be there in a minute. Don't shoot anybody."

"I won't," she promised.

The Story on Ginger

THIS WAS THE story on Ginger as Ray had put it together from Peanut and Ginger herself.

Ginger had come from a little Georgia town, had been sort of dumpy with hair colored like a wharf rat, and had made bad grades at the worst high school in the state. This meant that her lot in life was to marry some beer-drinking shit-kicker and raise children in a trailer house that smelled like baby piss. As plans go, she thought this one SUCKED with capital letters.

She knew that if she didn't get out of town, she'd end up in women's prison or the insane asylum. All she wanted to do was yell "Fuck" in church and start food fights at American Legion pot luck dinners.

With increasing frequency, the sheriff's deputies began showing up at her parents' home every time there was an act of senseless vandalism in the area. This was a bad sign, since by Ginger's reckoning she was responsible for no more than half the incidents she was being blamed for.

Two days after graduation, she took her savings out of the bank and told her parents, "I'm going to Atlanta."

They both cried. Her father was still crying when he took her to the bus station. He hugged her and shoved another five hundred dollars in her shirt pocket.

Ginger almost cried herself, because this was a lot of money for her parents.

"You take care of yourself, baby," her father sobbed.

"I will daddy. I just want something different for myself."

As soon as she got to Atlanta she took a MARTA bus to Little Five Points, bought a black leather motorcycle jacket, a can of pepper gas, dyed her hair platinum blonde in the Zesto bathroom, and moved into an abandoned automobile.

"Forget all the high school heroes," she said. "From now on, I'm the star of my own movie." She lost weight, fucked guitar players, and became a fixture in the music scene. She even put together a band of her own, notorious for having touched off a brawl which ended in the burning of the Northside Drive club where they were performing.

Then she met Peanut and decided that gangsters were more fun than musicians. Shortly after this she was accosted by three shitheads in the alley behind the Euclid Avenue Yacht Club. They demanded sex for all until she pulled a pistol from the back of her jeans and shot one of them in the foot. She had been aiming at his groin, so the next day Peanut took her to a target range.

Since her aim had improved, there wasn't any doubt that if given good reason she not only would, but could, send some poor peckerwood to redneck Valhalla.

The Dykes Kick Some Butt

DUE TO HIS natural caution, Ray parked behind a welding business a few hundred feet from the bookshop and walked behind a thin ribbon of trees planted as a buffer. He came up on the near side of the store so the building hid him from the parking lot. He rapped once on the door.

"It's me."

Ginger opened the door a crack and then let him in.

"Jesus, are the cops here yet?"

"Cops? I don't know. I came around the side. What happened."

"The college kids were outside parading with these signs that said things like, 'You are degrading to women', and there were some dykes getting liquored up in the Cheshire Beach, and they thought the signs were about them. So they got pissed and went outside and beat hell out of the demonstrators."

"Oh man, what a mess," Ray said. "I'm going to go take a look."

He went outside and leaned his head around the corner of the building and was astonished by what he saw: eight police cars, three EMS ambulances, twenty people handcuffed and squatting on the ground, EMTs ministering to a half-dozen wounded, and three television crews.

"There's somebody!" One of the camera crews had seen him.

He dashed back into the store.

"We got a giant cluster fuck moving in our direction," he said.

He walked to the back room and began tearing open a box containing copies of *Sweethearts of the Rodeo* and Bendix appliance repair manuals.

"Make yourself as straight-looking as you can," he yelled.

She brushed her hair back, looked at it in a mirror, then gave up and wrapped it in a scarf.

There was a frenzied knocking at the door.

"Just a minute," Ginger yelled.

"The white lab coat," Ray suggested.

"And the horn-rimmed glasses," Ginger added. Both were artifacts from a costume Peanut had worn to a party and had been folded behind the counter ever since. She slipped them on. Ray couldn't help but laugh.

"Do I look anal retentive enough?" she asked.

"Pinch your face up," he suggested. He put the books in her arms.

"I don't know how you can do it, but try to shift the attention away from us."

"I'll think of something."

He retreated to the back room while she let herself out, then returned to the door to see if he could hear anything.

At first there was mumbling, then loudly, "I'm Ginger Loudermilk. No, I'm not the owner, but I am the manager."

More mumbling . . . then, "I don't have to claim anything. This is not a pornography shop and never has been one. We sell collectors' books."

"What sort of collectors' books?" The questions were getting louder and clearer. Ray thought it probably meant they were recording now.

"They would mainly be in the area of cultural irony," Ginger said. "I'm going to hand some out so you can get a look at them. It's an idea that's hard to explain, but easy to understand when you see some examples."

"The demonstrators claim they were here to protest pornography."

"Are those the same people who were just arrested for public riot?" Ginger asked. "What happened here is that they had a homophobic demonstration, it backfired, and now they're trying to blame it on the little guy next door."

"You're saying this was not a demonstration against pornography?"

"Look, aren't college students supposed to be smart? If you're smart, and you want to demonstrate against pornography, where are you going to do it? In front of a pornography shop or in front of a lesbian bar and a store that sells old washing machine repair books? You figure it out."

"Do you think the cowgirl look is coming back?" Somebody must have gotten a look at *Sweethearts of the Rodeo*.

"I hope so," Ginger said. "As long as both the skirts and the boots are shorter," Ginger said.

"Goddamn right," a drunken, husky female voice yelled.

"This is for . . . press . . . uh . . ."

"Don't push me motherfucker."

"This is . . . help."

"I'm gonna kick your skinny ass."

Ginger came back in the store.

"Holy shit, Ray, they started at it again. The dykes that didn't get arrested in the first go round are beating crap out of the reporters."

"Sounds like a good idea," Ray said.

"How did I do?" she asked.

"You were beautiful."

"The cultural irony thing was something I got out of a magazine." She seemed a little embarrassed.

"Don't sell yourself short. You're smart as a whip."

He was surprised when she blushed.

Princess Naughty

THEY CLOSED DOWN the shop and were almost to Ray's apartment when Ginger began rummaging through her purse.

"I've been digging through the back room, Ray. Look what I found." She held up a worn tome with nothing printed on the cover.

"Listen to this." She began reading. "'Who was the mysterious woman who lived in the hacienda on the hill? Some said she was the widow of a rich American, others a poet destroyed by love. No one knew for sure, but to the men of the pueblo she was known as Princess Naughty.'"

"Oh yeah, I remember that one now. The guy who sold it to me thought it was the stupidest book ever written. I though it might be funny just to put it on the shelf and let somebody discover it. Who knows? They say books change lives."

"You got a deep sense of humor, Ray. You'll wait years to deliver a punch line to someone you don't even know."

"Life's hard. You got to laugh at something," Ray said.

They pulled through the gates of the apartment complex and parked in front of the building.

"It's been a long day. Do you mind if I take a shower?" Ginger asked.

Ray tried not to think about what was going on in the bathroom as he listened to the water crackle against the plastic shower curtain. He fixed a drink and walked to the porch as he fought back the brain flashes of being the water as it slid down her body.

He heard or felt footsteps, he wasn't sure which, so he went inside. Ginger was standing in the middle of the room naked.

"Sorry, I didn't know," he said.

Instead of covering herself with a towel, she walked toward him then put her arms around him.

"I know how loyal you are Ray, but Peanut and I broke up."

She tilted her head back and looked into his eyes. "I can't help how I feel."

"Me either," Ray said.

Ginger and Ray on the Sofa

GINGER AND RAY were propped up on throw pillows at opposite ends of the sofa looking at each other. They were naked, and her legs, crossed at the ankles, rested on his thighs. He held her feet in his hand and rubbed them slowly.

Much of Ginger's experience with sex had not been good. Most of the time it felt as romantic as a dog humping her leg. Usually, the pleasure came after the guy left the room and she masturbated.

Sometimes it was worse than bad because the men had been so removed that she was sure they were fantasizing about someone else while they lay with her – thinking about some woman in a magazine while they used her as a blow-up sex doll.

Of course, lately she had been guilty of the same thing herself: sleeping with Peanut and imagining it was Ray. Peanut had been someplace else, too.

"I've pretended I was making love to you."

"Oh man, that's painful to think about – all those expectations. I hope the real thing didn't disappoint you," he said.

"No. You were better."

Ray chuckled like he didn't believe her.

"Really," she said.

Ray cocked his right eye.

"It was like we were in the same room," she said.

"We were in the same room," he agreed.

"I mean you were right there."

"I usually am wherever I am," he agreed.

She laughed. "I know. That's why I love you."

He didn't say anything.

"How do you feel about this?"

"I guess I'm worried about Peanut," Ray said. "I hate to say it, but he's been acting so pathetic lately, I've been feeling sorry for him."

"I know. Me too."

"What's going on? Is he bummed about the break-up?"

"No. We parted friends. Mostly, he was so hinkey over the other thing that he hardly noticed."

"Other thing?"

"You know, that shitass he's been following."

"The Shitass Ronnie Gordon?"

"That's him. Gordon got busted on some bullshit grand theft auto situation, and he snitched Peanut out for armed robbery. Peanut did better than five years."

"That's very fucked-up."

"You know he was married?" she asked.

"Yes. His wife died."

"She died when he was inside. I think it hurt him a lot more than he admits. Then there's something else, too."

"You mean it gets worse?" Ray asked.

"Peanut would be really pissed if he knew I told you."

"You don't need to, baby. I know how it goes. Peanut was a young and skinny kid when he went in and some guys made him their punk."

"He cried when he told me about it." Ginger said. "I think he's working himself up to kill the Shitass Ronnie Gordon."

You Want to be a Criminal?

THE DOOR BELL woke Ray from a sound sleep. He put his feet on the floor and looked at the clock: 3:00 AM.

Ginger stirred on the bed beside him.

"What is it, Ray?" she asked.

"I don't know. But it's fucked up."

"I bet it's Peanut," she said.

He pulled on his slacks and stuck a .380 in the back of the waistband.

"Jesus, Ray . . . You expecting something that heavy?"

"No. I always do this," he said. "If I was expecting something heavy, I'd use the nine."

"I like that nine."

"That's nine millimeters," he said and threw a shirt at her.

"Just another night at gangster central," she said as she slipped it on.

It was Peanut, and he was cleaned up and wearing a suit.

"What the fuck?" Ray said.

"I had an inspiration. Let's talk."

"Okay, man. But before you come in I got to tell you Ginger is here."

"I figured that. No problem. Ginger and me came to an understanding that we don't understand each other."

Peanut was putting on a good imitation of no problem, but Ray didn't believe it. He'd have to be careful not to rub it in and hope that time healed.

He heard the shower start in the back of the apartment. He opened the door and Peanut walked over to one of the chairs by the fireplace and sat down.

"Here's my idea, Ray. Let's go toss that building near Lenox

Square where we saw the Shitass and see if we come up with anything."

Ray thought it over. If Ginger was right, he needed to help Peanut get off his obsession with the Shitass Ronnie Gordon. Maybe if they ripped him off and roughed him up, it would be enough to keep Peanut happy. If not, it could roll back on all of them. They could all look like co-conspirators in a master plan to kill pinhead ex-cons.

"Are you fucked up?" Ray asked.

"No."

"Sounds like a good idea, then. Let's toss it and see if we come up with an angle on the Shitass. Give me a couple minutes."

Ginger was sitting on the edge of the bed looking gorgeous in Ray's robe.

"You might want to put your clothes on, baby," Ray said. "We're going to break into an office. You can come along if you want."

She grinned. "You're going to let me do a B&E with you?"

"Sure thing. I been thinking for a long time that your talents are wasted on the store."

The robe fell open as she stood, put her hands on his shoulders, stood on tiptoes, and kissed his lips. She whispered in his ear.

"Thank you. I really wanted this. I'm going to give you the best blow job you ever had in your life."

"You already have," he said.

"Then you know what you've got to look forward to."

"I'm thinking about it already. Only thing is, you get involved in this part of the business, you got to promise not to get killed."

"Anyone gets killed, it isn't going to be me."

There was fire in her eyes, and he believed her.

Ray took a quick shower and slipped on a suit. Ginger and Peanut were talking comfortably but sitting in chairs across the room from each other, establishing a comfortable distance.

"Everybody here want to be a criminal?" Ray asked.

"Yes." They both laughed.

"In that case, we got to break the law," he said.

"I thought we'd never get around to that," Ginger said.

"Since we got a lady with us I think we ought to ride deluxe," Ray said.

"Hot damn, the Voodoo Cadillac. You got the Jerry Lee CD in the car?"

"Yep."

"I just ate a couple cat head biscuits, and I'm feeling sane as Al Gore. It doesn't get any better than this. Let's roll."

Breaking and Entering

GINGER WAS OPENING the car door as Peanut walked around to the passenger's side with the attaché he had retrieved from his car. She realized that he was probably expecting to ride shotgun.

"Mind if I ride up front with Ray?" she asked.

"Course not," he said and slid into the back.

She sat primly in front, looked over her shoulder to see Peanut sunk low where he couldn't see anything, then let her skirt ride up to give Ray something to think about.

She saw him smiling and realized he had been watching her and knew what she'd been doing.

She smiled back.

Ray had "Great Balls of Fire" cranked up on the Eldo's CD, and they rode with the windows down enjoying the cool night air.

"Jerry Lee Lewis is one of the six great geniuses of history," Peanut said.

"Oh yeah, who might the other five be?" Ginger asked.

Ray looked at her face, then his eyes dropped to her legs. She turned toward him and spread them a bit more, then their eyes met again. Ray was trying to keep a straight face, but she saw the smile lines around his eyes.

"The other five would be Sam Colt, Jesse James, John Dillinger, D.B. Cooper and the man who invented the indoor shitter."

"Good list," Ray said. "You checked this place out?"

"It's a five-story building with a parking deck in the basement. The place doesn't have much security, no TV or anything, but there are two guards at a lobby desk who take turns making rounds.

"I figure we go in through the garage and just act like we belong there. If we get caught, we kill the guards, skin them and make it look like the Satan worshippers done it."

"How many of those biscuits did you eat?" Ray asked.

"Not nearly enough," Ginger said.

They parked in the basement garage, and Peanut handed Ginger the attaché.

"She's been practicing with this at the store. Let's see if she can get us in."

It was true, she had been practicing, but both Peanut and Ray were pros so she felt self-conscious when she took the kit. She gave each of them a penlight, latex gloves and an inspection mirror, took the wallet of picks and slid it in her bra, slid the slim jim up the arm of her blouse and handed the case back to Peanut.

"Peanut, why don't we leave that in the trunk?" she said.

"McLendon Building" was stenciled in black spray paint on the fire door. She popped the slip lock with the slim jim and they were in.

"Let's start at the top and work down," Ray whispered.

They climbed the stairs quietly to the fifth floor landing where she silently opened the door to the inside hall just a sliver.

Ray pulled the mirror from his pocket, extended the handle, threaded it through the crack and looked both ways down the hall.

"Clear."

He stepped through the door, listened carefully, then stepped aside and held it open for Ginger and Peanut. The carpet and dark paneling absorbed the sound much better than the concrete stairwell had.

They walked halfway down the hall where opposite two elevators and the rest rooms they found a wall of glass and on its other side a large open office. With twenty desks on an evenly spaced grid, it had the old fashioned floor plan that was common before movable partitions. On the wall of the far side of the room, a series of doors led to what were probably the bigwigs' offices.

The door held the painted sign, "Johnny McLendon, CEO, The McLendon Company, Timber, Textiles, Manufacturing."

The glass wall and the openness of the room made Ginger nervous. She glanced at Ray and Peanut but they didn't appear concerned so she slipped on her gloves, hoping this didn't make her seem paranoid, and was grateful to hear them put on theirs as well.

It was a cylinder lock so she took the picks from her bra, went down on her knees and slid the two narrow wires of spring steel into the keyhole.

Ginger had developed a good sense of touch, but locks could be unpredictable. She was afraid it would take long enough that she would get nervous and screw up, and Ray would make her quit.

Having felt her way along the cylinder twice she gave the second pick a slight turn and was surprised to find it moving. It had taken two seconds.

"In," she said softly, stood and pushed the door open. She saw an amazed look on both their faces.

"You got a gift, baby," Ray whispered.

The light from the hall created a perma-dusk in the front work area, so she could easily see the dark-wood desks and English prints on the wall with red-coated, drunken squires being catapulted through the air on horses with bodies like foot-long hot dogs.

The office doors on the far wall were open but the rooms were dark. They turned on the hooded penlights, small flashlights with dark metal shrouds to contain the light beams, and briefly looked in each until coming to the last office which was much larger than the others and bore a sign which said, "Mr. McLendon."

"Let's start here," Ray said.

He pointed the light toward an old free-standing safe in the corner.

"I wonder where they keep the money?" he said.

They walked into the room.

"Think it's a decoy?" Peanut asked.

"Could be. If it is, we aren't going to find the real one. Their main security is probably that nobody would think they had much cash around."

"You any good with safes?" Ray asked Ginger.

She realized it was both a joke and a compliment.

"I've been reading up on explosives," she said. "So far, I think I know enough to blow up the building and kill all of us."

"In that case, we might want to try something else. I bet they wrote the combination down someplace," Ray said. "Why don't you two look under the desk drawers, behind the pictures, in the potted plants . . ."

"And what are you going to do while we crawl around on the floor?" Peanut asked.

"I'll keep watch so we don't get busted."

"A good job for upper management."

Ray pulled a visitor's chair around so he could see the entrance. Peanut was under the desk looking under the drawers. Feeling very silly, Ginger picked up a philodendron plant and pulled a white plastic stick out of the pot and looked at it.

"Damn, Ray," she said "They better put you on that television network with all the psychics."

"You got something?"

"Looks like a combination."

Ray was still looking out the door toward the hall.

"Shit, we got a problem," he said. "Somebody's out there."

He slid the chair back and got on his knees on the floor, moved back from the door, and held the mirror near the office floor pointing back out toward the entrance.

"A guard," he said.

Ginger got on her hands and knees and crawled quietly beside him and looked down at the mirror. At first she couldn't make it out, then she saw him with his gawky face and high water pants.

She whispered in Ray's ear, "He looks like the poster boy for the Save The Hillbillies Foundation."

"If he comes toward us, sit at the desk and act like you're sick. When he comes to check, I'll knock him out."

She heard a key going into the door lock.

"He's coming in."

The guard opened the door, crept into the office, and slowly moved his head about, as if he was listening. Ginger began creeping toward the desk chair, but Ray grabbed her ankle. When she looked again, she saw the guard move more confidently to a desk in the center of the large open office.

He pulled a pocket knife from his pocket, opened a small blade and began jimmying the lock on the right-hand side drawer. When he had it open, he pulled out a small metal box, opened it, pulled some currency from it, counted it out, put some in his pocket and the rest back in the box.

His radio crackled.

"Otis, where the hell did you go, buddy?"

The guard didn't respond. He placed the metal cash box back in the desk and locked the desk drawer again with the pocket knife.

"Otis, where the hell are you?"

The guard pulled the radio from his waist and spoke into it.

"Hold your horses, Lamar. I was sitting on the damned john. I'll be there in a minute."

The guard went back to the hall, re-locked the door and left.

They didn't move or speak until he was long gone.

"Used to be sort of exclusive being a criminal," Peanut sniffed. "There are so many people stealing these days, we're stumbling over each other."

"What's the world coming to?" Ginger agreed.

"While we're trying to figure that out, we might want to get the safe open," Ray said.

"Good idea."

Ginger pointed the flashlight at the plastic stick with the combination written on it, tightened her face in concentration, then bent over, turned the safe dial back and forth and pulled the door slowly open. Ray and Peanut pointed their penlights at the safe.

"There's nothing in here Ray, except a big pile of some weird pieces of paper."

Ray reached into the safe and pulled one out.

"Currency wrappers," he said. "They're moving a lot of money through here."

"I told you. The Shitass Ronnie Gordon really is moving money around."

"What the hell is McLendon up to?"

McLendon in Panama

JESUS IT WAS hot. Not only that, but people had been laughing at him all day because of his stupid fucking outfit. Stupid fucking shirt, stupid fucking shorts and the worst part was the hat, a cheap pink straw pork pie with a large plastic dinosaur attached to the top. He guessed that was the point though.

He was hoping to take a James Bond wardrobe: tux, flashy sports clothes, then he would rent a hot car and flash some money around the casino, and generally set the stage.

As he thought about it, he realized Schiller knew best. Why tip off the enemies of America by dressing like a spy? Then they could neutralize him, extreme prejudice, the whole bit. Nobody would suspect anything if he dressed like a total fool.

As his taxi stopped in front of his hotel, he couldn't believe it. What a dump. The stucco was stained and peeling, and two of the iron balconies had begun to fall from the side of the building.

"What a shit-hole," he said.

"Not a place of much health," the driver agreed in English.

As he paid the driver, the man laughed at him. He carried his own bag to the registration desk.

"Hah," the room clerk said.

McLendon pounded his fist on the desk.

"What's so goddamn funny?" he asked.

"Nothing, Sir,"

"I have a reservation for Buster Crab," he said.

The man laughed again and handed him his room key.

"You going to carry my bag up?" McLendon asked.

The clerk seemed startled by his question.

"Alas, there is no other help, and I must remain here."

"I don't think you and I are going to get along, are we, son?" McLendon asked.

"No, Sir, I don't think so," the clerk cheerfully agreed.

McLendon made his way to a dirty stone curved stairway whose steps were smooth with wear. Halfway up, it broadened to a small landing occupied by a dead woman with a fly crawling on her face.

"Jesus, please save my poor white ass," McLendon said.

He was undecided whether he should step over her or run for help. He was even less sure who needed help the most, the dead woman or him.

She stirred and brushed the fly away. She wasn't dead after all. Just asleep.

He prodded her with his toe. She grunted but didn't wake up. Didn't look like she was asleep either, probably on some drugs. He stepped over her and climbed to the second floor stairway.

The hall was even dirtier than the stairs had been. In places where water had collected the thick dust looked like mud, and a used condom lay at his feet. Sounds of sex came from a room with an open door down the hall. The bed squeaked and in the same rhythm a woman made a soft uh, uh, uh sound. It was as mechanical as the bed, like she was having to remind herself to moan.

As he grew closer he heard a guttural grunt in time with the creaking box spring.

A mestizo soldier, fully dressed in green fatigues and black boots, lay humping a naked woman, her legs spread wide. He concentrated on a spot on the pillow next to her, while she stared fixedly at the ceiling.

She looked American or maybe she was a city girl from some place around here. He couldn't figure her for a low dollar hooker. She must have heard him, because she looked in his direction.

Her face was expressionless as she watched him watching her fuck the soldier.

Jesus, she's on dope too, McLendon thought. She probably doesn't have a clear idea what's going on — maybe a tourist drugged into white slavery.

He wondered if maybe he should rescue her, but decided it might interfere with his mission. He let himself into his room instead.

The place was a mess. The bed looked like it had been slept in and when he looked in the bathroom he almost threw up.

The clerk was chuckling at him again as he pounded his fist on the desk.

"I no understand, Sir," he kept repeating.

"You need to clean up my room. Put new sheets on the bed. Unclog the goddamn toilet."

"No understand."

"Okay, let me put it this way then." He reached into his back pocket for his wallet and pulled out a hundred dollar bill. The clerk looked at it hungrily.

"I'm going to go for a walk," McLendon said. "When I return, if my room is clean I will give you this hundred dollar bill. If my room is not clean, I will give this money to someone else with the instructions to beat you within an inch of your life."

"Very good, Sir. I will take care of it. And congratulations on having understood our system so quickly."

Rendezvous

THESE WERE THE instructions: McLendon would walk a mile to a plaza where a man wearing a baseball hat would pick him up in a blue pick-up truck with a stenciled sign on the sun visor saying HOTEL. The truck would circle the plaza once an hour beginning at 12:10 PM.

The final instruction – be sure you aren't being followed – was the hardest.

Almost as soon as he left the hotel, he attracted a half-dozen rowdy young boys dressed in a pathetic selection of frayed cheap pants and dirty T-shirts who giggled, pointed and shouted in Spanish at him.

"*La rana.*"

"*La rana.*"

"*Oye señor, pon una rana en el sombrero!*"

He wasn't sure what would be the best method to keep them from following him. He thought about paying them to go away but as soon as he pulled out his wallet the crowd tripled, all of them with outstretched hands.

He would just have to try to lose them. He hoped that they would lose interest as he walked from the poor section surrounding his hotel.

He kept a brisk pace hoping to tire them out, but they ran past him and circled him like a swarm of bees. They turned it into a game. Shouting, "*La rana. La rana.*"

He wondered what it meant. Maybe he could use it as a secret code name.

They hit the edge of the commercial district with three-story stucco buildings nestled next to the occasional chrome and glass high-rise and bright plastic signs that proclaimed Aiwa, Sony and Nikon. The crowd had grown if anything.

He tried a quick double-back but the kids took it as a game and began jumping and yelling.

It was 12:15. He had already missed the first meeting time. He took a quick series of aimless lefts and rights hoping they would lose interest but they followed with even greater fervor. He guessed there wasn't much going on this afternoon other than him.

After twenty minutes of this, he realized he was lost, and if he asked anyone for directions he would tip off where he was going. He desperately tried to find his way back to his route, and in the muddle missed the 1:10 meet as well.

At last he found a familiar street and regained his bearings but the crowd had grown to thirty or more.

Shitfire, it looked like he was leading a class field trip for the Dead-End Kids.

He ducked into four Indian trade shops before he found one with an exit to the next street and scurried through it, but the children raced through the shop to the accompanying yells of the merchants who came out from behind the counters to shoo them out the back door with McLendon.

Finally, he just gave up and walked to the plaza with just a few minutes to spare before 2:10.

He saw the blue pick-up with the HOTEL sign on the visor immediately. The driver with the baseball cap had pulled to the side of the road and was checking out the old men sitting on benches in the park at the center of the plaza.

McLendon caught his eye, and the man nodded.

"Jump in," he said.

McLendon opened the door to the pick-up and slid onto the seat, shut the door and rolled up the window as the children jumped and squealed at the side of the truck.

"Get the fuck out of here!" the man yelled, and the kids screamed and ran in every direction, more amused by the yelling than frightened.

"I'm Plank," the man said as he climbed into the driver's seat.

"McLendon."

"What happened? I've been driving around for hours."

"I was followed. I couldn't shake them."

"Followed?" Plank looked around sharply as he pulled into traffic. "How many?"

"About forty."

"Forty? Christ on a crutch. Where are they?"

"The children."

"Oh, the children . . . I wouldn't worry about them."

"But you said not to let anyone follow me," McLendon said.

"Yes, but I still wouldn't worry about them."

"It was the hat."

Plank glanced at the pink pork pie with the plastic dinosaur.

"I can see that the hat might draw a crowd. You should take it off," Plank said.

"But Schiller said I should wear it."

"He did? Well, I'm telling you that you can take it off."

"Thank God." McLendon took the hat off and slapped it on the seat next to him. "What does *la rana* mean, by the way?"

"The frog."

"Damn, I should have known."

The Road to Rio (Hato)

"WE'RE TRAINING THE cadre at Rio Hato. It's an old Air Force base," Plank said.

They had driven across a huge bridge and seemed to be making for the sparsely populated regions outside of the city.

"Training?" McLendon asked.

"It's for sharpening up," Plank explained. "We all, at the least, had ranger training. Before an operation we sharpen the skills."

"I see."

"We thought we'd run you through the course to give you a taste of what's involved."

"That would be great." McLendon pictured himself shooting from the waist, unloading a clip on the sneering shits back at the Driving Club. No more Mr. Frog Boy . . .

"You have any experience with weapons?"

"No. Not really."

"Ever fired an M-16?"

"No. Uh-uh."

"Ingram, Uzi?"

"Nope."

"A handgun?"

"Nope. Not that either."

"No firearms experience of any sort?"

"No. I used to go hunting with my father."

"Well, what did you use?"

"Nothing. I just watched. He wouldn't trust me with a gun. He said he thought I would shoot him."

Plank smiled. "Would you have shot him?"

"Fuckin' A."

"Good man. Looks like you got the instinct. Just need a little training."

"You think so?"

"Sure," Plank said. "You can teach anyone to point a gun. But if you are going to kill somebody with one, you got to have the inclination."

"You think I could make the grade?"

"You got what it takes," Plank assured him. "We used to have a saying: If you kill for money, you're a mercenary. If you kill for pleasure, you're a psycho. If you kill for both, you're a Green Beret."

"I can see that."

McLendon had been glancing out the window and knew they were moving toward open country because the small cement block homes with green tin roofs and glassless windows of filigree brick were further apart. There weren't many cars, but they passed people walking along the side of the road who gave a friendly wave.

"I'm supposed to give you a briefing, but first I need to give you this." He handed McLendon a pill in a small ziplock bag.

McLendon took the bag, pulled it open, and was about to pop the capsule in his mouth when Plank started screaming.

"Shit. Don't do that. Stop. It's a suicide pill."

McLendon was shaken. "I thought you wanted me to take it."

"It's in case you're captured. I can't give you the briefing unless you promise to take that if you're captured."

"Oh sure, no problem." He put the pill back in the bag and put it in his shirt pocket. "I'll keep it right here."

"Be careful you don't leave it in there when you do the laundry. Those pills play hell with your clothes. Eat holes right through them."

"Sure," McLendon said, but he wished Plank had kept that last detail to himself.

"The other thing I need to explain is that we operate on a need to know basis. Which is another way of saying you and me don't need to know much, so we aren't told shit."

"They don't trust us?" McLendon asked.

"No, it isn't like that. Too much information is a burden. Say you get captured and you can't get to your suicide pill fast enough, they hook electricity to your balls and shock hell out of you for two or three days. At that point you give them everything you got, but if you don't got shit you don't have to worry about it."

"Sure. That makes sense. Don't tell me shit," McLendon said.

"Just the general outlines."

"I may not even need to know that."

"Well, you got to know where your money is going."

"Not really."

"Schiller wanted me to give you this much, so you'd know the reason for some of the preparations."

"I understand."

"What we got here is your basic problem in today's post–cold-war world picture. We got terrorists who want to gas the shit out of the United States and a congress who has lost their guts and won't give us funding."

"Those sons of bitches."

"So we have to look toward other funding sources."

"And that would be me," McLendon said.

"That would be you. But instead of coming to you to float the whole boat, we have a neat scheme. We're going to use your money to buy drugs from the Colombians, then unload the deal on the Russian mob. That way we get to support our friends in South America, de-stabilize the former Soviet Union, finance our operation, and provide a nice profit for our investor."

"That would be me again."

"Correct," Plank said.

"Now we got another cadre training someplace that's going to take out the terrorists. I don't know shit about who they are, where they are, what they are up to, none of that. Could be the terrorists are a cover story and they are going to kidnap some

Japanese bankers or some shit. I don't know, and I don't want to know."

"Me either," McLendon agreed.

"That's the spirit. The thing you got to keep in mind is that handling the money and the drugs is going to be dangerous, maybe more dangerous than the actual operation. It's a lot of money, and we are going to be dealing with some very scary people.

"They may not operate on a need to know basis, and some of the people who know may not be team players. You got the picture?"

"There's a good chance somebody's going to get their ass shot off," McLendon said.

"I'd say you got the picture."

They drove over a ridge and looked down to a landscape of semi-arid broken hills and a breathtaking view of a bay with gently curving coastline and the Pacific.

McLendon felt like the condemned man who's mind had been focused, and he felt something as close to serenity as he had ever felt in his life. For once the pack of ferrets that tore away at his self-confidence were sleeping. The beauty of the moment almost brought him to tears.

Plank left him alone in his thoughts until they hit the bottom land at the coast. He stopped at an unmanned traffic stop.

"You want to get out and lift the barrier?" he asked McLendon.

It was a counter-balanced swivel arm like a railroad crossing guard back home. It stopped the truck just short of an enormous concrete ribbon that crossed the highway at right angles. On the far side he saw a line of two-story stucco buildings with red tin roofs.

"What the hell is that?" McLendon asked.

"It's the runway."

"It crosses the highway."

"No shit."

McLendon laughed and shook his head in disbelief.

"Welcome to Rio Hato," Plank said.

The Mango Beret

PLANK DROVE THE truck up a bare dirt track away from the airbase, over a small hill. McLendon saw five men in jungle fatigues standing around three long tables holding the wildest collection of guns he'd ever seen.

"Here's our cadre," Plank said proudly.

They climbed out of the truck, and the men walked toward them and shook Johnny's hand in turn.

"Meet Johnny McLendon. He's the man who's financing our little war."

"This here is Arizona, Hardendorf, Krog, Harold and Bass."

The men slapped him on the back, and he felt almost like he was one of them. They looked pretty much the same. Short hair, well–built, in their late twenties or early thirties. The only one who stood out was Arizona, who was a black man with three parallel scars on each cheek and who spoke with an accent.

Plank slipped on a black nylon harness with aluminum clips all over it, and a shoulder holster holding what looked like a ray gun.

"We're going to walk you through our range. Here, take this."

He handed Johnny something he wouldn't take to be a gun. "What is it?"

"A Mac 10. Here . . . you hold it like this. Here's the safety. We're going to walk down this ravine and when a target pops up you just point and pull the trigger."

They walked down a shallow ravine and it wasn't long before a target popped up. He pulled the trigger but lost his grip on the handle as it fired and began rotating in his hand.

The members of the cadre leapt behind him throwing themselves on the ground. He was sure he was going to shoot himself, but he couldn't make it stop firing. Finally the gun fell silent.

"What happened?" McLendon yelled.

"Just a little glitch at the start of training," Plank said as he stood up and brushed the dirt from the front of his shirt. "You need to get a better grip with your right, then put your left up front there."

"Like this?" McLendon asked.

"That's great. Look at how fast he picks this up?"

"He's a champ," Krog said.

"We'll have to show him how to jump without a chute next," Harold said.

Johnny didn't think that was a skill he wanted to learn any time soon.

Plank showed him how to put in the next clip, and they moved down the range. He didn't lose control of the gun exactly, but he could tell he was shooting wild and didn't see any evidence he had hit a target.

"Okay, we're going to change the drill. I'm going to give McLendon here a different load and we'll do team firing." Then he explained to McLendon. "Some people find this load I'm giving you easier to handle. I don't, but you just may be one of the men who does."

They walked in an open parallel line down the ravine and when the first target popped up, McLendon and the others began to fire. Plank was right. He was holding it steadily on the target, and he could see he was slaughtering it.

"Yeehaw," he yelled.

"That's the way, Johnny," the men were yelling.

It was hard work, and after a while they took a water break. The men were grinning at each other and Plank pulled something from a thigh pocket.

Damn. It was a beret. It was sort of tie-dyed looking and colored like a ripe mango, peach melting into a dull apple green.

Plank cleared his throat.

"For services rendered to his country in time of need, I'd like to present this beret to Mr. Johnny McLendon."

He stepped directly in front of McLendon, placed it on his head, then stepped back and gave a sharp salute.

"Welcome to the cadre."

The other men saluted McLendon. He was nearly in tears for the second time that day. This was the life for him, all right.

"Now, it's time for you to meet Bill Schiller."

Commandante Bill

SCHILLER HAD LONG ago learned to recognize incoming fire, so when the round sizzled past his ear he dove under the table.

Thwap! One of the poles supporting the roof took a direct hit.

He lay there wondering what sort of deranged incompetent had been turned loose with a firearm, but thought of the answer as soon as he framed the question.

It had to be McLendon.

As he lay under the table, he thought of six million dollars and recovered his capacity for patience. The qualities which made McLendon attractive as a victim could also make him difficult to handle.

The picture that had emerged from Bart Oakes's briefings over the years was one of a severely damaged human being. He was capable of being infantile and insecure and at the same time was prone to vastly overestimating his talents and acting rashly and without reason.

As a result he had an army of advisors who presided over a family trust and would never allow him to invest in a scheme as hare-brained as the one Schiller was proposing.

The whole point of bringing him to Panama was to separate him from the meddling hands of people who were looking out for his interests, and fill his imagination with dreams of glory and the conviction that he knew what he was doing.

Once he thought it was safe, he crawled from under the table and made ready for McLendon. He had arranged a laptop computer, two black boxes which were actually avionics packages from a recently crashed airplane, and a small satellite dish on the table to give the impression of a high-tech communications rig, and more importantly to give the impression that there was someone to be in communication with.

Luckily, they hadn't been hit by the wild gunfire. He booted the computer and loaded a communications simulation program used for training, and it looked like he was tearing up the airwaves between his lowly cabana and major world capitals.

He took a fresh bottle of scotch from the case, and dusted extra glasses for Plank and McLendon.

Schiller loathed Plank, but because he was such an accomplished liar he was sure that Plank didn't suspect.

In the distance, he was leading an oddly proportioned man in his direction. He hadn't believed Oakes when he had said McLendon looked like a frog. He had written it off as one more example of Oakes's disgust with everything about the man, but Bart had been right. He had almost no neck, and he was all legs.

He was wearing a hideous pair of checkered shorts, an incredibly stupid-looking print shirt, black plastic nerd glasses, and a beret that looked like an LSD flashback. It had a patch on the front, a trident impaled on some sort of leaf.

McLendon grinned widely as they drew closer. Then as Plank was about to introduce them he stepped forward with an outstretched hand.

"Johnny McLendon. I'm very pleased to meet you."

"Schiller." He held out his hand, and McLendon pumped it vigorously.

"I feel like I've known you for years, even though we just met," McLendon said.

"Don't think I haven't been aware of your contribution to our cause," Schiller said. "I'm afraid they don't give out medals for our work, but you certainly deserve one."

McLendon beamed. For a moment, Schiller almost felt ashamed. This was going to be too easy. If the Russians had been like this, the cold war would have been over in 1948.

"You did a superb job of disguising yourself," Schiller said.

"What do you think, Plank, does this man look like he's involved in a secret operation?"

"I was just following orders," McLendon said.

It was the first time Schiller had heard the Nuremberg Defense applied to one's choice of clothing.

"The black plastic glasses are the perfect touch," Schiller said.

"They are my regular glasses," McLendon said.

"They cause your enemies to underestimate you," Plank said.

"They do indeed," Schiller agreed. "We should get a pair for every man in the cadre."

"That would be a good idea," Plank agreed.

"I'll take care of it," McLendon said. "I'll place the order with my optician."

"My God, you're fast off the mark. There's no holding him back, is there Plank?" Schiller said.

"He tore up the combat firing range."

"Well, I'm not surprised. After all, he's no stranger to the dangerous side of the street. Although we've never met, we do have a history, don't we Johnny?

"Please, have a seat. Let me fix everyone a drink. We've got scotch and more scotch," Schiller said.

"I'll take more scotch," McLendon said.

Schiller poured him three fingers as he settled into a comfortable, folding camp chair with a leather seat and arm slings. Plank sat next to him and Schiller handed both men a drink then poured one for himself and sat opposite McLendon, eye to eye.

"You've done a patriotic service to your country through the years, Johnny. When congress lost it's taste for covert ops, our country would have been overrun by those who would destroy us, if patriots like you hadn't stepped up to the plate."

"It's been a pleasure," Johnny said. "And at last we get to work together directly, without that prissy geek, Dunbarton Oakes."

"Bart was a useful front man in his day," Schiller said.

"But his day has passed," McLendon said.

"That's right, Johnny, and now you're the man."

McLendon glanced down at the beach and beyond to the horizon.

"Beautiful place you got here. My hotel is a real shit-hole."

"I know, but we use it for a reason. The DEA, the drug cartels and probably half the governments in the region, have bugs all over the first class hotels. We don't want you turning up on a tape transcript, do we?"

McLendon slapped his hand on the chair's arm sling. "I knew it. I knew there was an explanation. Don't worry. I'm a good soldier. I can put up with hardship."

"I know you can, Johnny. And there could be more hardships before the operation is over. It's good to know you're ready. Plank gave you the suicide pill?"

"Yes. And I'm ready to use it if captured."

"Good. Now that you've been briefed and received some weapons training, it's back to Atlanta. We'll strike camp and join you in a few days. Plank will make contact and begin planning the funds transfer.

"We'll need the money in two deliveries. The three-hundred-and-fifty thousand right away, and the six million as soon as you can get it together."

"That second one will take a few weeks," McLendon said.

"I understand."

"I have a driver, Gordon, who I'd like to handle the money at my end. He's an ex-con. I have him delivering cash off the books to various politicians. He's dependable."

"As long as you trust him," Schiller said.

"Yes, he's a good man. In fact, he had a question he wants me to ask you, if you don't mind."

"I'll be happy to answer it if I can."

"Good. He wants to know if it's true that spies get a lot of sex."

Schiller nodded thoughtfully, trying to appear to be giving the question careful consideration when actually he was trying to hide his astonishment.

"Our lives have to be rather circumspect. We don't get to know a lot of people on a social level unless our cover requires it, and that doesn't happen often. No. I'm afraid spies probably get far less sex than your average individual."

"Damn. I was afraid of that."

Debriefing

JOHNNY MCLENDON HAD driven Plank insane, and that meant the first part of the plan had fallen into place.

Arizona had left with McLendon in the truck to drive him back to town, and Plank after seeing him off and reminding him to wear his straw hat for the remainder of his stay in Panama, was pacing the sand floor of the cabana and raving.

"I thought he was going to kill us on the course. Eventually, we put blanks in his gun and sprayed the targets for him. He thought he was a marksman."

"He managed to hit one of the poles." Schiller pointed to the corner support furthest from the ocean.

"Holy shit, I wonder what else he hit. There could be someone dead in the bushes."

"The beret was a nice touch," Schiller said.

"What a dumb fuck. He almost cried when we gave it to him."

"I've never seen one like it. Where did you get it?"

"It was a screwed-up dye job. We got them for about a nickel. The patch is from a cook's outfit in the Paraguayan army."

"So that wasn't a trident, it was a fork and lettuce?"

"Right. And you should have seen the hat he was wearing when I picked him up – pink straw with a plastic dinosaur on top."

"That's incredibly bizarre," Schiller said.

"He said you told him to wear it."

"I told him?"

"Yes."

"That's even stranger . . ." Evidently, someone at the Foundation who had handled the coded message disliked McLendon enough to want to humiliate him. More good news. The whole operation was going much better than Schiller had anticipated.

"I gave him the suicide pill, and he almost popped it in his mouth."

"We don't want that to happen."

"And now he wants to involve an ex-convict. That's a major security risk. I can't imagine why we are using McLendon in this operation."

"Six million dollars."

"Money or not, he could put everyone at risk."

Purposefully, Schiller looked bored and it pissed off Plank. He let him stew while he tossed back his scotch, stood up and poured another.

"You might as well strike camp and take the cadre to Atlanta. I'll get in touch once you're settled. Look into the chauffeur. McLendon as much as confessed to violating the federal election laws and using him as a bag man. Get some proof. We can always blackmail him if he gets out of line."

Plank smiled. "I knew you'd have it covered, Sir"

As Plank walked away, Schiller threw the knife into the table and it stuck straight up. He didn't look up. He knew he had played Plank well, pushing him to the edge of anger then reeling him back.

Manipulating Plank was an important part of the plan. It wasn't hard, because Plank was stupid, and Schiller knew many things that Plank could not.

For instance, he knew that there was no second cadre in training for the operation because there was no operation, only his intention to steal six million dollars from McLendon.

At the right moment, he would push Plank until he exploded and took the cadre down with him. Then he would kill him, frame him, and happily steal the money, while anyone who cared searched for Plank and his confederates.

There was a tidiness to this. Plank was a monster. He needed to be put down like a mad dog.

Schiller had discovered this after noticing a cryptic statement in his military record about Plank needing close monitoring of his off-base activities. He had called the man who had entered it, the former C.O. of the unit Plank had served in.

It seemed that Plank was suspected in a series of brutal rapes. The man was convinced that Plank was guilty, and as convinced that he would never be caught. He was too good at what he did to ever be caught. Schiller knew that killing him would be a public service.

The Frog Boy Punch-out

MCLENDON WAS DROPPED off at the same square where he was picked up. As he walked the streets back to his hotel, a wild American go-juice vibrated the recesses of his subconscious igniting a hunger for revenge from a thousand insults, spits at American tourists, embassy bombings, hostage seizures, not to mention his father's compulsion to humiliate him at all of his birthday parties, school visits and any time he was unlucky enough to be caught with the man in public.

All these damn foreigners and traitors burned the flag and his father called him Frog Boy. It was all part of the same menace, people tearing apart the country and the family from without and within.

But now McLendon was in a position to do something about it, to strike back, and he knew just how he was going to start his campaign; with that goddamn sneering Spanish-speaking clerk at the hotel who was probably a traitor.

He picked a variety store run by an Indian merchant at random, pulled the Godzilla hat low on his forehead to hide his face and purchased a pair of socks and a large bar of soap.

On the street outside the shop he placed the bar of soap inside one of the socks, tied two knots to keep it in place, and hid it in his right back pocket. He had seen this in a movie.

He returned to his hotel room, and noticed the soldier and the American whore were back at it. He slipped out of his stupid fucking spy outfit and slipped on more normal sports clothes, then packed his suitcase and walked down the dirty staircase to the registration desk.

"You must be about to leave us, Mr. Buster Crab," the desk clerk sneered.

"Yes, I am indeed, but there is one more task I'd like to hire you to do," McLendon said.

"Yes?"

McLendon glanced around. "It's rather delicate."

"We could step into my office," the clerk suggested.

"That might be best." McLendon agreed.

He followed the clerk into the small office, took the soap blackjack out of his back pocket and swung it hard. His plan was to knock the man out so he could pull down his pants and write God Bless the US of A on his ass in indelible black ink, but unexpectedly the clerk turned toward him.

The sap connected hard to the jaw, and McLendon heard a crack as it snapped.

The clerk's face went blank, his knees wobbled, but miraculously he remained standing. McLendon stood with the sock at his side for a full ten seconds not knowing what to do next, till the man's eyes cleared and his hand went to his jaw.

Then McLendon pulled his wallet from his back pocket and counted out ten one-hundred-dollar bills and handed them over.

"Will this cover it?"

The clerk's eyes were a balance of disorientation and frightened incredulity, and he blew blood bubbles as he spoke.

"Yesh, Mishter Bushter Rab."

"Thank you very much," McLendon said. "I enjoyed it very much. It was a pleasure doing business with you."

On the street in front of the hotel, he was so overcome with joy, he began loudly singing, "I'm a Yankee Doodle Dandy." As luck would have it, three off-duty US service personnel with buzz cuts heard him and began singing along.

"God Bless the US of A," McLendon yelled. "America is coming back."

The men yelled too, then the yelling turned sarcastic and became jeering. McLendon looked at them more closely and realized they were drunk, and probably on their way to his hotel to seek the services of a prostitute.

The Shitass Apartment

EARLY THE NEXT morning, Peanut called Ray.

"What you doing?" Ray asked. "You still following the Shitass Ronnie Gordon?"

"Found his squat. I was going to do a B&E this morning. Figured I might find something there."

"I better go along to keep you out of trouble."

"I thought you'd say that."

"Are you high?"

"No man, I'm as clean as the day is long."

"If you're thinking of clean days as being long days, you're developing a problem," Ray said.

"Don't worry about that, my man. It's under control."

"What's it like out?"

"It's nice out. In fact, it's so nice out, I think I'll leave it out."

"I was talking about the weather, not your goober."

"In that case, it's hot already," Peanut said. "Dress cool."

"Dress cool, but dress up," Ray said.

This was part of Ray's business philosophy. You should always dress like a businessman when you're breaking the law. If people see a guy in a conservative suit doing a B&E, they assume he's the landlord.

A lot of guys, especially the young ones, dressed like villains on television shows. Ray imagined this was an expression of gangster pride, but to his way of thinking this came close to being the perfect definition of stupid.

The Shitass's apartment was an attic efficiency on Monroe near the park. An iron staircase climbed from a backyard which once had been a garden. It was surrounded by two huge oaks obstructing the view from the neighboring houses.

They passed a birdbath filled with green scum.

Peanut looked at it and said, "Why am I not surprised? The Shitass has even got a shit birdbath."

Ray followed him up the shaky staircase to a rusted landing where he worked the slip lock with a short plastic ruler.

Inside, the apartment smelled like dirty socks. It was one room with a little galley kitchen and water-stained drapes. A cat jumped from the sink, strolled across the floor and rubbed against Peanut's leg.

"Check out the art collection."

Ray pointed to a windowless wall which contained two pictures. One was a cheap color portrait of an older woman primped and dressed in her best clothes. The word "Mom" was written across the top of the blue background in block printing, and Gordon had drawn a bullet hole in her forehead.

The other picture was a crude pencil drawing on lined note-book paper. On the bottom of the sheet, the name "Ronnie" was proudly scrawled.

"I can't make out what that's supposed to be a picture of," Ray said. "Looks sort of like a pop-up toaster. Why would somebody want to draw a picture of something like that?"

Peanut studied the drawing.

"I think it's a car," he said.

"Doesn't seem to be a lot to search here," Ray said. "Just this one little closet."

The door was ajar. He opened it all the way.

"Here we got a chauffeur's uniform, two pairs of blue jeans and three T-shirts. Seems like he goes for the ones with slogans on them. One says, 'Party till you puke.'"

He pulled the second one out where he could see it.

"You'll like this one, Peanut. It says, 'What drinking problem? I get drunk, I fall down, no problem.' Looks like you and him have one thing in common."

"Fuck you. We don't have nothing in common. Look it here."

"Right, this is one of my all time favorites," Ray said, 'Yea though I walk through the valley of the shadow of death, I shall fear no evil . . . for I am the meanest son of a bitch in the whole damn valley.'"

"That third one is a joke, but the other two are right on target," Peanut said.

Ray began pulling open the drawers of a small orange desk. "Nothing here. Wait a minute."

He saw two pieces of paper in the bottom drawer and reached to get them.

"Exhibit one is a copy of a letter on the stationery of The McLendon Company. It says that Mr. Gordon is Mr. McLendon's chauffeur."

"I figured that the guy that looked like a frog was McLendon. Sort of a shame, being that rich and looking like that," Peanut said.

"This second sheet is Ronnie's financial plan."

"That should be good."

"Listen to this:

Things to buy
1. a stereo and CD that girls like
2. clothes to attract women and get them naked
3. pussymobile"

"This guy is pathetic."

"You're right." Peanut walked to the bed and unzipped his pants.

"What the fuck you doing?"

"I'm going to piss on his bed," he said.

"He's not supposed to know we've been here."

"He'll blame it on the cat."

"Yeah, but think of the cat."

The cat jumped on the bed to see what he was doing.

"I'm not worried about the cat," Peanut said. "The cat ain't like him. It ain't a snitch, and if it has to do time, it'll do it right."

It was too late to argue since he was already at full stream so Ray looked around the apartment for something else of interest. There wasn't much. He walked to the trash can and looked in it.

"He likes canned beef stew."

Peanut was zipping up his pants.

"You through, or you want to crap in the ash tray, too?" Ray asked.

"No, I think that should do it for now," he said.

Ray believed him because he looked like a satisfied man, which meant Ray had a serious problem on his hands.

Mother at the Driving Club

PEOPLE THOUGHT MCLENDON was floating in a lake of thousand dollar bills, and that was one way of looking at it. Another was that he was too broke to even pay attention unless he engaged in the humiliating act of begging in public.

True, he had made money from his escapades with the Foundation, but most of it had been spent as quickly as he made it. Being rich is expensive.

His father had been a determined man who through the work of clever lawyers had seen that the everlasting hell he had visited on his family while alive would continue in perpetuity after his death.

His estate was left to a trust which his wife, Johnny's mother, would oversee until she remarried, Johnny died, or was placed in psychiatric care, at which point the money would pass to a collection of charities evaluated on the basis that they would do nothing to make the lives of the "common working man" better.

As a result, his mother had entertained herself with a series of escorts who looked like central casting's idea of investment bankers, while Johnny extorted money from her with periodic threats of voluntary commitment or suicide.

The one bit of freedom allowed him by the will was an allowance to hire a chauffeur. His father, J.T., had been convinced that it would be a dark day for the American Republic if his son ever learned to drive an automobile.

Johnny, of course, has used this freedom wisely by hiring the grossly inappropriate Gordon, and it had irritated his mother endlessly, just as he had hoped.

He had called his mother.

"I need some money," he said.

"You know I prefer to discuss this at the Driving Club."

"In the middle of the dining room."

"Yes, the view is better there," she said.

"The view is better by the window," Johnny said.

"It's a different view."

She was waiting at her favorite table, a small bird-like woman in an ancient rust-brown Evan Picone suit. Johnny suspected that if you went to sleep on a beach, she might peck your eyes out.

"Where's Henry?" McLendon asked.

"Who?"

"The one with the big handkerchief."

"Oh, Henry . . . It's been an age."

"If you're looking for someone, my chauffeur is free . . ."

McLendon was talking loudly, on purpose. As long as his mother made him beg in public, he would make her pay for it.

"Don't be silly."

"He's hung like a horse," McLendon said.

An older couple with white hair shifted uncomfortably and pretended to ignore him.

"If you want money, you're doing a poor job of appealing to my generosity."

McLendon knew she was going to shit when she heard the amount, so this was going to require all of his tricks.

"It's my mental illness. You know that Dad used to take me hunting with his friends. They convinced me that it would be fun to pretend I was a dog. They used to make me retrieve sticks and point quail."

"We've been through this all before," his mother said. "And frankly, I don't believe you. I know your father was cruel enough to do that, but he didn't have enough imagination to think of anything that bizarre. I think pretending to be a dog was your idea."

There was some truth to this. Johnny had always considered it better to be treated like a dog boy than a frog boy.

"You probably suggested it to him," McLendon said.

"No," she said. "I never cared enough about you to think of anything like that."

"That's why my life is so bleak and meaningless," he said. "Some days, I feel like chucking the whole thing. I wonder if the waiter could get me a razor blade so I can cut my wrists here in the dining room."

He knew he had her.

"How much do you want?" she asked.

"Seven million, cash."

"Are you insane?"

"I suspect so. I probably should have myself committed to an institution," he said.

"What is it for? I hope this isn't another one of your schemes to sell forest products in Central America. They have plenty forests of their own."

"But they always buy, don't they?"

"Yes, although I can't imagine why," she said.

"Because I bribe them."

"Surely you can find someone to bribe for less than seven million dollars."

"This money isn't for a bribe. I'm going to buy narcotics from the Colombian cartel and sell them to the Russian Mafia."

"Yes, of course, dear . . ."

"I'm serious," he said.

She was pretending not to believe him, but he could see the adding machine running in her head.

"It will take several weeks," she said.

"I need three-hundred-and-fifty-thousand now."

"Fine," she said. "Now lets talk about my percentage."

Schiller and the Shitass

THEY HAD BOOKED two suites in the Buckhead Ritz. Schiller was sitting at a small desk in his bedroom absorbing the information in a dispatch.

McLendon had broken the jaw of his Panamanian desk clerk. Interesting, Schiller thought. This both simplified and complicated the situation. It provided one more piece of blackmail information.

It also meant that McLendon could respond both unpredictably and violently, most probably to situations which he felt were frustrating, demeaning and beyond his control.

They would have to be very cautious about triggering this behavior, unless there was a situation where it could be used.

There was a gentle knock at the door.

"It's Plank, Sir."

"Yes, come in Plank."

Plank shut the door after him and stood stiffly next to the bed.

"Have a seat. Take some weight off your legs."

Plank sat stiffly in a upholstered chair.

"I'm afraid we may have a problem."

"Do tell."

"It's with security."

"How so?"

"There's been a break-in at McLendon's Atlanta office, and the chauffeur thinks he's being followed."

"Could be serious, could be nothing. Tell me what you have."

"They had a problem with missing petty cash at the office so they set up a surveillance camera."

"And?"

"They got pictures of a security guard rifling the desk. He did a sloppy job of it."

"What does the security guard have to say?"

"Somehow he got wind of it and took off."

"Doesn't sound too complicated," Schiller said.

"They think someone got into one of the safes. This guy does a bad job of jimmying a lock with a penknife, then he cracks a safe? It doesn't make sense, does it?"

"I bet they have the combination written down somewhere. The guard probably found it," Schiller said.

"Yes, Sir. I'll check on that."

"The guard and the chauffeur, have they had contact?"

"Yes, Sir. The chauffeur goes into the building all the time."

"I suspect there may be something in that."

"I have the chauffeur here. Would you like to talk to him?"

"Yes. What was his name again?"

"The Shitass Ronnie Gordon."

"That's not a common name."

"No, Sir. It isn't."

"Very well. Bring him in."

"Yes, Sir."

Plank opened the door and said, "Gordon, get in here."

Gordon shuffled in awkwardly, like he was in shackles, and held his hat in front of him in both hands, a shabby man who looked like a fat rat with a skin disease. Judging from his reaction to authority, Schiller guessed he must have spent a lot of time in prison.

"They call you the Shitass Ronnie Gordon?" Schiller asked.

"Yes, Captain, that's right," Gordon said.

"Why is that?"

"Well, because that's the name my folks gave me."

"They named you 'the Shitass?'"

"Well, no. They named me Ronnie, they just called me 'the Shitass.'"

"And why was that?"

"I guess it's because I'm a shitass."

"I suspected as much," Schiller said.

"It caught on with everybody. I hated it at first, but afterwards I started using it because it made people fear me."

Schiller had trouble imagining anyone being afraid of this pathetic, self-deluded little fool.

"You think you're being followed?" Schiller asked.

"Yes, Cap'n. I do."

"Why?"

"I was caught in traffic the other day, and I seen this guy I did time with over in South Carolina."

"Why do you think he was following you?"

"Well, that would be because he was behind me."

"That doesn't mean he was following you," Schiller said.

Gordon thought it over.

"I see your point, but if he had been in front of me, I would have been following him. But he was behind me, so it was him that was doing the following."

Schiller saw pressing the point wasn't going to do any good, so he asked, "Name?"

"The Shitass Ronnie Gordon."

"Damn it, I know your name. What's his name?"

"They call him Peanut Shoke. I don't know if Peanut is his real name or a street name," Gordon said.

"You got that, Plank?"

"Yes, Sir."

"He broke into my apartment, too," Gordon said.

"How do you know that?" Schiller asked.

"He pissed on my bed. Discovered it when Plank went over to my place with me to drink a couple brews."

"He has a cat," Plank said.

"How do you know it wasn't your cat," Schiller asked.

"It wasn't no cat. It didn't smell like it."

"Any other signs of a break-in?"

"He didn't take nothing or anything like that."

"Why would this Peanut break into your apartment, leave everything undisturbed, but urinate on your bed?"

"He don't like me none."

"Anything specific?"

"I turned him in to the duly constituted authorities."

"He went to jail?"

"Yes Cap'n. They sent him up to the joint, and he got made into a punk and had to go down on everybody."

Schiller stood up quickly and laid a sharp open-hand slap across Gordon's face, splitting his lip and knocking him to the floor.

"You're making a false report because you're afraid to admit you're a bed wetter, aren't you?"

"No, I ain't," Gordon pleaded.

"It's a physical problem. Some people have it. It's nothing to be ashamed of. Just act like an adult."

"I didn't piss my bed," Gordon whined.

"You know this security guard who's gone missing, don't you?" Schiller barked.

"No. I don't know him at all."

Schiller nodded to Plank who kicked Gordon in the side.

"Oh, man. I thought I was a secret agent now," Gordon moaned.

"I did too, but secret agents are supposed to tell the truth."

"I met him at work," Gordon said. "I didn't know him personal."

"Help him up, Plank," Schiller said. "Technically, this is McLendon's problem since we haven't had the hand-off yet, but we should look into it. Have Krog and Hardendorf find out if anyone is following him."

Gordon was dusting himself off. It was more a non-verbal complaint at his treatment than anything else, since the floor wasn't dusty.

"Get out of here," Schiller said.

*　　*　　*

A few minutes later, Plank came back to the room alone to see what Schiller thought about the interview with Gordon.

"It sounds like the Shitass and some of his hillbilly friends may have planned a robbery."

"Yes, Sir. That's was I was thinking too," Plank said.

"Find out who's involved and take care of the problem."

"Yes, Sir."

Schiller saw a suppressed smile on Planks' lips. He was a man who couldn't wait for the killing to start.

Shitass Tag

PEANUT AND RAY were playing tag with the limousine using the old brown Honda. They had picked up the Shitass at the McLendon Building and followed him south on Peachtree.

Some geniuses from the City had decided to drop traffic cones and drill holes in the asphalt during lunch hour so traffic was inching along. Gordon, stuck six cars ahead, talked on the cell phone.

They were caught in the blow job district around Eighth. The lack of appeal of sidewalk sex in a heat wave had dried up business, so the girls were driven by desperation from the side streets to seek potential johns in the snarl of traffic. They weren't being very discriminating either.

Ahead, a dirty blonde in cut-offs, a tube top and combat boots was pounding on the window of a car full of tourists, silver-haired men and women, yelling, "You want I suck you?"

Seeing she wasn't having much luck and figuring Ray and Peanut for better prospects, she stumbled toward them.

"You want I suck you?" she asked.

"You want I set you on fire?" Peanut said.

"Cool off, sweetheart. All I did was offer to suck you."

"I had better sex in the joint," Peanut said.

Ray pulled a twenty from his wallet and held it out to her. "Get lost."

She grabbed the money and was gone.

"I was just kidding about sex in the joint," Peanut said.

"I understand," Ray said. "It was a joke."

"Right . . . Wait a minute. He's breaking free of this mess. We're going to lose him."

"Looks like he's talking on the phone some more," Ray said.

"We're going to drive past him. You better hold back."

"There, he's moving again."

They followed the limo across town to Northside Drive then wound over to Howell Mill near the waterworks, turned on a side street and began wandering aimlessly on littered semi-paved streets, past derelict warehouses with collapsing roofs and a pen with goats.

"We're getting near your garage, Ray."

The garage was a building Ray had bought on the cheap many years before. It had housed at one time or another a taxi company, an ambulance service, a heavy-equipment repair shop, and now a flock of guano happy pigeons.

"What's he up to?"

Ray was thinking out loud as much as asking a question.

"Think he's spotted us?" Peanut asked.

"I don't think so, but he's pulling something. Maybe he's just being careful. Why don't you call Ginger and tell her we'd like some back-up?"

Peanut pulled the cellular phone from the glove box and dialed. After about thirty seconds he pressed the hold button.

"I got her machine."

"Go ahead and leave a message."

"Ginger, me and Ray need a hand. Give us a call on the mobile . . ."

"Don't know if it's anything," Ray said.

Ahead the limo made a turn.

"I can see him talking on his phone again," Peanut said.

For much of the morning they had been chatting to pass the time. Ray also had his own agenda. He wanted to understand just how crazy Peanut was over the Shitass situation. They slipped back into the conversation.

"Ginger let drop the other day that your wife died while you were doing time," Ray said.

"That's right."

"Something you want to talk about?"

"No problem. It was a long time ago. We married real young."

"Ever think about doing it again?" I asked.

"No man, once was enough. Getting legally hitched was a lot like my other brushes with the law. She was a lot of fun, but then she'd start riding my ass about how I wasn't making nothing of myself. Said I ought to be more like her brother.

"Shit, that guy is crazy. He keeps losing whatever cash is left from drinking in schemes like chinchilla ranching. Spent all the money on the cages and the food and the animals and everything, then he'd get drunk and forget to shut the doors and all them over-priced vermin would run off. Thanks to my brother-in-law the bayous of Florida are filled up with them damn coat rats."

"It gives the gators something to do."

Peanut chuckled.

"There is that."

"Hold on, it looks like he pulled in that skinny little alley ahead. I'm going to drift by real slow, see what you can see."

Peanut rolled his passenger side window down.

"Whole family was a bunch of drunks." He went back to the conversation. "When I was in the joint, she took serious drunk. One night she was feeling sentimental, and she told her brother she's going to go outside and sing a love song to the man in the moon. That way her sweet husband up in the penitentiary could hear it. Well, she was singing away, only thing was she was standing in the middle of the highway, and this dump truck comes along and runs right over her. I didn't hear a damn thing, of course. I was a couple hundred miles away."

Ray slowed as they approached the narrow alley between two decaying brick buildings. He didn't see the man, just a movement in the corner of his vision and a voice.

"Don't try anything assholes. This shotgun will take care of both of you."

Ray took his word for it, keeping his hands high on the

steering wheel, but turned slowly to look at the barrel of the twelve gauge just in case the man was having them on.

"Just sit tight."

Another man walked in front of the car. He had his right hand in his pocket. Either he was playing pocket pool or he had some sort of weapon. He opened the car door and stepped back.

They looked like clones, nearly shaved heads, plain dark suits, black T-shirts, black running shoes, black nerd glasses, both about six feet and built like athletes. It was like they came from a thug factory that only had one model.

"Keep your hands where we can see them and get out of the car."

"No problem."

Ray wasn't thinking "no problem." He was thinking he was already dead.

Body Count

SOMETIME BETWEEN NOW and when they took their weapons away, they had one move, and from the way these guys were operating, it wouldn't be a good one.

The Shitass Ronnie Gordon came striding from the limousine.

"Now we got you stupid pukes," he said.

"Shut up, Shitass," the man with the shotgun said.

"I see you're held in the same regard by your co-workers as you are by everyone else," Ray said.

"I'm going to enjoy hurting you, you bush league puke," Gordon said.

"Move back in there," the man behind them said.

Peanut and Ray looked at each other. Ray knew Peanut was looking for an opening too.

They walked slowly into the alley.

Thwaap!

Peanut went down on his knees. The man behind them was swinging a sap. He wasn't going to take their weapons away and kill them. He was going to beat them into brain damage, take their weapons away and kill them.

Ray started going down, leaning his head forward, trying to take as much force out of the blow as he could. And then it hit.

He fell on his knees and caught himself with his hands cushioned by a mattress of fat air. He didn't feel a thing, and time was either very slow or very fast. He wasn't sure. He was noticing everything including the song of the crickets, but he couldn't understand what any of it meant.

"You got 'em good."

He heard this.

The shotgun was prodding at him. His hands were stinging. Something funny was happening because Peanut was standing back up. He didn't like the damned shotgun one bit, so he reached up and grabbed the barrel with his left hand and pushed it over to the side. The man was looking at Peanut. Ray was up on his left foot and reached back and pulled the lightweight Smith and Wesson from the ankle holster and pushed it as hard as he could into the groin of the man in front of him and pulled the trigger three times.

The shotgun fired, and the blast ripped past. The heat burned, and he thought the side of his head was on fire. The sound roared for a half second, and then it seemed like someone had turned the volume off, and he couldn't hear anything.

What the fuck was Peanut doing. He looked like a dancing bear trying to kiss the man with the sap. He held the man's head with both hands and butted his face several times then delivered a savage punch to the neck, and the man stepped back. Ray emptied the gun into the man's chest.

Ray was standing up now, and the first man he had shot was writhing on the ground. Ray kicked the shotgun away. The Shitass Ronnie Gordon was running back to the limo. Ray couldn't have shot him, since he was out of ammunition, but didn't see the point in it anyway. It was Peanut's grudge.

"What the fuck's going on?" He shook his head. "I don't think I can hear anything."

"You hear me?" Peanut asked.

"Yes, but you sound funny."

"That shotgun knocked out your hearing in your left ear."

"I guess so."

"The Shitass is getting away," Peanut said.

"Let him. We got enough problems."

He looked at the man on the ground, who was moaning and calling for his mother.

"We ain't going to take him to the hospital. I guess we ought to put him down," Peanut said.

"We need to get these guys out of here."

Ray bent down next to the man on the ground and turned his good ear to him. He reached out and grabbed Ray's hand.

"Get it over with," the man said.

"How did you pick us up?"

"Following . . . we were following the driver, they said he was . . . followed . . . said he's not a bed wetter."

"Who said?"

"F . . . f . . . fuck . . . fuck you. You really fucked me up, buddy."

"Nothing personal, man. I was just returning the favor," Ray said.

'That's . . . that's a good one. Only . . . you're as dead as me. I guess we did each other." His laugh turned into a spasm and then he was quiet.

"I don't guess he's going to say no more," Peanut said.

"He's dead."

"Other one too."

They hadn't been paying much attention to the Shitass Ronnie Gordon, except to notice that he had driven the limo out of the far end of the alley and left.

"We got to get out of here and take these guys with us."

"I don't think they are going to fit in the trunk of the Honda," Peanut said.

"No, I think we're going to have to put them in the back seat."

"They're seeping blood."

"We can get rid of the car. Wash it out with a hose, then get it crushed for scrap."

"What you want to do with these two?"

"We can take them over to the garage and figure it out later, but let's get moving. Those gunshots are going to attract cops."

He grabbed a body under the arms, and Ray held it by the heels. He slid across the seat of the Honda, leaned the corpse back and slammed the door. Ray pushed the feet into the leg well, its head resting on the ledge.

The cellular phone rang. Peanut retrieved it from the glove box.

"No time to explain," he said. "We had an emergency. It's very fucked up. Meet us at the garage and bring lots of plastic tarps. Leave a bay door open."

Peanut picked up the man who had swung the sap and pushed him into the seat. He tried to make him sit up but he fell forward with his face in the other man's lap.

"Looks like he's going down on his friend," he said.

"Let's don't worry about how they look. It's not far to the garage. Let's just get the hell out of here."

There wasn't much traffic. Ray took it easy as he made his way to Howell Mill. His brain wasn't working worth a damn, so he was driving on mental auto-pilot, but he was good at looking cool with a twenty-five to life felony in the car.

"You're doing fine, Ray. How you feeling?"

"Still can't hear worth shit. How 'bout you? You took a hell of a shot."

"My brains ain't no more scrambled than usual."

"One thing I need to tell you, Peanut, is we can't get caught with these bodies. Ordinarily you're much better off just taking the bust and paying somebody off or running out on bail, but this is different. You get what I'm telling you?"

"Yeah. I was thinking along those lines myself."

"Reload my piece."

"Right."

"The other thing is I'm pretty fucked up. Tell me if I'm about to do something stupid."

"So far so good."

As they entered Howell Mill, a Buick station wagon with Cobb County plates and a "Family Values" bumper sticker pulled up beside them. The driver looked in the car and began yelling and shaking her fist.

Ray looked at her and rolled down the window, but couldn't understand what she was saying.

"I can't hear you," he said. "You got to yell louder."

She yelled and shook her fist again.

"Can you understand her?"

"She said something about unnatural lust and a cold shower." Peanut looked at the back seat. "It's them guys back there. I told you it looked like he was giving head."

"Lighten up. They're young and in love," Ray yelled at the lady.

She spluttered and quaked. Ray thought she might run them off the road. He considered firing a shot across the hood of her car and then was amazed that he had considered it. He was messed up for sure.

She was still yelling and shaking her fist as he pulled onto the street to the garage. The bay door was open.

"Jesus, Ginger is here."

"I called her, remember?"

"No."

They pulled in the building, and Ginger closed the door behind them. As Ray got out of the Honda, he felt woozier than he expected and leaned against the car roof to get his balance. Ginger looked terrified.

"Ginger. It's very fucked up. I wish you didn't have to see this."

"Just tell me you're okay, and I won't worry about the rest of it."

"I took a good shot, but I'm all right."

"What the hell happened?"

"The Shitass Ronnie Gordon set us up. These two guys got a start on beating me and Peanut to death."

"They're onto us?"

"They knew we were following Gordon."

"They tried to kill you?"

"Yes."

Peanut was busy with the corpses. He spread out a big blue plastic tarp and pulled the first body from the back seat, laid it on its back, then got the other.

It was the first real look Ray had at them when they weren't shoving a gun in his face.

"These guys look like they just got out of the army," Peanut said.

"Yee-oow. Who shot this one in the nuts," Ginger asked.

"That would be Ray 'I don't believe in violence' Justus."

"I don't believe in violence," Ray said. "But if you're going to use it, it helps if you're good at it."

"Cheap suits," Peanut said.

He pushed a suit coat open and pulled the wallet from the inside breast pocket.

"No labels, nothing in the wallet but money, no ID. He's got a piece in a fancy shoulder rig."

He pulled the gun from the holster and held it in front of him.

"Never seen one like this."

It looked like a custom-made job, short and compact with a fat silencer.

"Never seen one either, but I've heard about them," Ray said. "It probably uses subsonic .22 rounds, quiet. You use it up close. This is what they were going to kill us with."

"I don't like this a whole lot," Peanut said.

"Me either. Looks like your friend the Shitass Ronnie Gordon runs with an unusual crowd."

"We need to get rid of the bodies. You got any good ideas?"

"Let me think about it," Ray said.

"I know where I could put them through a wood chipper," Peanut said.

Ginger and Ray looked at each other.

"Wood chipper sounds like a good idea," Ginger said.

"I go for wood chipper," Ray agreed.

"Okay, later I'll take these suckers out to the country and put them through a wood chipper, but first I got a plan." Peanut said.

"A plan?"

"Yeah, it's based on a principle you taught me. When the shit hits the fan, they move the money."

"That's generally true."

"In that case, let's go steal it."

Shitass on the Run

"I NEED SOME air," Ray said.

They were driving the old white van from the store. Ginger was at Ray's apartment.

"You doing okay?"

"Brains are still mush."

"You going to puke?"

"I don't think so."

"Still deaf?"

"No, my hearing seems to be coming back."

They laid back a half block from the drive to the parking lot of the McLendon Building. Ray pulled a steel-gray, straw hat with a silk band low on his head, slipped on sunglasses and traded a hop-sack blazer for his suit coat and felt disguised enough not to be noticed.

He left the van and walked down the street talking to Peanut on the cellular and tried to spot the limo. It wasn't hard. Gordon had pulled it into the fire lane in a covered portion of the drive, near a walkway to the front entrance.

"He's here," Ray said. "I can see the car real good."

"My bet is he'll head south. Cross the street and head back north as far as you can still see him. That way you can give me the word, and I can pick you up as he leaves."

"Got you."

Ray walked a half block up Peachtree, stopped at a MARTA shelter and took a seat on the bench. He could see Peanut up the street.

"Nothing yet," he said to the phone. "Can you see me?"

"Yes."

"There are some citizens walking toward me, so I'm going to hang up. I'll stand up if we got to go."

"I'll call you."

A couple walked past but didn't stop. A black man wearing a dark-gray suit and nerd glasses, carrying an umbrella and an attaché, stopped in front of the bench. He looked up and down the street then sat next to Ray.

The man pulled a cellular phone from his pocket and spoke.

"I'm calling to confirm my appointment," he said.

Ray's phone rang.

"Yes?" Ray said.

"You still able to drive?"

"Yes."

"Bye."

"Amazing inventions," the man said.

"Pardon?" Ray asked.

"Mobile phones . . . they are amazing inventions."

"Yes, they are," Ray agreed.

"In my country there are many places where phones are rather scarce."

Ray nodded.

"I'm from Nigeria," he said.

"Yes," Ray agreed blandly.

"Have you ever been there?" he asked.

"No, I haven't."

"In my country we have giant rats that are fifty feet long from nose to tail," he said.

Ray looked at him, but didn't speak.

"You don't believe me?" he asked.

"No."

"But you said you've never been to Nigeria, so how would you know?"

"I don't know Nigeria for shit," Ray said, "but I do know rats."

"Are you looking for one now?" he asked.

Ray's mind came into focus with the same urgency as a driver who finds a cement mixer in his path. He figured either this guy is crazy, he wants to suck my dick, or he's with them . . . whoever they are.

He looked at the man like he thought he might start foaming and shaking at any moment.

"Are you feeling all right?" Ray asked. "You're dressed a bit warm for the weather."

"I'm used to much hotter," he said.

Ray guessed the man hadn't made up his mind if he was watching the building yet. There weren't any obvious bulges of guns. Was he covered by someone Ray didn't see?

He tried not to react, but the Shitass Ronnie Gordon was walking from the building carrying a large molded aluminum suitcase. He stood up.

"Sit here with me, my friend," the man said.

Ray's phone rang.

"Yes."

"You got company?" Peanut asked.

"Yes."

He saw the white van pull into traffic and head toward him.

"Why must you leave just now?"

"A friend has offered me a ride."

The van pulled next to them, and Peanut leaned over and opened the passenger door.

The man reached down to open his attaché, and while he was off balance Ray punched him in the face. He put his weight behind it and the Nigerian crumpled over. His cellular phone clattered to the pavement. Ray grabbed it and the attaché case and got in the van.

"I either just mugged one crazy son of a bitch Nigerian tourist, or we got company."

He worked the clasp of the attaché.

"Which one is it?" Peanut asked.

"Bunch of electronic bullshit and another one of these." He held a pistol similar to the one they had lifted from the corpse so Peanut could see it.

"Damn . . . who are these guys?"

"You see anybody following us?"

"No."

Ray looked back and saw the man he had hit struggling to get up. Blood ran from his nose. No one was coming to help him. He didn't see any cars following them.

"You got any ideas?"

"Maybe they are looking for us, but they're missing men and are spread thin. They had a man out front of the McLendon Building to see if we showed up. They probably have people near here. He was talking on the phone when he sat down, but I don't think he had made me yet."

Peanut was closing on the limo. Ray pressed re-dial on the mobile phone.

"What are you doing?"

"Quiet."

The phone rang once, then a man with a mechanical clipped voice answered.

"What have you got?"

Ray spoke into a cupped hand.

"In front of the building . . ."

"Say again. I can't understand."

"In front of the building . . ."

"Yes, go ahead."

"It was nothing."

"Very good." He hung up.

Peanut grinned.

"Hand me that gun," he said.

The limo was caught in traffic, and they were catching up fast.

"I might just bust a cap in the fucker right here."

"Don't even think about it."

He took the gun.

"Hold on, I'm going to ram the son of a bitch."

Ray fastened the seat belt and held his palms against the

dashboard. He was tossed forward as they made contact. He saw Gordon's head and neck whiplash. He doubted he would live long enough to visit a chiropractor.

Peanut put the van in park.

"Take it. I'm going after the fucker."

Gordon was out of the car and moving angrily toward the van. He hadn't recognized Peanut yet. Peanut opened the door and slid to the ground. Gordon froze, and Peanut shot his left thigh. Ray didn't hear much more than a hollow thump, but saw the leg spasm and begin to bleed.

The little pissant was having a gun-crazed mental meltdown on the street in Buckhead, and it was going to get them both killed or busted.

"You crazy fuck. You're not supposed to shoot him in the middle of Peachtree."

Either he couldn't hear or he wasn't going to listen. Ray jumped out of the van.

"You shot me you crazy son of a bitch. You can't touch me. I'm a government man. I'm a secret agent," Gordon yelled.

"Secret snitch is more like it," Peanut said.

"No man, I'm an agent. I got a badge."

"If you got a badge let's see it."

Gordon dug into his back pants pocket and pulled out a leather wallet. He flipped it open showing a stainless-steel shield engraved with "Special Agent" in its center.

"That thing don't mean shit. It doesn't even say special agent of what."

Ray reached into the limo and pulled the silver suitcase from the back.

"You can't take that," Gordon said.

"Fuck you," Peanut said.

"You shoot him again, and I'm going to kill you," Ray said. "You understand what I'm telling you?"

"Yes," Peanut gulped.

Ray slid the suitcase in the van.

"I told you, you can't kill me. I'm with the government. They'll never rest until they avenge my death. Same thing if you steal their money."

"Shut the fuck up," Peanut said.

"Why you got this punk for a partner?" Gordon asked Ray. "Hey Peanut, you ever tell him how you fucked for the bad boys in the joint?"

"Next time we meet, I'm not going to stop him from killing you," Ray said. "Meanwhile, I told your friends you helped us out, so they're looking for you too."

"No man, don't do that."

"Already done. Now get out of here."

They got back in the van and followed the limo till the Shitass found a turnoff.

"Let's see if we got a parade," Ray said.

"Gotcha."

He didn't see any sign of anyone following them.

The Nigerian's phone rang. He bit his tongue as he talked.

"Yellow."

"Can't understand you."

"Hell yell no."

"Did the money get off okay?"

"Headed north," Ray said.

"North . . . why did he go that way?"

"Don't know."

"Shit."

He hung up.

"They still don't know. We better haul ass."

"I'll drop you at your car, then I can take care of those guys at the garage."

"You know what I said about killing you was bullshit," Ray said.

"I know that, Ray. You were just trying to get my attention."

"Good. I'm glad you saw that."

"Right, and you know that thing the Shitass said about me being made into a punk."

"Oh hell, I knew that was bullshit. Who would believe the Shitass?"

"Nobody but another shitass."

The Nigerian's phone rang, and Ray answered it again.

"Yes."

"You're a dead man, you dumb son of a bitch."

He threw it out the window.

"Peanut, they're onto us."

Damage Assessment

SCHILLER SAT AT the desk in his suite at the Buckhead Ritz humming absent-minded fragments from the overture of *The Magic Flute.*

Flipping through the pages of a travel magazine, he thought, Tahiti is too crowded – I need some place where a strange face will be noticed. I don't want any unexpected guests.

It was odd that in spite of all the meticulous planning for his retirement, he hadn't picked a place yet. It probably meant he wasn't ready to let go of his professional life. Maybe he would wander until he found a spot that felt right.

Plank, out of breath, lurched into the room without knocking.

"There's a problem, Sir."

"Have a seat, Plank. You look tired. You can give your report sitting."

"The operation is fucked up beyond all recognition."

"How so?"

"Krog, Hardendorf, McLendon and the Shitass are MIA. Arizona has a smashed face."

Schiller wondered if Plank could tell he was stunned. No, he decided after a twenty second silence. He's thinks I'm being cool.

"Explain."

"As directed, we set up an operation to trap the people who were following Gordon. We believed the outcome would determine if the chauffeur was involved. The plan was to lead them into a two–man trap."

"That would be Krog and Hardendorf?"

"Yes. We got a call from Krog saying the trap was about to be sprung. Then a few minutes later the Shitass reported they were themselves ambushed by a large gang of about twenty men."

"You say twenty? It doesn't seem likely that Gordon would know anyone who could organize twenty people."

"I thought about that and came to the same conclusion. Since Gordon knew the location of the ambush, it wouldn't have taken many people to take it out. If they were good enough."

"We have to consider that possibility," Schiller agreed. "The Shitass's confederates may not be clever, but they could be very good at the street level violence they trade in. Please continue."

"We dispatched Arizona to keep an eye on the building. He saw Gordon return and had a man pegged for one of his accomplices. Gordon emerged from the building alone. He was carrying a large silver Haliburton which held the money."

"The money – how much?"

"Three-hundred-and-fifty thousand."

"Just the seed money?"

"Yes."

"Good, go on."

"At this point, the accomplice broke Arizona's nose and took his cell phone, gun and attaché."

"It sounds like he knew what he was doing."

"Arizona was impressed. The man moved fast enough to sucker punch him and afterwards kept his wits in taking the phone and the gun."

"Was this Peanut Shoke?"

"No, too old to be Shoke . . . He's in his forties. A man that could be Shoke picked him up in an old white van. The plates were stolen from another vehicle. They left following the Shitass.

"After this our information is sketchy. McLendon disappeared. We found the limousine abandoned. There was blood in it."

"Blood? Where?"

The driver's seat and the driver's side floor."

"Hmm . . . That's interesting. There's no indication that McLendon left with Gordon."

"No Sir, none at all."

"Conclusion?"

"Gordon set up the robbery with some of his hillbilly friends. Maybe the missing security guard was one of them along with Peanut Shoke and the fourth man who assaulted Arizona. Gordon lied about the animosity between himself and Shoke, but they probably did know each other in prison. My bet is that they double-crossed Gordon and shot him. McLendon has probably gone to earth and will come out when he knows it's safe."

"A very good job of intelligence analysis," Schiller said. Plank beamed at the praise. Actually, Schiller didn't think the facts, if they were the facts, indicated much of anything yet. But he knew from experience that it was good for morale in the ranks if the troops had the impression that someone knew what was going on.

"Assuming we've had losses, we need to generate some perspective. Krog and Hardendorf are soldiers. We are all soldiers. Sometimes soldiers are killed on risky operations."

"That's understood, Sir."

"If they are dead, we can't let grief or anger cloud our judgment. This is easier said than done."

"I see your point," Plank said.

"Our overriding goal is to find McLendon and get him safely back on board. Until he has delivered the money, McLendon is the operation and without this operation our country is weakened."

Schiller bent down and picked up a portable green plastic file box and flipped it open. Shuffling through the manila folders, he selected one with Maggie Donald written on the tab and pulled out a four by six color photograph.

"This is Bart Oakes's secretary. Harold has been following her, among others. She's an attractive woman."

Plank took the photo and looked it over.

"Yes, she is."

"She's sleeping with McLendon."

"So if he's in hiding, he might want company?" Plank asked.

"Yes."

"I'll pay her a visit."

"Convince her it would be wise to work with us. That will be all."

As Plank turned to leave the room, Schiller added the afterthought, "When you convince her, no rough stuff. Just talk to her."

"Yes, Sir."

"I'm very serious about that."

Schiller was exhausted. He lay on his back on the bed and put one pillow behind his head and covered his eyes with another.

He needed to think about possibilities. The more he considered Plank's scenario for the loss of the men and the money, the less likely it seemed. But now he needed sleep.

He imagined himself lying in a hammock. Soon he was dreaming about life on a sandy island, rocking on the front porch of an open bungalow, a cool breeze tickled the back of his neck.

He walked to an open deck and looked down and saw a woman walking on the edge of the surf. She saw him and waved. It was a wave that a person in love would make.

He waved back, but he couldn't tell who she was.

Maggie Has Company

As SOON AS McLendon had called to say he was going to hide at his apartment, Maggie had Frippo, the security guard at the Foundation, follow her home to her town house on a side street off Piedmont and wait while she recovered from the top shelf of her closet the revolver her husband had given her.

Frippo had examined the handgun, cleaned it and then loaded it.

"It's in good working order, and, with this ammo, it's going to stop them if you hit them."

She had thanked him and after he left, gone upstairs to relax in the small whirlpool in the master bath, putting the gun and the portable phone on the shelf behind her head.

As the turbulent water massaged her muscles and the tension slipped from her body, she felt she could drift off to sleep. She imagined the island paradise where she would live once she had her share of McLendon's money. A place without cares where you could pick food from the trees . . .

Then, without thinking, she grabbed the gun and the phone and stood up.

The bath pump had stopped and the lights were off. No electricity – it was too coincidental to be an accident. She tried the phone. It didn't work.

Of course, she thought, the portable needed power to work. She slipped on a heavy terry cloth robe and walked to the bedroom. The phone there was dead also.

The downstairs door shut quietly. The entry floor creaked. Someone was in the house.

She had wondered if something like this happened, would she be so frightened she couldn't protect herself. She had never thought she was brave and was surprised to be coolly appraising the situation.

As she saw it, if the intruder was looking for her he would come to her. If she lay in wait, she would have the advantage, because it is always easier to hide than to seek.

Maybe like Scarlett O'Hara with the Yankee looter, she would shoot the intruder and bury him behind the house.

She crept back to the bathroom and hid beside the doorway.

He was moving quietly through the house. She had no idea where he was for five minutes and then she heard the stairway banister click as it shifted with weight, stocking feet on the carpet outside the bedroom, and fabric brushing against the door.

She gave it a beat then stepped into the bathroom doorway, holding the pistol in both hands and hissed, "Freeze."

The man's back was turned toward her. He raised his hands slowly and she saw they were empty.

"Turn toward me, slowly."

"Yes Ma'am."

As he turned, she saw he had the body of an athlete. His face was handsome but didn't show much intelligence, and oddly, he wore glasses identical to Johnny McLendon's.

"If you're a good boy, we can talk and you can leave. If you're a bad boy, I'm going to kill you and pull your pants around your ankles. Then I'll call the police. Do you understand?"

"Yes Ma'am."

"Now, lace your fingers together tightly behind your head, and drop to your knees."

"Yes Ma'am."

"Very good."

"Ma'am. I'm with the CIA."

"How very interesting. I thought you weren't supposed to admit that."

"I work for Schiller, and he's working with Bart Oakes."

"What a disappointment. I'm not going to get to use all those nice interrogation techniques my husband taught me. You're giving up without a fight."

Actually, her husband hadn't taught her much at all. She was improvising, but it seemed to be going well.

"Husband?"

"If you're actually Company, you might have known him – Rick Donald?"

"Yes Ma'am. I knew him. I'm just telling you this because you're one of us."

"One of us? How odd that you disabled my power and phone and broke into my home. If I was 'one of us,' you could have simply made an appointment."

"I should have done that."

"What's your name?" she asked.

"Plank."

"Well Plank, why have you broken into my home?"

"To send a message to McLendon. Tell him Schiller will guarantee his safety."

"I will certainly do that," she said.

Plank's face seemed to go blank and she wondered what was happening. He didn't say anything and she was frightened again. She tightened her finger on the trigger in case he rushed her.

"Anything else?" she asked.

"You know there is."

"I don't think so."

"You want me to put on your clothes don't you?"

"What are you talking about?"

He seemed to be in a fugue state – not moving, listening to distant music.

"You want me to put on women's clothes . . ."

"No. I don't know what you are talking about. I just want you to leave."

"You always do."

"Always? We've never met before. You're crazy. Come back to earth and leave."

She cocked the revolver. His concentration returned as he looked at the pistol.

"I'm going now."

"On your way out, reconnect the power and phone," she said.

Plank Reports

"SHE'S RICK DONALD'S widow."

"Jesus. Why wouldn't Bart tell us something like that?" Schiller asked.

"I don't know, but I had the feeling I was dealing with a highly trained operative. She saw me coming. I killed the power and phone and checked for signs of a security system, but she still caught me red-handed."

Schiller couldn't tell why, but he was certain there was something about the encounter Plank wasn't telling. He seemed embarrassed. Maybe it was just that he was caught when he shouldn't have been.

"Plank, let me be candid. This is a major, possibly dangerous development in our unfolding operation. We don't know who she might be working for, perhaps the CIA Inspector General's Office or even the FBI. We are operating without charter and are not in a position where we can afford to have our operatives holding back facts."

"How could you tell?" Plank asked.

"It's what I do and I've been doing it since before you were born."

"Yes, of course, sorry . . . this won't go any further, will it?"

"No," Schiller reassured him.

"Well, when she had the gun on me, she told me she wanted me to put on women's clothes."

"Are you serious?"

"Yes, I'm afraid so. I told her I wouldn't and she said, 'You can go now. Oh, and on the way out, reconnect the power and phone.'"

"Amazing. She's a cool one," Schiller said, but he suspected he was catching a glimpse of Plank's peculiar madness.

"Yes, Sir. After the operation, I'd like to give her back every bit of that and more."

"You'll do nothing of the kind until we know who her friends are." So this was how it worked, Schiller thought. Plank imagined some humiliation that justified his brutality.

"And if she doesn't have any?" Plank asked.

"Then it's between the two of you. None of my affair. But only after the operation."

It was a safe enough concession, since by the end of the operation Plank would be dead. The phone rang and Schiller picked it up.

"Schiller here."

"This is Maggie Donald."

"Yes, Mrs. Donald."

"Call me Maggie, Bill."

"Yes, of course, Maggie."

"I've spoken with Johnny. He'll be at his condominium this evening if you'd like to visit. I'll be with him."

"Yes. I'd like that. Shall we say eight?"

"That would be good," Maggie said. "And Bill, you know I really didn't appreciate that visit this afternoon. We aren't going to have any more of those, are we?"

"No, of course not."

She hung up.

"That was your girlfriend," Schiller said.

Plank curled his lip. He looked like he was contemplating pain he hoped to inflict on her.

"I don't know who she's working for, but she's bringing McLendon in."

Get Outta Town

RAY DIDN'T HAVE any idea how hot he was. He didn't want to take any chances, and even more important, he didn't want to lead anyone to Ginger. Ordinarily, he would fade away, but love was making life complicated.

He picked up the Voodoo Cadillac, then found a pay phone on Ponce in front of the Clermont Hotel and called her.

"Hello." She sounded frightened.

"It's me."

"Thank God. I've been worried sick. Are you okay?"

"Don't worry about me, baby. I'm doing good. It's done."

"I need to see you."

"You will, but first you need to listen to me. Have you got your clothes together?"

"Yes."

"You know where I keep the nine and the vests?"

"Yes."

"Grab them and your clothes and get out of there. Head north and find an out-of-the-way motel. When you leave take Piedmont. Get a room for Peanut too. Leave your cell phone. Call me to let me know where you are. You all right with that, baby?"

"Yes, but please hurry. I need you."

"I love you," Ray said.

Ray drove up North Avenue to Rio and cut through the parking lot so he could see Piedmont. Traffic was light so it was easy to spot Ginger as she drove past in her beat-up orange Tercel.

She wasn't being followed – the first hint that they might still be anonymous.

Keeping Busy

RAY DIDN'T LIKE the idea of driving back to the garage. It was too close to the scene of the gunfight and could be crawling with men in their funny thug suits and nerd glasses. Still, it didn't seem like there was much choice. He had to make sure Peanut was on top of the body situation or the whole problem could get even worse.

He got out of the car and walked upstairs to the Lambda Pharmacy and bought some hair dye and headed to the house.

He could still feel Ginger's presence at the apartment. He took his shirt off to color his hair, then had an idea. There was a big box of Ginger's belongings in the bedroom which she hadn't yet unpacked. He shuffled through it and found her clippers, slipped on the half inch comb, and gave himself a buzz cut.

He rubbed the dye into his hair, waited ten minutes and showered. His plan had been to match his lighter facial hair and maybe grow a mustache or a Van Dyke. He had done a fairly good job of matching the colors, but it still looked shocking to him.

He figured he was about to discover if it was true that blondes had more fun.

He tried to imagine a look that would say, I'm rich – don't fuck with me, and decided to pose as a rich real-estate developer. That meant Polo slacks and knit shirt, Cole-Hahn slip-ons, five-hundred-dollar belt, three-hundred-dollar shades, and a large gold watch.

One of the advantages of being a thief is that you never pay full price.

"Jesus, Ray . . . I almost shot you." Peanut was peering around the garage door. "The hair and the outfit really threw me off. Didn't know it was you at first."

Ray slid inside.

"What you doing?"

"Keeping busy."

"You got any clean cash?"

"I got a couple stashes," Peanut said.

"At your squat?"

"No."

"Good."

"You need some?"

"No, I was wondering if you were covered. Ginger got away clean. Nobody has picked me up yet, but I don't know if I'd go home if I was you. I think the Shitass probably made you."

"I've been thinking along those lines myself. I might check it at a distance to see if they're there."

Ray looked around the garage and didn't see the bodies.

"Our friends are in the back of the van. I've got them covered up real good."

The van was partially masked for painting.

"How long is that going to take?"

"Another hour. No sense in you hanging around."

"I think I'll stick."

"Ginger will be wanting to see you."

"Peanut, I think I'll stick around."

"I know I screwed the pooch. You don't have to tell me that. I don't blame you for not trusting me. I've really been acting stupid, but I'm back on track."

Peanut was talking sincerely and acting sane.

He wanted to say, "Peanut you've been fucking-up big time," but this wasn't the time for therapy.

Instead, he said, "It isn't that I don't trust you, man. But when you move these guys, you're going to need some back-up."

"Yeah, okay. Why don't you take the money and hang out someplace. I'll call when I'm ready to roll."

"Call me on Ginger's cell phone. I think it's the least likely to be intercepted."

"Sure."

He crossed over behind the van and picked up a nylon duffel.

"I switched bags."

"Good plan."

"Gave it a quick count. There's better than three hundred thousand."

"All right."

"Ray, I know you're going to think I'm crazy, but I really fucked-up. I think I got us in over our head. I've been looking at these guys. I'm afraid they're probably government. It's too heavy for us. I think maybe we should find a way to give the money back."

"That may be the best plan," Ray agreed.

"Here."

Peanut pressed something into his palm. He looked down and saw it was a pair of black nerd glasses.

As he drove away, Ray felt much better about their predicament. Peanut was recovering both his sanity and his sense of humor. Together, they could work their way out of this mess.

Waffle Time

RAY DECIDED TO camp at the Waffle House on Howell Mill. As soon as he sat at the booth he realized he hadn't eaten, so he ordered a short stack, eggs and sausage.

The waitress, a young, good-natured country girl with short black hair, thought he was the bee's knees and made a fuss over him. As a result, his table was very clean, the salt, pepper, syrup and utensils were well organized and his cup was full.

Ray suspected that if he made a move he could get more than his coffee warmed, then wondered what he was thinking about that for. He was in the middle of a job that had blown up and had a girlfriend to think about. He guessed it was proof that old habits die hard. Nothing wrong with entertaining thoughts.

He had put the cell phone on the table, and it rang. The waitress raised an eyebrow and smiled.

"Busy man," she said.

Ray picked up the phone and put it to his good ear.

"Yo."

"It's me." Me was Ginger.

"What's up?"

"You ready for a night in the Motel Deluxe."

"Sounds like a big time."

"Roll on up in the Gaines de Ville."

"Gotcha."

She hung up.

Ray fished change from his wallet and walked over to the pay phone.

"Information for what city?"

"Gainesville."

"What listing?"

"Motel Deluxe."

A machine voice returned a number and Ray hung up and dialed it.

A man with Appalachian diphthongs answered.

"Moe-teyull Dee-la-ux."

He made each word sound like it had twelve syllables.

"This is Randal. I'm going to meet my little lady up there. Wonder if you could spot me some directions, podnuh."

"I'd be most de-lighted."

As the man finished a rhapsodic rendition of the way to the Motel Deluxe, the cell phone rang.

"Ready to roll," Peanut said.

"I've never seen anyone talk on so many phones at once," the waitress said.

"Got to run, darlin', but this should cover it."

Ray handed her a twenty. From the sparkle in her eyes, he could tell she was in love.

"You come back," she said.

In the Pines

FOLLOWING PEANUT UP North I-85, Ray admired the paint job he'd done on the van. It was a shade Peanut called silver leaf, a light green, that made the van look much newer than it was. It blended into traffic so you didn't really notice it.

This was the reason he'd gone partners with Peanut in the first place. Your average criminal imbecile would either have not bothered to paint the van or done it in a plain dark blue that said, just painted by a nitwit. But Peanut was subtle.

It reminded Ray of a story. When Peanut was in the joint he'd worked his way into the auto shop and was hell with a spray gun.

It seemed like every guard and sheriff's deputy in the state had a shit beater they needed painted. Peanut suspected they'd buy'em then sell'em for much more once he'd painted them.

Anyway, when Peanut was a short-timer he invented a special paint mix that would fade in six months revealing messages on the undercoat like: I SUCK DONKEY DICKS or WANT TO FUCK MY WIFE?

This was another reason Ray liked Peanut. He might be a psycho, but he had a good sense of humor about it.

His mind wandered as he followed Peanut for about thirty minutes without seeing a tail, but it snapped back into focus as the van's blinker went on. They exited to a secondary highway and followed it west past a large asphalt field holding a gas station, truck stop, restaurant, motel, cat house.

Four miles further and they turned left on a county road, then a gravel drive with "Posted, No Trespassing" signs. It turned to dirt, then a pine straw padded track through dense woods.

The chipper was in a clearing next to a small corrugated shed with a padlock on the door. As Ray stepped from the car to the soft forest floor and smelled the sweet resinous air, he thought, it's been too long since I've been in the piney woods. I need to go to a place like this where I can wash the dirt off my soul.

"Place belongs to a friend of mine who's out of town for a while until a situation cools down. Nothing to do with the law . . . a pissed-off husband."

Peanut unlocked the shed and stepped inside. Ray heard him moving things around and finally he emerged carrying a chain saw, a Husky 90.

"This will cut them boys like butter."

"Best to use the right tool for the job," Ray agreed.

"Follow this path through the trees and you come to a fishing pond. I figured if you could help me fit it on the trailer hitch, I can pull the chipper over there and shoot them boys' shredded meat over the water so the fish can have a big meal."

"I know it would make them feel much better to know they were being put to a good use," Ray said.

"They're returning to the great circle of life."

Peanut got in the van and began backing as Ray gestured with his hands, bringing him within six inches of the tow bar of the chipper.

"Good job," Peanut said.

"I'm not one for unnecessary wrestling with machines."

They lifted the front of the chipper and rolled it slowly forward till they could drop the socket over the ball of the trailer hitch. Peanut screwed it tight.

"We're only going about a hundred feet at low speed so I'm not going to mess with the safety chains. Hop in. Let's ride."

"I think I'll walk it," Ray said.

The van rolled slowly down a path through the pines. As Ray followed behind it, he saw a break in the trees ahead. In another fifty feet he saw the pond.

Peanut did a wide U-turn, then backed to the edge of the shore. He opened the side doors from the inside and stepped

out pulling the tarp with the corpses after him. It hit the ground
without bouncing.

Ray shuffled along not trying to make any time, enjoying the
walk in the woods until he caught up with the van.

"These guys must weigh three-fifty wrapped up like this.
Help me drag them away from the van."

"Sure."

"There's not much point in you sticking around," Peanut
said. "I got us into it, I don't mind cleaning up the mess. I'll
take care of the Honda. Get everything squared away."

"Ginger got you a room at the Motel Deluxe in Gainesville."

Peanut smiled and nodded his head in appreciation.

"Deluxe – that sounds like Ginger," Peanut said.

"That's what she is – deluxe all the way," Ray agreed.

As Ray walked back to the Voodoo Cadillac the chain
saw began to whine. Then the throaty sound of the chipper
kicked in.

He had to get out of this place. The rotting leaves on the
ground of the clearing smelled like the grave.

He drove toward Gainesville and thought about how being
in love with Ginger was complicating his life. It wasn't just that
she was beautiful or fun. She felt like part of him that had been
missing for as long as he could remember.

Loving a person that much can change the way you look
at things.

He felt sick over the killings, but there wasn't a damn thing
he could do about it.

Oakes Loses His Shit

THE CRUISE CONTROL for his brain was broken. Ever since McLendon had called Maggie with the news that twenty well-armed hillbillies in blue bib overalls were about to attack, Oakes' mind had raced so fast that it was useless — like tires spinning in the mud, no contact with terra firma, no movement, just a frantic whine and desperation and the claustrophobic panic at being trapped.

To make matters worse, Frippo had escorted Maggie home, leaving him alone in the building. He had bolted the steel core front door and retrieved a riot gun from the case in the guard room.

He didn't know if he would know how to use it. He wasn't even sure how to hold it. In the end, it made him feel more ridiculous than safe, but he carried it anyway.

He started by searching the ground floor. There were bars on the windows, but he made sure the windows were locked anyway.

Then he searched the second and third stories. He went into rooms he hadn't seen in years. The building was an enormous empty tomb — no, he didn't want to think about dead people, it was an abandoned theater, a theater of war, a theater for private dramas, a casino where the stakes were lives and countries. Mostly it was empty now.

What if? What if they had changed the Constitution and Reagan was still President? What if the congress had quit fooling around and made him king or emperor? None of this would be happening now. By now you would be hearing the cavalry's hoof beats. Ride the villains down. Cut them with a well-swung saber. Blood on boots and saddles.

What if the army of villains showed up now? What if they

blasted the door open and came in? Should he call the police and blow the secrecy of the operation and his chance at the money? What chance?

He wished his mind would stop. He pulled the two-liter bottle of cheap scotch from the bottom shelf of the credenza behind his desk. Normally, he poured it into a crystal decanter to convince himself it was better than swill, but today he filled a water glass and took a series of large gulps. His mind wasn't working sober, so why not?

Elation. The sense of well-being was almost comic. Here he was, feeling on top of the world in the middle of a collapsing tower of shit. As he laughed out loud, the phone rang.

"Yes?" he answered tentatively.

"I'm calling for Oakes."

"Who should I say is calling?"

"Cut the shit. This is Plank."

"What's going on?"

"Shut up and listen."

Oakes was silent, and after a few seconds Plank asked, "You still there?"

"I was listening," Oakes said sarcastically.

"Any more smartass and I'm going to take a knife to your face. You understand?"

"Yes."

"We need to meet."

"Why?"

"That's not a valid question."

"Okay," Oakes said.

"You know where Ponce de Leon Avenue is."

"Yes."

"Meet me at the Blue Lantern on Ponce de Leon at eight."

"Tell your boss, Schiller, I need to know what's going on."

"Schiller doesn't know about this meeting, and you're not going to tell him. You understand?"

"Yes."

"He's an old man, and he's getting slow on the uptake."

"I see."

"You tell him I said that, and I'll call you a liar. Then I'll filet you."

"But I'm about to be attacked by the hillbillies," Oakes whined.

"Throw a teapot at them," Plank suggested as he hung up.

Oakes didn't have a feeling of well-being any more. He felt drunk and stupid. God help me, he thought, I need to sober up.

He heard a knocking at the door and almost wet his pants. The knocking was still going on when he got back from the bathroom. He went to the guard room to see who it was on the security monitor.

Maggie Strokes Oakes

MAGGIE DONALD KNEW that Bart's mental railroad was probably going off the rails, so she decided to stop by the Foundation before she met Johnny McLendon.

She pounded at the door, but nothing happened.

Each time she had been tested in the last weeks, she had surprised herself at her cool reactions and mastery of each situation. She had come to the conclusion that she didn't need Dunbarton Oakes to stage a robbery. In fact, she was certain that he would be a liability, an expensive liability since he would end up with half the money.

She knocked again. Nothing happened for several minutes, then she thought she heard steps on the other side of the door. It burst open suddenly.

"Come in, quick," Oakes said.

He's a mess, Maggie thought. He's drunk, and it looks like he's falling apart. I think I'd better give him a blow job.

He bolted the door as soon as she was in the large entry hall.

"We're going to be attacked by an army of crazed hillbilly convicts."

"Bart, darling, you need to relax."

She put her arms around him and pushed her hips into his. Their lips met, and he thrust his tongue deep into her mouth. It tasted stale, like cheap scotch.

She hiked up her skirt and went down on one knee in front of him. He was already hard when she unzipped his fly and took him in her mouth.

This was the part they never showed in Vivian Leigh's movies when she was being the sexual adventuress, but she imagined it was about as romantic as this.

He pushed much harder and deeper than she intended and when she broke away for air, he took her hand, pulled her to her feet and led her to the sofa in his office.

It looked like a blow job wasn't going to do it. Given his mental condition it didn't seem like a good time to argue so she quickly took off her clothes, lay back on the couch and spread her legs.

As usual, he came down on top of her quickly, entered her before she was ready, and began pumping. About all she could do was gasp and think of six million dollars.

As far as she could see, the only thing Bart Oakes had going for him as a lover was a hair trigger. After less than twenty thrusts he began making his customary peeping sound, like a chicken, then fell forward onto her with his full weight.

"God, that was great," he said.

"Oh, yes, yes," she agreed, "but I can't breathe."

"Sorry," he said.

He rolled onto the floor and sat with his back against the sofa running his hand over her breast.

"That was so good. Let's do it again."

"It was so good, I think I'd like to remember it for a while. You know, enjoy the glow. Anyway, I need to go see McLendon."

"I hate to think of that."

"It's hard. But together the two of us can get through this. We have to remember what this is about. We don't just want the money. We need it. In fact, we deserve it.

"We don't have any idea what happened. We only have a hysterical story told to McLendon by the chauffeur. Johnny McLendon was frightened, and he acted stupidly."

Oakes perked up as he absorbed the idea.

"You're right about that. We only have the chauffeur's word, which isn't worth much."

"You know what I think happened?" Maggie asked. "I think Gordon shot Schiller's men and went back to McLendon with a crazy story. Johnny handed him the money. He ran off with it. End of story. Not much to it."

"That makes sense."

He was thinking it over. Maggie noticed with alarm that his hand was no longer stroking her breasts, but was inching toward her groin.

"I really want to do it again," he said.

His face was distorted with a crazy neediness. Whatever the cost, she had to keep him from imploding and ruining her chance for the money.

"Sure, baby, come on up."

At the moment her entered her he looked at her as if he was about to speak, but had decided not to.

"Uh . . . What is it . . . uh . . . darling?"

"Before you got here, I got a call from Plank."

"Tell me more."

"He's going to meet me tonight."

"More . . . more . . ."

"Schiller doesn't know about it," he gasped.

Maggie moaned.

"He told me . . . Oh God . . . he told me not to tell Schiller."

He collapsed on top of her.

"That was so wonderful."

"I can't breathe."

As she slipped on her clothes, she needed a shower – not only for her body but for her peace of mind.

He was acting distant, almost hostile. She had always felt that Bart was a friend until they started having sex. Now, she thought he didn't like her very much. He was one of those men who hated the vulnerability they showed when making love.

It was odd, but she had almost come to enjoy the affair with Johnny McLendon. He was so pathetic that he could be lovable in a grotesque and perverse way.

It related to a theory she had about meat: the stupider the

animal the better it tasted. Johnny even liked to think of himself as Spike the Dog. Now that was stupid. She couldn't imagine anything much stupider and yet he was surprisingly good in bed.

Bart could compare interpretations of a Monteverdi opera and he was terrible at sex. Of course, she was smart herself and thought she was good at it, so maybe the theory only applied to men. Her husband was smart, but that was love. This probably just applied to casual sex. Casual sex was best with stupid men.

For years, she had heard Bart whine about his round-heeled wife who ran off with the carnie artist. Maggie had reevaluated the legend after learning something about Bart's use of his ding dong. The poor woman had been lucky enough to find a man with swivel hips and a sense of humor in bed, who was also fun to talk with at breakfast.

She wished Plank would beat the hell out of Bart Oakes. Too bad that for her own good she couldn't let it happen.

"Plank paid me a visit," she said.

Oakes was putting his clothes on dreamily. This caught his attention.

"Yes?"

"He broke into my house."

"Good God. What did you do?"

"I had a gun. I questioned him then let him leave."

"Oh no."

"Do you have a gun, Bart?"

"No."

"Plank is dangerous. Why don't you call Frippo? When you meet Plank, have him go along."

All Aboard

JOHNNY MCLENDON HAD a sheepish look as he opened the door.

"I guess I sort of ran off the rails," he said.

"No problem, Johnny. You were protecting yourself. You need to do that. Without you, there's no operation," Schiller said.

Schiller followed McLendon through a short entrance hall to a spacious living room whose far wall was floor to ceiling glass with a spectacular view of the midtown skyline.

"I've got scotch and more scotch," McLendon said. "Oh, and I've got ice and water too."

Pretending McLendon had been clever, Schiller said, "Hard choice but I'll go with scotch on the rocks."

McLendon was clumsily fussing around at the wet bar.

"Maggie thinks Gordon was in on it," McLendon said.

"So do I."

"I never would have guessed that. He was always honest with me."

"People can fool you, Johnny."

"I'm usually a good judge of character."

Schiller heard movement in the back of the apartment. He guessed it was Maggie Donald.

"Did you know he is called 'the Shitass Ronnie Gordon'?" Schiller asked.

"No . . . you mean the whole thing? Shitass and all?"

"Yes?"

"Why do they call him that?"

"I asked Gordon that very question. He said it was because he is a shitass."

"I wish I'd known that."

"Don't worry about it, Johnny. We need to get back on track.

That's the important thing."

Maggie Donald walked into the room, glanced at Schiller and smiled.

"I was just making Bill a drink."

"Let me take care of it," she said.

She looked at the one McLendon was making, poured it out, and started again.

God, she was beautiful. She had just washed her hair and blown it dry and it hung around her head like a gold halo. She wore a black silk robe that draped her body giving provocative hints but no more.

She gave Schiller his drink and looked directly at him.

"Johnny, I left my suitcase in my car. Would you mind getting it for me?"

"I was thinking, I'd like to be called Spike from now on. Spike McLendon sounds more like the sort of guy I am."

"All right then, fetch, Spike," Maggie said.

Schiller saw a look pass between them. McLendon had a stupid expression on his face, one that Schiller had never seen outside of chemical interrogation. He understood then that Maggie Donald had power over McLendon.

"Sure Maggie," McLendon said. "Arf, arf."

Maggie followed him to the door, then made sure it was shut.

"I'm glad we have some time alone," Schiller said.

"It's not accidental."

"I suspected not."

"Have a seat."

He sat on a long beige leather sofa. She sat next to him.

"Who are you working for?" Schiller asked.

"I've been working for the Foundation. You know that, but I'm afraid Bart Oakes has turned out to be a disappointment."

"How so?"

"He's more a whimper than a bang."

"I see, and McLendon?"

"A temporary arrangement."

"He seems quite taken by you, and he has an enormous amount of money."

"He could never have enough to make it a permanent arrangement."

"Who then?"

"I could work with you if you were nice to me."

"With me?"

"Yes."

He slowly slid his hand to her knee. She put hers on top of his.

"What would you bring to the partnership?"

"Let me see." She pretended to think. "Did you know Plank is seeing Bart Oakes tonight?"

"No. Should I?"

"Evidently not. Plank threatened to hurt him if he told you."

"Yes. I see."

"Looks like little Mr. Plank is going off the reservation."

"And what do you think that means?" he asked.

"Nothing is as it appears to be."

She had that right. Things were even less what they seemed than he had imagined. If Plank was melting down this soon, he would have to move faster than he had thought.

"Would you like to know what they talked about?" she asked.

"Certainly."

"I'll find out tomorrow and let you know."

"It can't get back to Plank."

"No, of course not."

"Sorry. I guess that was obvious."

"Don't worry about it."

"You have to get Johnny . . ."

"Spike," she corrected him.

"Spike. You have to get Spike back on board. He needs to have the money together as soon as possible."

"Not a problem," she said.

"No, I'm beginning to get the idea that it won't be."

Oakes and Plank on Ponce

FRIPPO SAT BESIDE Bart Oakes in the front seat of the ancient Volvo. At work, he was a practical nonentity, a man who disappeared within the blue guard uniform.

Tonight he was a different, much tougher man. His salt and pepper hair was combed back and held in place with pomade. He wore discount store running shoes, old chinos, a cheap golf shirt, and a dark-blue windbreaker whose sleeves were pushed up to his elbows, revealing a Special Forces tattoo on his left forearm.

It wasn't that cool out tonight, so Oakes suspected the windbreaker was to hide a gun.

"Are you armed?" he asked.

"Yep. I'm carrying a high-cap nine and a back-up."

Oakes didn't have any idea what he was talking about, but it sounded impressive so he felt more secure.

He pulled off Ponce and parked in front of the building. Frippo climbed out of the passenger's side and stretched, allowing Oakes a glimpse of a holster with an ugly automatic.

"The Blue Lantern, huh? This place used to be a real joint. A low point even for Ponce de Leon." Frippo pointed across the street toward town. "That used to be the Army Induction Center."

Frippo led the way inside. They had arrived a half hour early, and once they found Plank wasn't there yet they studied the menu. They both settled on the Jerk Chicken Muffaletta and iced tea, got their drinks and sat down in the last booth by the utensil dispenser.

"Here's the plan," Frippo said. "When he comes in I'm going to stand up and make my presence felt, then I am going to go

up to the front of the place and find a seat. You slide to the
outside. Don't let him sit beside you and force you back in
the corner.

"That way he sits with his back to me and the rest of the room
and gives us the psychological and tactical advantage. Otherwise,
he's got some friends out there, he's got you trapped and me
caught between them.

"Not to say something's going to happen, but this way if it
does we do all right."

"Thanks," Oakes said. "That's what I brought you along for,
and you haven't disappointed me."

"Just what I do," Frippo said. "What's he look like?"

"I don't know that I've ever seen him."

"Don't worry, I'll spot him. I can spot a jumper at a
thousand yards."

Oakes wasn't sure he knew what sort of man to expect. He
was sure he couldn't spot him at a distance, but Frippo seemed
unconcerned. The waiter brought their sandwiches and while
Oakes picked at his, Frippo ate with enthusiasm.

"Want to finish before he gets here," Frippo explained.

He was examining the crumbs when an athletic-looking man
strode through the front doorway. He wore a dark suit and
black T-shirt and, oddly, black plastic framed glasses similar to
the stupid-looking ones favored by the cretin McLendon.

Frippo stood up.

"Slide over," he said.

Oakes slid to the edge of the bench seat and watched the
two men lock eyes like they were each aiming a weapon. Plank
walked toward them briskly.

"Beat it, gramps," Plank said.

Frippo looked at him like he thought he was a bug on the
linoleum.

"Pathetic, the pussies they're giving berets to these days."
He let the statement sink in, then said, "Son, I'm giving
you a pass because you don't know who you're talking to,

but if you ever speak to me like that again I'm going to rip your fucking head off and piss down your throat. You understand?"

The words hit Plank like a granite curbstone. He blinked then forced a smile.

"Yes," he said.

Silently, Frippo picked up his iced tea and walked to the opposite wall at the front of the room. He quickly turned to the window and scanned the street, then evidently satisfied Plank was alone, sat at a booth facing them.

"Slide over," Plank said.

"No. I think I'll sit here."

"I like the outside."

"There's an outside seat on the opposite side of the table."

"Slide the fuck over," Plank snarled.

Oakes looked at Frippo and nodded his head toward Plank. Without making a big deal over it, Plank sat down across from him, his back to the door.

From the reaction to Frippo, Oakes thought he understood something about Plank. He searched his inventory of poses to find the right fit for the situation and decided on the military-industrial colonel interviewing a rowdy platoon sergeant. He shouldn't try to challenge Plank's macho aggression, but instead be very casual about it. Imply his own inability to physically challenge Plank was irrelevant. The system would grind Plank into mush for him.

Oakes spoke softly but leaned forward to add force to his voice.

"For the future of your career there's something you need to understand. There are political operatives and there are military operatives.

"To put it more personally, I am political, and you are military. People like you often have contempt for people like me because you see us as weak. On occasion this leads to a foolish miscalculation.

"You are in the middle of making one of these miscalculations. You assume that because you are younger and more fit, you can intimidate me. Instead, you are about to land on the shit list of your nightmares.

"The reason for this is that while you may control the guns, I control the money. If you want to quickly lose all of your friends, all you need to do is inspire a good up-your-ass investigation by some congressional staff feminist-from-hell, followed by a loss of funding. Do you understand?"

He was blowing smoke and was scared as hell, but Plank seemed to be going for it. As he suspected, the man didn't have a clue about how things were done beyond the most basic operational level. The beauty of the situation was that if he was going behind Schiller's back there was nobody he could ask to explain further.

"Yes, Sir. I understand."

"Fine. Now how can I help you?"

"I had a few questions I was wondering if you could answer."

"I'll answer what I can."

Plank didn't say anything, and Oakes wondered if he had intimidated Plank too much.

"Go ahead," he prompted.

"Have you noticed that something is very different about the way that Schiller has organized this operation?"

"Tell me what you mean."

"For starters, he isn't involving the Foundation."

"Yes, of course I noticed that since I'm it's Director. What else do you have in mind?"

"His allowing McLendon to use the Shitass Ronnie Gordon was an amazing lapse in security that cost us two men."

"The Shitass what?"

"The chauffeur," Plank explained.

"Yes, the chauffeur, of course. I'd never heard him called that. You're right. It was an appalling lapse."

"Then, of course there's the way the operation is set up. Schiller says it's because we're using drug money, and he needs absolute deniability to protect the agency. But the set up is too odd for that to be the only reason."

"Explain," Oakes said.

"Well, supposedly we have two teams. One is responsible for organizing the black bag job. There were six of us collecting McLendon's funding and setting up the administrative function. The other team is running the actual op. No contact between the two. I haven't seen any evidence of a second team."

"How has Schiller explained this?"

"First the need to establish deniability. Also, he said that we had to isolate McLendon from his financial advisors. He didn't think they would stand for him investing in such a risky endeavor."

"He may have a point there. From what I've seen, bringing McLendon to Panama was a brilliant tactic and it worked," Oakes said.

"Yes, but the reasons still don't remove the stink."

"So what do you suspect?"

"I think Schiller's off the reservation."

"Working for someone else?" The thought seemed silly. "There's no one else to work for."

"I think he's working for himself," Plank said.

The idea was so obvious he was surprised he hadn't thought of it himself.

"That's a very interesting and very dangerous idea," Oakes said.

"Yes, Sir, I know."

"If you force the issue and you're wrong, you're in trouble, if you don't and you're right, you're in trouble."

"I know. It's a double bind."

"Either way, you're going to need a friend who can massage the bureaucrats."

"I realize that now," Plank said.

Oakes considered his options for a moment. He could exploit the situation as long as he could sustain Plank's indecision.

"Here's what I want you to do," Oakes said. "Watch Schiller closely. Gather information. Don't act. Report to me instead. If you're right, we need to handle this very carefully, because if you're right, Schiller will have you by the balls. Don't think he isn't good at it."

"I've seen him work."

"You need a friend."

"Yes, Sir. I do. I'll watch him and report to you."

"Good man."

"About the other thing. I didn't mean to come on so rough."

"No explanation is needed, Plank. I understand. You found yourself in an untenable situation, and you had to test me. You had to see if I was the real thing."

"That's it exactly."

Oakes thought it wasn't the truth. Plank was cruel by nature and he only knew how to dominate or submit. There was nothing in the middle. The trick was in making him think he couldn't dominate. Then he'd submit by choice.

Plank had come to find information and had given it away instead.

"You've made all the right moves," Oakes said. "Just keep it up, and you'll get out of this mess with your career on track. You've seen men who were drummed out, haven't you? Always hanging around the edges, never able to be players again."

Oakes reflected that the description could well apply to him.

"Yes, I have, and I don't want to end up like that," Plank said.

"Don't worry. You won't."

Frippo gave Plank a few minutes to clear the parking lot, then he walked over to Oakes' table.

"You handled him real good Mr. Oakes. You whipped his ass."

Maggie the Spy

MAGGIE WANTED TO talk to Oakes about his meeting with Plank the night before, but she didn't want to appear too interested so she sorted and opened the mail until he leaned through the door of her office and said, "We need to talk."

He handed her a cup of coffee, and they sat in the wing chairs with the butler's table between them.

"I need you," he said.

"Me too, darling."

"We could shut the door."

"Bart, really . . ."

"Sorry."

She wanted to say, What do you take me for? but given her involvement for profit with McLendon she thought he might offer a characterization that was accurate but not very complimentary.

"I understand, Bart. Now tell me about your meeting. You seem very calm this morning."

"I put Plank in his place."

"Bravo!"

"He gave away some interesting information."

She waited till she realized he wanted her to ask.

"Tell me."

"Plank thinks Schiller is off the reservation."

"Who is he doing the operation for?"

"Nobody."

"I'm not sure I understand."

"There is no operation. It's a scam to steal the money from McLendon."

She considered the implications, and all the ones that came immediately to mind were good.

"What do you think we should do?" Oakes asked.

"Nothing."

"Nothing?"

"Don't you see, this is the best thing that could possibly happen. We don't need to do anything any differently than we had planned. The only thing that's different now is that we don't have to worry about the Agency looking for us afterwards, and that's a tremendous break," Maggie said.

"Yes. I know it is. What I meant was, what do we do about Plank?"

"I have some ideas about that. Let me think out loud, okay?" Maggie said. "I met Schiller last night, and he was making overtures. He wants me to help him manage Johnny who, by the way, wants to be called Spike now."

"Spike?"

"Yes. Anyway, let's imagine I meet with Schiller. I tell him I'm tired of working for the Foundation, I want to work with him. As proof, I give him Plank."

"Work you as a double?" Oakes asked.

"Yes. That way we could feed Schiller anything we wanted and get information in the process."

"Brilliant."

"You approve then?"

"Very much so."

"Why don't I give him a call?"

"His number at the Ritz is on the Rolodex next to my phone."

She crossed to his desk and sat on its edge, flipped through the cards until she found the entry for Schiller – Ritz, and dialed.

After being passed through the operator, she heard Schiller's voice.

"Schiller."

"Hello Bill. This is Maggie Donald."

"What can I do for you, Maggie?"

"I'm afraid Spike is being a very naughty boy. I need to talk to you about it."

"Of course. Why don't we meet downstairs for lunch? Will twelve-thirty work for you?"

"That would be fine."

"I'll look for you in the lobby."

As she hung up the phone, Oakes looked at her with admiration.

"The trap has been set," he said.

"Yes, it certainly has," she agreed.

Plank Is Stupid

SCHILLER WAS WEARING an attractively-frayed dark-blue linen blazer and white linen slacks. Maggie thought it interesting that without much effort he pulled off the arrogantly shabby style Dunbarton Oakes was always striving for, while Oakes worked at it desperately and only managed to look down on his luck.

Maybe that was the secret. You couldn't really do the look on purpose. It sprang from your assumptions about the world and it spoke more eloquently about class and background than a resume of the right schools.

Schiller acted at home as he led her into the main dining room and helped her to her seat after the maître d'hôtel showed them to their table.

After he had ordered scotch for both of them, he observed, "We may as well cut to the chase."

"Plank has convinced Bart that you're operating on your own. That the only operation is to take money from McLendon."

"Why do you think I involved Plank in the operation?" Schiller asked.

"I'm not really sure. He's so much more primitive in his approach than you are."

"The choice was intentional. It's because he's stupid and barely under control."

Maggie laughed.

"I thought he would probably figure that out and go to Oakes. I just didn't think it would take him this long."

"You expected this?"

"Yes, of course."

"You expected me to come to you?"

"That was unexpected."

"And it's true that the only operation is to take money from

Johnny . . . Spike McLendon."

"It's true."

"Oh."

"What's the problem?"

"It bothers me that you admit this easily."

"It should," Schiller agreed.

"It makes me think it's not true."

"That's the beauty of this line of work. You can admit to anything you damned well please and everyone thinks it's a cover story. That's because it always is."

"You're not helping me very much."

"Same for you, Miss Innocent. The other night you said you're not working with Oakes or the Company, but you could work with me."

Maggie smiled.

"Another cover story?"

"No."

"Why?"

"I think that should be obvious. If you were picking a partner in crime, who would you choose: Oakes, McLendon, Plank or you?"

Schiller leaned back in his chair.

"How do we act with so many possibilities?" Maggie asked.

"My suggestion is that we proceed as if we are both telling the truth but watch each other very carefully."

"Agreed."

"We need to decide how we're going to handle Oakes."

"The most serious problem with Bart is that he comes unglued when he's frightened," Schiller said.

"So we need to make him think he's in control . . ."

"Yes, for the time being."

". . . by feeding him bogus information."

"Exactly."

"At the same time it needs to be inconclusive enough that he won't act."

"What I would suggest is that you tell him that I immediately admitted to you that I was working for myself, and this made you think that I wasn't. That should keep him from doing anything."

"And how do we give him a sense of being in control?"

"Tell him you think you can find the truth if you have more contact with me."

She nodded.

"At the same time, we need to isolate him so he'll depend on you more. Who else is working at the Foundation?"

Frippo, the security man, and two part-time administrative assistants."

"Tell Bart to give them time off."

When lunch came Schiller ate slowly and savored each bite. Maggie wondered if this was the way he made love.

"Could I ask a crazy question?" she asked.

He was amused. "Certainly, the crazier the better."

"Do you think I look like Vivian Leigh?"

"I'm afraid I don't know her."

"The actress."

"An actress? Sorry . . . I don't get to many movies."

"You've never seen *Gone With The Wind*?"

"No," he said. "I know that must seem incredible. Did you want me to say you looked like her?"

"No, I don't think so."

Yes – No – Maybe

WHEN MAGGIE RETURNED to the Foundation, Bart met her at the door.

"What did Schiller say?" he asked.

"He came right out and admitted that he was on his own and was planning on stealing McLendon's money."

"He did? That's incredible."

"I agree," she said. "Think about it a minute. Doesn't it seem a bit too easy."

Bart struck one of his melodramatic thinker poses that he used from time to time to convince people that his mind was still a finely-tuned instrument. He stared into middle space, leaned his head back slightly and stroked his chin.

"You're right. He'd never say that if it was true . . . unless it's a double bluff."

"Which means we don't have enough to go on yet, but we do have an edge."

"And what's that?" Bart asked.

"Schiller trusts me."

Bart smiled. "It's that movie-star face of yours."

She hoped he wasn't about to lapse into his sexual neediness again.

"I had an idea," she said.

"Yes?"

"Since we don't really have a clear understanding of what Schiller is up to, I think we should limit all of our potential security risks."

"How so?"

"Give Frippo and the administrative help a few weeks off," she said.

Bart nodded slowly, but his pose was disintegrating under the stress. He stood and began an aimless pacing.

"I've got to get out of here and get some air," Oakes said. "Why don't you talk to them. Tell them we're closing down for a few weeks."

Chest Clamp

OAKES WALKED AIMLESSLY up Peachtree trying to find the courage to act. The realization that he was trapped had registered first in the recesses of his reptilian brain. It was less a thought than the feeling that his chest was tightly clamped and if he didn't flee he would suffocate.

He had felt this before, the sense that he was about to be crushed to death by forces as primal as an advancing glacier, and it always meant that Schiller was at work.

Why did he carry this curse? Was he an imperfect seer who only saw the future when it was too late to change it? Or was it simply that he didn't have the guts to act?

Either way it amounted to the same thing: he would watch his life collapse and live in whatever was left.

He couldn't tell yet what Schiller was doing, but this much was clear, he was isolating him and he had turned Maggie. She had been too damned glib. He heard Schiller speaking with her voice. Thinking about that hurt.

He found a pay phone on the street and called Plank.

"Plank here."

"Oakes."

"Yes, Sir."

"You were right. Schiller is on his own."

"I knew it. What are we going to do?"

"Expose him for a traitor," Oakes said.

"I'd love to be the one who brought him down."

"He's turned Maggie."

"That bitch."

Oakes was surprised at his vehemence.

"The first problem we're going to have to overcome is funding. When is McLendon going to have the money together to replace the amount that was stolen?"

"Four or five days."

"Don't do anything 'till then, but when he has it tell him there's been a change of plan. Have McLendon deliver the three-hundred-and-fifty-thousand to you, then bring it to me.

"I doubt it will do any good to tell him not to let Maggie know about it. Is there any way you can see that Schiller is out of touch?"

"I'll work on it," Plank said.

Oakes wandered until he realized he was near Peachtree Center. He found a bar he'd never been in before and proceeded to get drunk.

He didn't know what Schiller had planned for him, but he knew it was going to be awful. He didn't have a plan other than get the money from Plank and run like hell.

Anal Aliens at the Motel Deluxe

GINGER SAT BY the motel room window. She had been there for two hours splitting her attention between the driveway to the motel and absent-mindedly turning the pages of a stack of fashion magazines.

It was almost dark when headlights raked across the window. She looked outside and saw Ray open the door of the Voodoo Cadillac. The dome light yellowed his face and his hair was almost blond. He looked tired.

She opened the door and waved to him. He saw her and drove to their unit. She met him at the car.

"Hey, good lookin', what you got cookin'?" Ray said.

"I'm getting all cooked up over you, baby," Ginger said.

"Best damn news I've had all day."

She watched as he carefully climbed from the car.

"Damn, you get hit in the head and you go blond," she said.

"That guy caught me pretty good, but it was hair dye that did this. I don't think he did any permanent damage, but I'm feeling pretty woogly."

"Now you're making up words on me, Ray baby. I think you got hit harder in the head than you think. You come inside."

"Yes, Ma'am."

She led him inside and began taking his clothes off as soon as the door was shut.

"The television has triple-X movies piped in from the office. Why don't we turn it on and see if it gives us any ideas?"

She picked up the remote control, turned on the tube then finished undressing him. She was wearing a long T-shirt dress and he pulled that off, and they were both naked.

"Hey, look at this," Ray said.

She turned to the TV. In close up, a nude woman ran down a beach. The camera pulled back and Ginger saw she was being chased by five men in cheap plastic alien Halloween suits.

After many shrieks and giggles they finally caught her. Four men grabbed her by her wrists and ankles and carried her to a large rock where they held her face down with her butt in the air. The fifth produced a contraption that looked like a broken television antenna with Graham crackers taped to it and began probing her ass.

"What's this shit?" Ginger said. She couldn't imagine who watched crap like this.

She threw herself across the bed and picked up the phone.

"Desk, can I help?"

"What's that on the television?" Ginger asked.

"Uh . . . let me check. That would be *Anal Aliens*."

"I don't go for that *Anal Alien* crap. You got anything that just has two people enjoying fucking each other?"

"I don't know if we have anything like that."

"Well look. Okay?"

"I'll look right away."

She slammed the phone in its cradle.

"Glad to hear you don't go for that," Ray said. "For a minute there, I thought you were going to make me go out and find four other guys and some outfits and one of those solar-powered enema rigs."

She rolled to her back and gave a come-hither finger wiggle.

"Not a chance. Now you get yourself over here."

He looked so tired and pathetic.

"You don't have to do nothing, baby, but lay your head right here so I can make it better."

Anal Aliens on the March

RAY WANTED TO sleep all day, but he had work to do so he put his feet on the floor and sat on the edge of the bed waiting for his mind to clear.

Ginger popped up.

"You awake already?"

Jesus, he wished he could wake up like that. He held his head in his hands.

"Peanut wants to give the money back," Ray said.

"Do you think it's the best idea?" Ginger asked.

"Maybe. That's what I need to find out."

"How are you going to do that?"

"I got a plan, baby. I always got a plan."

"You're so smart, Ray. You've always got things worked out ahead."

"Yeah, everything except getting the shit kicked out of me and having to kill those two dressed-up weirdoes."

"Nobody's perfect. I think you need to get some breakfast in your stomach, then you'll feel better about yesterday. You hear Peanut come in during the night?"

"No, I must've slept through it."

"He's got the room next door. I heard him come in and bang around during the night. Think we ought to wake him up to go to breakfast with us?"

"No, man, let him sleep. Old Peanut had a rough day of grinding up corpses and shit. He needs his rest."

Breakfast was surprisingly good. They ate at one of those country places where the tables are old dinettes, the waitresses hold court, and the servings are enormous.

Ray got pancakes, Ginger a couple of eggs. Ray hated the

sight of eggs in the morning, but could survive the experience as long as they were on someone else's plate.

He took a pen and began drawing on the back of a paper place-mat.

"What are you doing?" Ginger asked. "Can I see?"

"Just a second."

He finished with a flourish and handed it to her.

"There you go, Princess Naughty."

"Mmm . . . I like that name."

She studied the place-mat and laughed.

"This is fucking nuts," she said.

"Right, I figure they won't know what to make of it. If they're the government, they got all sorts of forms and shit, but nothing like this."

"I'll say."

This is what Ray had written:

HAS SOMEONE YOU KNOW BEEN ABDUCTED
BY THE ANAL ALIENS?
More Incidents Are Reported Daily!
As incredible as it may seem
the Anal Aliens favorite victims are
CHAUFFEURS with SILVER SUITCASES
particularly shitass chauffeurs
who they consider the perfect test subjects for their solar
powered butto-scopes
as a result we have a special this month
on the recovery of
CHAUFFEURS with SILVER SUITCASES
unlike other services with phones and offices
we can only be reached
with a personal advertisement
in the
ATLANTA JOURNAL – CONSTITUTION
You Advertise – We deliver

"That should give their little minds a good twist," Ginger said.

"We have to look for a place to fax it. One of those copy and mailbox places. We need to get the fax numbers."

Ginger waved their waitress over, "Ya'll got an Atlanta business phone book we can look at?"

"Sure, hon', just a minute."

She went to another table, took their order, gave it to the cook and returned with a well-worn phone book. Ginger thumbed through it quickly.

"They've got phone numbers, but no fax."

"Looks like you get to call them up and play secretary."

"Oh . . . that sounds like fun."

"I love that girlish enthusiasm."

"Mmm . . . I got a little outfit that might help you with a little boyish enthusiasm."

"Ooh . . . Tell me about it."

"It's a little garter belt with stockings and a nice five shot .22 derringer I can slip in the top of them. I didn't get the pistol for the fire power. I just thought you might like to see me get it out. I call it my gangster girl outfit."

"Let's send this damned fax, then take that little ensemble out for a spin," Ray said.

Please Pass the Scissors I've Been Abducted

THE LADY BEHIND the counter had blue hair and a sergeant-major jaw that Ray suspected meant she didn't have much of a sense of humor. He guessed she was sixty-five.

Ginger was at the pay phone in front of the store.

"You got some scissors?" Ray asked.

"Yes, Sir."

She reached into a cubby-hole behind the counter and pulled out a pair and handed them to him. He began cutting the place-mat to the size of a single sheet of paper.

"The mail box business doing pretty good around here?" Ray asked.

"Yes, Sir, it's doing right well. We got a lot of your criminal element around here. They got no fixed address, or else they don't want nobody to know where they are living at. Then we got your construction drifters, the crooked preachers, your scooter trash and the drifter scum. Business is doing pretty good."

A regular Ma Barker, Ray thought.

"They all good boys that are just misunderstood?" he asked.

"They ain't all that good, and I understand them pretty well," she said.

Ginger finished her phone calls and came into the store.

"Can I help you, missy?" the lady asked.

"I'm with him. Here's those fax numbers, Elrod," she said to Ray.

"Thank you, Gorlene,' Ray said.

He handed the cut-down place-mat and the piece of paper with the fax numbers to the lady. She glanced at the writing.

"Damn," she said. "This happened to me."

"What?" Ray asked.

"I got myself abducted by them aliens."

"No shit," Ginger said.

"No shit, Missy."

"It must have been awful."

"It was terrible what they done to me. I wasn't even one of them chauffeurs with a silver suitcase, but they took me anyway. So terrible, I still hate to think about it. This is a wonderful thing you are doing here with this service. We didn't have it back in my day. We just had to get back from an abduction the best way we could."

"Thank you for saying that," Ray said. "Sometimes it's a thankless and dangerous job."

"You don't have to worry about a thing. Them aliens show up asking about you, I won't tell them a thing. In fact, I'll have my boys whip 'em."

Ray reached in his pocket and found the glasses.

"Let me show you something. I got these off one of them. We've run into a lot of this."

"Just a minute." She yelled to the back, "Billy, get out here a minute."

A young man wearing blue bib overalls came from a back room. He looked like he might have been cloned from Haystack Calhoun, although he also had a little Latin in him.

She pointed toward Ray. "He's one of us, Billy. Mister, show him what they're wearing these days."

Ray held out the glasses, then slipped them on.

"You see anybody with glasses like that, Billy, you beat his ass for Momma."

"I'll do it, Momma. I'll beat his ass."

On the way to the car Ginger said, "Jesus, Ray . . . you ever get the feeling that life is a lot stranger than you imagined?"

"Nope," Ray said. "I always thought life was crazier than anything I could think up."

What the Fuck?

THE PERSON ON the other end of the phone was barking like a dog.

"Spike?" Maggie asked.

"Arf."

She heard the fax machine behind her cycle on.

"What is it, Spike boy?"

"I just got a weird fax claiming Gordon was kidnapped by a gang called the Anal Aliens for asshole experiments."

"Just a minute."

She turned to the credenza behind her desk and grabbed the paper as it dropped into the paper tray.

"Oh Jesus."

She picked up the phone.

"We just got one too. Listen, keep a lid on this. Don't tell anyone. Understand? I'll get back to you."

"Before you go, you know, I was thinking it would be good if you had a dog name, too."

"You think so?"

"How about Queenie?"

"No thanks, Spike. I think Maggie will do."

"But that's already your name."

"That's right. Why change it? I'll only get confused. I need to go now."

She speed–dialed Bill Schiller and waited for him to answer while she turned around and put the fax in the machine to send.

"Schiller."

"Is your fax secure?"

"Yes."

"Hold on."

She hit the send button.

"What is it?"

"It's something crazy about the chauffeur. Johnny McLendon got one too. I want to see what you think."

"Okay, I've got it. Oh no. What the fuck?"

"I know. It's so weird I don't know how to react."

"Is your voice line secure?"

"Bart is out of the office. Frippo does sweeps before we open."

"Good. Don't let Oakes see this yet. Get Johnny . . . er . . . Spike, to keep it to himself."

"I already jerked Spike's leash," she said.

"Good job," he said.

"By the way, Bill, Spike thought up a dog name for me," she said.

"Do tell."

"He wants to call me Queenie."

She heard an anguished moan from Schiller's end of the phone.

"Queenie, Anal Aliens," he said. "God how I long for the cold war. Everything was so much saner then. No one cared who the President had sex with, and all we had to worry about was blowing up the world."

"Goodbye, Bill."

"Goodbye, Queenie."

Gangster Girl Fashions at the Motel Deluxe

"I'M GOING TO check on Peanut," Ray said.

"Sure darling, I'm going to fix up that little fashion show for you, so don't take long."

"You put it that way, I don't guess I will."

He knocked on Peanut's door and saw the window curtains move slightly and then the door open.

"Come on in, Bubba," Peanut said.

"Just for a minute."

Peanut sat on the bed, and Ray pulled up an orange upholstered chair with worn wooden arms. Peanut was subdued.

"You doing okay?" Ray asked.

"Yeah, man. How about yourself? You still feeling that shot to the head?"

"Just sore, no real damage."

"Your eyes aren't dilated or rolling around like marbles or anything?"

"No. You depressed, man?"

"I think I probably got us in some shit."

"It might be a good idea if you asked around back home for any news on the Shitass Ronnie Gordon. But keep in mind he won't be anxious to hear from you."

"I'll ask real careful like."

"As for the giving the money back, I'm checking on it."

"I figured you would," Peanut said.

"Let me tell you a tale from my youth."

"I'd like to hear it."

"When I was a kid I used to play poker all the time. Used to win most of the time. Penny ante stuff ... you understand?"

"Yeah."

"Anyway, first time I got in a high stakes game, I kept thinking about all the money. It scared me to death."

"I can see that."

"Then I got to thinking about it. I said, 'Fuck these guys, it's the same cards, same rules, same odds. I'm going to take these motherfuckers,' and I did. I won all their money, then I went outside and pissed all over their cars."

Peanut laughed.

"What it really comes down to is, I don't give a rat shit who these guys are. If I think we can take them, I say, fuck it. Let's do it."

Peanut smiled.

Ray knocked gently on his room door.

"If it's Ray Justus, come in. Everyone else stay the hell out," Ginger said.

He went in and shut the door behind him.

Ginger wore a black stretch-knit skirt and a red zipper-front shirt.

"Ready to see me pull my gun?"

"Baby, I was born ready," Ray said.

She placed a high-heeled foot on the bed, and the skirt slid up revealing the black garter straps and a stocking top with a chrome derringer next to her skin.

"How's that gun of yours doing?" she asked.

"It's fully loaded," Ray said.

Our Chauffeur with a Silver Suitcase Has Been Abducted

GINGER KEPT RAY occupied with fashion shows for the next two days. On the third morning she decided to let the poor thing sleep in. She'd kept him up half the night bouncing like a kid on a trampoline, so he certainly deserved time to recuperate.

She drove the Voodoo Cadillac to the little restaurant they usually hit for breakfast and bought him a cup of coffee, a couple of bacon biscuits and a newspaper.

She wasn't sure how long it took to get an advertisement in the paper, but she figured if the plan had worked, it would be in the paper by today.

She fought her curiosity and didn't look in the want ads till she had gotten back to the room. Ray had taught her a lot about being careful in public, never let people see what you're interested in, never react, never show your emotions.

It was something that didn't come to her naturally, but as she got to know Ray better, she realized it wasn't natural for him either. But it was part of being a professional.

He stirred as she entered the room, opened one eye, then drifted back to sleep. She sat on the chair next to the window and looked at the paper.

"Holy shit, Ray . . ."

"Uh?"

"Ray, honey, we got an answer."

He sat up and saw her with the paper.

"There's an ad?"

"Yes, darlin'. I got you some coffee and biscuits here if you want them."

"They cat heads?"

"No, but they got bacon in them."

"Okay, just a minute."

He sat on the side of the bed with an unfocused look.

"Why don't you sit on the chair, baby? That way you can eat your breakfast at the coffee table."

They changed places. He took the chair and picked up the coffee. She lay back on the bed, flashed a lot of leg and saw his face brighten.

"You awake enough?"

"Sure, baby. Let's have it."

"'Our Shitass Chauffeur with a silver suitcase has been abducted by the Anal Aliens – we need your monthly special. Please call . . .' and then it's got a phone number. Shoot Ray, it looks like it worked. We better find us a pay phone."

"Just as soon as I eat my breakfast, Princess Naughty."

He took a bite of a bacon biscuit.

"You know, the way you look on that bed is going to make it real hard to leave here and do anything."

Is Your Refrigerator Running?

SCHILLER WAS IN the living room of the safe house. It was a small apartment on the Buford Highway he had rented six months ago – an anonymous complex that was teeming with hyperactive children.

The phone rang. The voice sounded like a young man who was drunk.

"How big is your dick?"

He hung it up. It rang again.

"I'm serious. If you want your Shitass chauffeur back I need to know the volume of your dick, that means I need the length and . . ."

He hung up again. The phone rang again.

"Look, do you want the Shitass chauffeur with the silver suitcase or not? If so I need to know . . ."

"I'm going to hurt you if you call again."

"Is that a promise?" the man asked.

He hung up and the phone rang again. This time it sounded like an older woman.

"I got myself kidnapped by them aliens twenty-seven years ago," she said.

"I'm sorry to hear that."

"It was terrible what they done to me. They took me to their planet. It's called Wheely-Roo." She pronounced Roo with an odd emphasis that made it sound like she was being goosed.

"Ah, I see," Schiller said.

"They did experiments on me," the woman said.

"I'm really sorry but . . ."

"They was breeding experiments. You know what that means, Mister?"

"I really need to keep the line open," Schiller said.

"You should see my boys, Mister. They are not of this world."

"In that case, I'm sure you can understand my anguish."

"Damn right. I understand that anguish. But there's something you need to know, Mister. You got to prepare yourself. Once they put that Wheely-Roo weenie to him, that Shitass Chauffeur might not be worth getting back."

"I'm sure we'll be happy to see him, no matter what."

"Yeah, well fuck you. My husband, he left me. He said I'd been out fucking the Mexicans."

She hung up and the phone rang. Silence.

Finally a voice said, "You want to talk?"

It was a voice you wouldn't want to meet in a back alley or insult in a bar.

"Yes."

"I may be able to help you find something."

"We need to meet," Schiller said.

"Yes."

"Name a place."

"I don't care. You pick," the man said.

"Cafe Diem on North Highland. You know where it is?"

"I can find it."

"Say two-thirty today."

"Fine."

The man was calm and self-assured, Schiller thought. By forcing him to make the decisions he had given nothing away – no favorite haunts or parts of town, but Schiller had gotten the strategic advantage.

Schiller doubted the man had given this up from naivety. It meant he had resources. It was likely the meet would be covered by triangulated fire. Schiller would be walking in naked.

"Two-thirty, then."

"One thing I'd like to make clear."

"Yes."

"I hate people that make threats."

"I do also," Schiller agreed.

"You tell me your reason," the man said.

"Because people with real power don't have to threaten."

"You got it, buddy."

He hung up.

That had to have been one of the most chilling exchanges Schiller could remember. He rolled his neck, and rubbed the bridge of his nose. Why did the last act of his retirement have to become a surrealist nightmare? Why couldn't he just engineer a simple theft and go to some island south of Tahiti?"

The phone rang, and without thinking he picked it up.

"Is your refrigerator running?"

He ripped the cord from the wall.

Peanut Is Crazy

RAY SHOULD HAVE been frightened, but he thought about Ginger's special outfits instead. Ginger, on the other hand, was so tense he thought she might break in half if he tapped her with a finger.

"Take it easy, baby."

"I wish I could, Ray. I'm worried. I just got you, and now you might get killed."

"Just think about how much fun we're going to have if I don't."

"I wish you wouldn't say that."

"What do you want me to say?"

"Why don't you say you'll let me and Peanut back you up? That's what we're here for."

"The way I see it, if there isn't a problem, I won't need back-up. If there is a problem it might be like some guy falling off a mountain, pulling everyone on the rope with him."

"I'm going to cry."

"Don't do that. That would be worse than getting shot. How's this for a compromise? You drive me. You can let me off near there, and I'll walk in, that way if I need to make a fast getaway, I can give you a buzz on the cell phone."

"That would be better."

Ginger was driving, and it was obvious she still had something on her mind.

"Still worried?"

"I'm putting it behind me, thinking about something better – like you taught me."

"What then?"

"It's just something I was thinking about."

She was quiet.

"Hey, pull the car over to the side a minute. I'll get down on my knees and beg you to tell me."

She laughed.

"You know, Peanut used to be my boyfriend and now I love him like a brother, but I'm afraid he's going to get you killed."

"Don't you think he's doing better?"

"I think he's on a death trip. I don't think anything short of a good dose of electroshock is going to fix it."

She spoke with a conviction that surprised him.

"He looks up to you, so he covers up a lot of shit when he's around you."

"You know the first thing that attracted me to you?" Ray asked.

"No."

"You are so smart."

She blushed. "I thought you were going to say my body."

"I was trying not to notice your body at the time."

She hitched her skirt to mid thigh.

"You can notice it now," she said.

Man to Man

A BLOCK FROM Cafe Diem, Ray slipped on the black plastic nerd glasses. He didn't know why he did it. Maybe it was the fact that he had no back-up, wasn't packing or wearing Kevlar. Might as well have some prop.

From the sidewalk in front of the apartments across the street he saw a man who had to be his contact. He had the look of a predator like a wild wolf among the livestock.

He sat at an outside table, and that was not a good sign. Ray scanned the possible lines of fire and thought that if he had to boogie it would be better to use the back exit. At least that way he wouldn't have a crowd watching him do something as personal as die.

He was probably fucked no matter what, and looking scared wouldn't help. He tried to think of something nice.

In his mind, he saw Ginger's face when she was having an orgasm. Now that was beautiful, and it worked. He was feeling damned relaxed as he crossed North Highland.

He walked casually toward the man's table. Ray made him to be sixty, but tough. He had an ascetic look, sort of like a monk.

The man blinked when he looked at him.

"You the man who's looking for his shitass chauffeur?" Ray asked.

"You can keep the Shitass, I want the silver suitcase," the man answered.

They both smiled. The man gestured with an open palm toward the chair next to him, and Ray slid comfortably into it.

Too Many Jumpers

SCHILLER ASSUMED HE was covered by several long guns. He hadn't worn a vest because he doubted it would do any good. Hadn't carried a gun for the same reason.

If they wanted to kill him, why do it here? If all they wanted was the money, why bother to contact him through the bizarre Anal Alien fax? For the first time in his career, he had to admit he didn't have a clue.

But then, this wasn't his career, was it? This was an area where he didn't really know the rules.

The man took off the black glasses, folded them and put them in his inside coat pocket. Schiller cursed himself for thinking the glasses were funny in the first place. They had been a stupid self-indulgence. An inside joke to humiliate McLendon and the jumpers.

"The glasses," Schiller said. The man was very relaxed.

"Sorry about your friends," he said.

"And where might they be?" Schiller asked.

"That would depend on your religious convictions," the man said.

"I have none."

"Then from your perspective, I guess they're shit out of luck."

Schiller smiled involuntarily.

"From the expression on your face, I'd guess there's no hard feelings," the man said.

"None at all. In fact, I've got more of them I'd like you to kill," Schiller said.

The man made a noncommittal nod.

"My name's Ray."

"Schiller."

"Sounds like you're over-staffed."

"Yes."

"You might just give them notice."

"That could be messy."

"I understand."

"How about you? Sort of unusual to rip somebody off, kill two of their operatives, then use an Anal Alien advertisement to offer to take a meeting."

"I'm an unusual guy," Ray said.

"I can see that, but it still doesn't explain why you're here."

"I've found it's useful to know who I'm stealing from."

Schiller noted the use of "I" rather than "we." Schiller knew there were others, but Ray didn't want to call attention to them.

"I see what you're saying. Sometimes it's better to kiss and make up."

Ray didn't react.

"I imagine you're wondering if I'm the government."

"No," Ray said.

"But I am."

"Don't waste your time."

"Let me explain. I have been part of the government. A part of the government that occasionally isn't part of the government."

"I don't give a shit."

"That doesn't frighten you?"

"Nope."

Schiller was amused.

"Why not?"

"I took your money and killed your buddies."

"Yes?"

"How come the police aren't here?"

"You've got me there."

"You may be government, but you're illegal. Same as me."

"As are any number of other people. That still doesn't explain why you're here. You want to kiss and make up? You want to give the money back?"

"No."

"Why then?"

"I don't know what you're up to. But anyone who would make the Shitass Ronnie Gordon a secret agent is running one piss poor outfit."

"I'm beginning to share that opinion," Schiller said.

"I figure you could use some help."

In a flash, Schiller saw the final flourish on the end game. It would cost him, but it would seal his exit with shatterproof deniability.

"That's brilliant," Schiller said.

"I know."

"So, when can you kill the rest of my operatives?"

"Not so fast."

"You can keep the money. There may be more."

"Killing's my style," Ray said. "But I got a painless way you can dump a few of them."

"Do tell."

"I'll send you another fax."

"Send it to the Foundation."

"It will have a fax ID. Let them go to the place where I sent it from. Make sure they are wearing glasses like this."

"They will be. How can I get in touch with you?"

Ray wrote his cell phone number on a napkin.

"Catch you later." Ray stood and left as the waitress came to get his order.

Alive, For the Moment

RAY WAS DRAINED. It was like his emotions had been spilled on the sidewalk and none were left – not even fear. He took two deep breaths and dialed the cell phone.

"Yo," Ginger said.

"I'm cool," Ray said. "Head east on North Avenue . . . down the street from Buddies."

He looked up the road and in less than a minute saw Ginger drive the Voodoo Cadillac past Manuel's. She crossed the intersection, then pulled to the side of the road until Ray got in.

"How you doing?" Ginger asked.

"I don't know," Ray said.

"You're looking real good, baby."

Ray laughed. He felt human again. Ginger was magic.

"We've stumbled into some weird shit," Ray said.

"Tell me."

"This guy is some sort of spy, but he's illegal as hell."

"No shit."

"Yeah, and the thing was, he told me I could keep the money, he just wanted me to kill all the people that work for him. His name is Schiller."

Ginger looked at Ray, rolled her eyes.

"He sounds like some kind of psycho."

"No kidding. The guy's a complete psycho."

"Maybe we should forget the asshole."

"He's got some plan. I think there could be a lot more money in this."

"This scares me," Ginger said.

"Why's that, baby?"

"You know why, Ray. It's dangerous."

"I thought that was the fun."

He could tell she was thinking this over.

"It's a big jump from painting graffiti on dumpsters," she said.

They were heading up North 85 when his phone rang.

"Yo," Ray said.

"This is Schiller."

"Hello Schiller."

Ginger mouthed, is that him? Ray nodded.

"You're probably wondering why I called you."

"Let me guess. You're trying to get a fix on my phone."

"No. Not at all. Nothing that sinister. It's just that I got an echo."

"What do you mean?"

"How should I know what I mean? Now if these damn rabbits would get out of the road everything would be okay."

They stopped in front of the mailbox/copy/fax store. Ray hadn't spoken for a long time.

"You going to tell me what he said?" Ginger asked.

"He said he had an echo and he couldn't drive because there were rabbits in the road."

"Where do you think he was?"

"Sounded like the drug highway to Mars."

"Great, a doper-spy."

"Hey, you got to take your victims as they come."

"Yeah, and he did hire the Shitass."

Ray opened the door for her and saw the blue-haired sergeant major mom surrounded by three identical sons – all well over six feet, weighing three hundred pounds, wearing blue overalls, with wild hair and beards.

"So, you're back."

"We got them on the run."

A cheer exploded from the room.

"Now, we're going to try to smoke them out." He handed her the fax. "I need to get you to send this fax."

"There's no charge for this one," she said.

"Thanks, but I need to warn you. They could show up here. It could be dangerous."

"Do I look worried?" she asked. "My boys will take care of them."

"That's right," one of the boys yelled. "We'll break their fingers and rip their arms off."

"And we'll hang them up by their underpants and squirt a fire hose at them," another said.

"Then we'll cover them with bar-b-que sauce and take them down to the smoke house and have us a family meal for what they did to our mom."

The Stuff of Dreams

SOMETHING HAD GONE terribly wrong with Schiller's brain. It was as if he had passed through the looking glass to a horrible, distorted, cartoon universe. His thinking was so crazy he couldn't piece together the clues to understand what had happened.

He drove down the Buford Highway trying to hit as few rabbits as possible. Mexicans and Vietnamese and Cambodians waved at him like he was at a party.

He couldn't figure out what he was doing that was so funny. Maybe it was this hat he had on. He couldn't remember where he had got it.

He took it off and looked at it. It was his underpants. How had they gotten up there? He tossed them out the window, then took the money from his wallet and tossed it out too.

More happy pedestrians stormed the street.

He was close to the safe house. He thought he could find it. The driveway was there. He managed to pull in and parked, it seemed like sideways. He was walking sideways, and the hyperactive kids were bouncing off each other like pool balls.

"Gnats! Gnats!" he yelled.

Inside the apartment . . . thank God. He went to the bedroom to collapse, but his ex-wife was on the bed dressed in a French maid outfit, his dead son stood beside her — wounds fresh from Vietnam, blood and guts dripping on the floor.

Schiller collapsed into the fetal position.

He opened his eyes at four-thirty in the morning and realized he had been poisoned. Plank had slipped a hallucinogenic drug into his thermos of coffee. The pathetic slug was about to learn a lesson. Unfortunately, it would be too late to become part of a self-improvement plan.

In the morning, he would kick ass. In the meantime, all he could do was drink water and detox.

Too Hungry for Dinner at Eight

RAY AND GINGER dropped by the Motel Deluxe to pick up Peanut. He sat in the back seat of the Voodoo Cadillac as they cruised down the county highway looking for a place to eat.

"Did we remember to pick up Peanut?" Ray asked.

"I don't know. I haven't heard a peep out of him. Maybe I should check and see if he's still alive."

"I feel too stupid to talk," Peanut said.

"It's not so bad, Peanut. We're getting it back together," Ginger said.

Ray saw a Thai–Mexican joint in a rundown frame building decorated with Christmas lights, and pulled into the gravel parking lot.

"What do think?" he asked.

"Great choice," Ginger said. "I can have basil shrimp and Peanut can eat a burrito."

A Thai hostess met them at the door and led them past a Mexican cashier to a table next to a wall decorated with sombreros and statues of Thai dancers balanced on tiny shelves.

"Looks like instructions for a Buddhist hat dance," Ginger said.

"You can't never tell these days," Ray said. "Maybe it's some new international exercise program."

"Anyway, I'm starving," Ginger said. "I am too hungry for dinner at eight."

"I like to play cards and masturbate," Peanut said.

"Any more talking, I'll puke on my plate," Ray added.

"That's why my leg has got a cramp."

"Doesn't sound like top forty material," Ginger said.

"I'll stick to crime," Peanut said.

"Got to go where your talents lead you."

"Maybe we shouldn't talk so loud about masturbation and puking, people are looking at us."

There was a sprinkling of Thai and Mexican families and long-haul truck drivers in the restaurant glancing furtively in their direction.

"They're just looking at you because you're so beautiful, darling."

"Why thank you, Ray baby."

"What I'm wondering is what are we going to do with our windfall?" Peanut said. "We going to keep it or return it? These guys government or what?"

"I don't know that it makes much difference if they are government as long as they are illegal. Who they going to complain to if we knock them over?"

"You got a point there," Peanut said.

"I think we ought to vote on what we want to do next," Ray said.

"You tell us how to vote, and we'll do it," Peanut said.

"First, listen to the way I got it broke down," Ray said. "Back in the old days when they could blame everything on the commies, these government guys could do any damn thing they wanted. They could act like they were doing us a favor by breaking the law. Thing is, I don't know that they understood how protected they were."

"I think I see where you're going with this," Ginger said. "They aren't protected any more."

"Now they're playing in our neighborhood," Peanut said.

"Our neighborhood and our game. The one we've been playing all our lives."

"Hot damn," Ginger said. "This scares the living hell out of me, but I still like the way it's going."

"So we keep the money?" Peanut asked.

"I don't think that's all he's saying, honey."

"Right," Ray said. "We keep the money and go back for more."

"Shitfire . . . You're the real thing, Ray," Peanut said. "You're a real gangster."

Trunk Money

"WE'VE GOT AN operation going." McLendon was so excited, he was like a child.

"I was wondering why you were jumping around," Maggie said.

"I've got a dog in my pants," he said.

"You leave Mister Doggy in his kennel."

"I don't know if I can do that."

Thwap! She hit him with a swipe of the rolled up newspaper. He yelped.

"What operation? Who is we?"

"Plank asked me to get some more money together to replace the stuff that was stolen."

"Not Schiller?"

"Plank. He's coming over in the morning to pick it up."

"You've got it here?"

"Here, in a place nobody will ever find it."

"Very good, Spike."

"But I'll tell you," he said.

"No. Don't."

"Don't?"

"Don't be a bad dog and tell all your secrets. Don't tell anybody until you give the money to Plank."

"Not even you?"

"No, Spike."

"Nobody could find it."

"That's because you are so smart."

"I know. Nobody could figure it out."

Maggie forced drinks down him, and he still screwed like a demon. She was almost to the point of smothering him with a pillow when he passed out in the middle of a mumbled sentence that ended in a snore.

She said, "Does Spike want to eat a little pussy cat?" He didn't wake up.

She tickled his side. He didn't stir.

She punched his side. He snored louder.

She went to the kitchen and called Schiller. It was obvious that Plank was pulling something, probably with Bart's help or even at his suggestion, which meant the little shit Dunbarton Oakes had cut her out.

Schiller's secure phone rang a dozen times before she gave up. She went to work.

She thought it likely the money would be in small denominations, so the package would be large.

First, she looked under the bed. Nothing.

The luggage in the master bedroom closet was empty. The shelves filled with folded blankets, hat boxes, shoes, stacks of sweaters, shirts, clothes she had never seen him wear, and she imagined he would never wear. Maybe he had someone buy his clothes, someone like the interior decorator who bought his furniture. Johnny had an odd habit of paying people to do things that people usually enjoyed doing themselves.

She checked the chest of drawers, a cedar chest, looked under a chair, behind the pictures and came to the conclusion the money was not in the bedroom. Then, just to be thorough, she gave it a quick once over again, this time checking the carpet for a hidden floor safe.

Next, she searched the living room. There were fewer hiding places here. The shelves beneath the wet bar were filled with identical bottles of the same single-malt scotch, a testimony to Johnny's single-minded conviction that his tastes were universal.

Turning over the easy chairs revealed nothing more than chair bottoms and dust. The search was not going well. Two hours later she had finished the dining room, the kitchen, the study, all three baths and the utility room and come to the conclusion the money was not in the apartment.

She tried to think this out. He had said, "The money is here," but not "The money is in the apartment." Maybe "here" meant "here in the building." She wondered if there was a storage room downstairs. That didn't feel right, but it was possible.

She returned to the bedroom, picked Johnny's pants off the floor and found the keys in the pocket. It didn't leap out at first, because she didn't immediately realize how odd it was. It was a new car key with an engraved BMW logo.

She had never seen Johnny drive. She didn't even know if he could drive. He was always being driven around in his limousine. The afternoon Gordon had disappeared he had hired a new driver. Maybe the car had been bought like the furniture and the clothes.

She slipped on her print rayon dress and a pair of flats, not bothering with underwear. Quietly, she shut the bedroom door, the apartment door and took the elevator to the basement garage.

She almost walked into a red BMW. It was too well-used and lovingly maintained to belong to Johnny. Same for the green one parked ten spaces to the left. She spotted it parked at the far end of the garage, in a spot nobody would pick, especially Johnny, if he actually was using the car.

It was new and high end. As she walked closer, she saw the tires still had an off-the-shelf finish, almost as if it had been delivered here on a trailer. She looked at the odometer: sixty-nine miles. Jesus, how appropriate.

She opened the trunk and saw an aluminum silver suitcase. A small brass key on the keyring fit the lock. The case was packed with currency bundled with tight red wrappers. She had never seen so much money in one place in her life – three-hundred-and-fifty-thousand dollars.

She knew she was taking a chance, but she couldn't let Plank and Bart get their hands on the money. She closed the suitcase and put it in the trunk of her Volvo.

Game Face

MAGGIE TOOK A shower and got dressed early.

The gun was a problem. Meeting Plank without one was not a good idea, and she didn't see a way she could hide a gun on her body without wearing a jacket. If she did, it would be so obvious that she might as well not hide it at all.

Putting it in one of the easy chairs was the best plan she could think of. For it to work she had to sit down at the earliest opportunity and not move.

Plank arrived thirty minutes early. She suspected this was a tactic to throw them off balance. It had worked on Johnny, but that wasn't much of an accomplishment since he was always off balance.

"You came too early. I don't have my clothes on," he said. He was wearing his boxer shorts made from a silk print fabric with large, goofy, slobbering dog heads.

"He can see that Johnny," Maggie said.

"Why don't you fix him some coffee or something?"

Plank watched her closely as she walked across the room. She didn't know if he was looking for a weapon or planning a rape. Probably both.

"You boys have your little secret operation going. You've got to cater it yourself. I'm going to sit this one out."

She sat in the chair and slid her hand between the seat cushion and the arm and felt the handle of the revolver. An ugly anger twisted Plank's face. She wasn't looking forward to what was about to happen.

"I don't care about fucking coffee, just get me the money," Plank said.

"Yeah, okay." Johnny started toward the door and had his hand on the knob.

"Johnny, where on earth are you going?" Maggie asked.

"Downstairs," he said.

"You can't go to the lobby dressed like that."

"I'm not going to the lobby. I'm going to the basement."

"I don't care where you're going. You must at least put on a robe."

"See the way she looks out for me," he said to Plank.

He retrieved his robe from the bedroom and left to get the money from his car trunk. As soon as he closed the apartment door, Plank's attitude went from hostile to homicidal.

"Once this is over you're mine," he said. "I'm going to hurt you real bad."

She pulled out the gun, cocked the hammer, and pointed the barrel toward the center of his chest.

"I guess it would be a good idea to kill you right now, then."

He blinked. "That wouldn't be a good idea," he said.

"And why not? It seems like self-defense to me."

"You know why."

"No, enlighten me."

"There are people who would . . ."

She interrupted, scolding him with the gun barrel. "Plank. Poor Plank. Don't you get it? You aren't connected to anything. Oakes is working for himself, Schiller is working for himself, even Johnny is in it for himself. You don't have any sanction or any protection. What do you really think the company's opinion would be about you threatening to torture the widow of one of their dead heroes?

"It's time to open your eyes. Far from being protected, you're an embarrassment. You'll be treated like a gangster. Do you think anyone will care if I kill you? They'll be grateful."

"All right," he said. It seemed like an odd response, but he likely couldn't think of anything else to say.

Johnny came running into the apartment screaming incoherently. She quickly put away the gun.

"Why? Why me? Why? Why? They got me. They got me again."

"Calm down, Spike," Maggie said.

"Shit, they got me. Always me! Why? Why?" he yelled.

"What the fuck is going on?" Plank asked.

"Some fuck stole the money."

"Oh, man. Who knew about it?" Plank asked. He looked at Maggie.

"Given his luck at holding on to money, I told him I didn't want to know anything about it," Maggie said.

"She's right," Johnny said. "She didn't want to know about it. I was willing to tell her, but she said it was a violation of need-to-know. There's no way she could have known where it was."

"Where was it?" Plank asked.

"In the trunk of my car."

"You're kidding. That's really stupid."

"No. Not really. Nobody knows I have the car."

"I didn't know he had the car. I've only seen him being driven in the limo," Maggie said.

"I don't drive it," Johnny said. "I had it brought here so I could use it when I learned to drive. My father never let me drive. Now I'm a grown man and I can't drive a car."

"And nobody knew about it?"

"No. I had my driver bring it over . . . Shit, my chauffeur knew it was here."

"You mean nobody knew it was here but the Shitass Ronnie Gordon?" Maggie asked.

"Yes." Johnny McLendon muttered. "God I'm stupid. I'm so damned stupid."

"You aren't as stupid as all that," Maggie said.

"Thank you, Maggie. You're too good to me. I don't deserve you."

Plank was appalled by Johnny's self-pity.

"Those goddamn hillbillies," he muttered over and over.

The phone rang.

Go Get 'em

OAKES COULDN'T THINK of a way to bluff past Maggie Donald when she picked up McLendon's phone.

"Hello Maggie."

"Hello Bart."

He paused. "I miss you," he said.

"Right."

Another pause, then he heard her say, "It's for you."

"Plank here. Jesus, we've been robbed by the Shitass Ronnie Gordon and the hillbillies."

"You're kidding?"

"Nope."

"Could it have been Schiller?"

"Absolutely no way. I dosed him."

"Maggie?"

"She didn't know where he'd put it. McLendon left the money downstairs in the trunk of his car."

Oakes heard Johnny McLendon grousing in the background.

"That was stupid."

"Yes, very stupid. The only person who knew about the car other than McLendon was the Shitass Ronnie Gordon."

Now, he could hear McLendon speaking, "Why me? Why does it always have to be me? I'm sick of it!"

"See if you can calm him down. He may be an idiot, but we need him."

"Yes, Sir." Plank was holding his palm over the receiver, but Oakes still heard his muffled voice, "Shut the fuck up, or I'm going to shoot you."

"Okay, he's quiet now," Plank said.

"Luckily, I've got a good lead for you on the hillbillies. I just got a fax from one of their confederates offering to provide information leading to the return of the Shitass chauffeur."

"That's good news," Plank said.

"Yes. I've got the station ID and the phone number. You get the cadre together and I'll find the location. Then I want you to go there and shake the truth out of them. Understand?"

"Yes, Sir."

"And do me a favor. Don't threaten Johnny McLendon any more. In fact, I want you to apologize right now."

"Apologize?"

"Yes, Plank. Johnny McLendon is rich enough to have both of us killed and pay Congress to pass a resolution thanking him for it."

"I understand, Sir."

Oakes didn't think it was likely Plank would ever understand.

Turn About Is Fair Play

HIS FACE WAS numb, and it wasn't light yet. The water had flushed his system, and he no longer saw his dead son swinging the eyeball that hung down his cheek in time with the Brandenburg Concerti.

Schiller's mind was clear enough, but his body felt like he had been beaten by croquet mallets.

He knew he had to act fast. Plank had lost control sooner than he had expected. It meant the plan could unravel if he didn't reassert control.

He laid out slacks and a knit shirt, then took a shower. Starting with the temperature uncomfortably hot to start a sweat, he turned it to ice cold to jar his mind awake.

After he dressed, he looked in a supply chest in the bedroom and retrieved a vial of a slow-acting hallucinogen that had been cooked up by the Agency. It was probably the same thing Plank had poisoned him with.

You dose somebody, and several hours later they begin hallucinating and become disoriented. Give it to someone's pilot, and they end up in a corn field.

Shit, his car was parked across three spaces. It was a wonder that he hadn't ended up in a corn field himself.

He let himself quietly into the jumpers' suite at the Ritz. The coffee had been prepared the night before and was waiting on the machine's timer to brew. He poured the drug into the water vessel then left the room.

Upstairs in his suite, he called the desk. It was time to figure out why he had been poisoned.

"Any messages?" he asked.

"Yes, Sir. You have a number. A Maggie Donald called at

2:45 AM and asked that you call her as soon as possible. She is at McLendon's apartment."

"Very good." Schiller said.

"Then you have seven messages from Mr. Johnny McLendon."

"Indeed."

"I'm afraid they are garbled. The night man said he seemed quite agitated."

"I understand. Go ahead and read them to me."

"Yes, Sir."

Schiller wanted to tell the man to hurry the fuck up, that he could have walked downstairs and read the messages himself faster. Instead, he waited politely.

The man read, "The money, the money, the shit ax robbed the trump."

"Did you say trump?"

"Yes, Sir."

"Go ahead."

"Why me? Why me? I'm not the soup did fog boy."

Schiller spoke without thinking. "What on earth is that supposed to mean?"

"I don't have any idea, Sir."

"Sorry, of course you don't. Nobody could. Go ahead."

"The next four messages are identical. They consisted of loud screams."

"I see."

"Then here's the last one. It says, 'Going to be a safe. They're coming on me. I've got the runs.'"

"It would appear my friend is having a breakdown."

"Yes, Sir."

"Thank you."

Luckily, McLendon was still in his apartment. He picked up the phone.

"I'm outta here," he said.

"No," Schiller barked.

"What?"

"If you leave now, I will hunt you down and kill you."

"I thought we were friends . . .' Johnny sounded hurt.

"True, but friends kill each other all the time."

"Yes. I know that."

"What happened?"

"The Shitass and his gang stole the money."

"What money?"

"The money you told me to get together."

"I told you no such thing."

"But Plank said . . ."

"Johnny, we've been penetrated. Plank has been turned. Don't trust anybody."

"I won't. Nobody but you and Maggie."

"Is she there?"

"She just left."

"Meet me outside of your building in fifteen minutes. We need to talk."

Hillbillies my ass, Schiller thought as he grabbed a pillowcase and a pistol. He recovered his car from the garage and once he turned onto Peachtree, he called Ray Justus.

Sweetheart of the Rodeo

GINGER WAS AMUSING Ray by walking around the room with nothing on but a pair of cowgirl boots.

"Am I the sweetheart of your rodeo, baby?"

"You certainly are."

Ray's cell phone rang on the bedside table.

"You may as well get it," Ginger said. "It's probably that dope fiend Federal man."

"As long as you don't mind." Ray picked up the phone.

Ginger watched his face change from irritation to curiosity to outright amusement.

"Yes. Yes. Sure thing," he said.

"What was that about?"

"He said one of his buddies dosed him with LSD and he wants me to break into some lady's house and steal another silver suitcase full of money that she stole from him."

"Jesus, Ray, what's this thing with all these suitcases?"

"I don't know, but I think it's all right. I hope this is a trend."

"I think this guy has got some pretty shitty friends, doping him up like that. I thought government people were supposed to be respectable. You know, real tight-asses."

"I don't know how tight their asses are, but they can't hold on to their money for shit."

"I think he's crazy – putting all his money in suitcases so people can steal them. If he'd just stay off the dope and quit driving down that rabbit fur highway, he might hang onto his money."

"Yeah, but we don't want him to hang onto his money."

"I hadn't thought of it that way. You're so smart, Ray."

As she kissed him, there was a gentle knock at the door. She looked through the peephole.

"It's Peanut," she whispered.

Ray slipped on his robe as Ginger shut herself in the bathroom.

First the Suitcase, Then the Shitass

PEANUT WAS STILL looking sheepish.

"Got a call from a buddy back home."

"Uh huh."

"He says he knows where the Shitass Ronnie Gordon is hanging out."

"Over in South Carolina?"

"Yep."

"Fucking outstanding."

"I though you might like that."

"You think you can handle it, or you want me to?"

"What did you have in mind?" Peanut asked.

"We need to get him back here alive, one way or another. I'd like to have him cooperating, if we can arrange it."

"What for?"

"I want to make him our Oswald."

Peanut grinned. "I like that," he said.

"Thought you might."

"What do you have in mind?"

"Cut out a wad of money, maybe twenty thousand. Give him some of it. Hire him some hookers. Tell him we re-thought the situation. All is forgiven. We need a man like him for the big score. Make sure he flashes cash.

"Get him to buy some guns, nice and legal. Make sure there's a paper trail and he's on it. Tell him we need the receipts for our expenses. Don't let him go back to his apartment, but you put the receipts there."

"I've always liked the way you think," Peanut said.

"The important thing is you can't kill him, even if he says you went down on Ronald Reagan."

"I'm working on that," Peanut said.

"Okay . . . we got some big news. I just got a call from the dope-crazed secret agent man. He wants us to steal another one of those silver suitcases."

"You're shitting me."

"Nope. Let's get ready to roll in ten."

"Sure, Ray."

"After we take care of the suitcase, you go get the Shitass."

Ginger was toweling off after a shower.

"You better dress straight," Ray said. "I figure since this is a woman's place we're breaking into, you should be the one to go in. Somebody sees it they'll just figure you're one of her straight friends dropping something off."

Ginger rolled a stocking up one of her shapely legs.

"How about straight on the outside, gangster girl next to the skin?" she asked.

"That'll give me something to think about," Ray said.

Put Your Head in This Sack

MCLENDON LOOKED LIKE a frog eyeing a frying pan. His eyes bulged with fear, and his lips were stretched thin with tension.

"Get in the back seat."

"The back?"

"Shut the fuck up and do what I say."

"The back . . . okay."

"Now lie down on the floor."

"Anything you say, but I got to explain."

"Put this over your head." He threw the pillowcase on the back seat.

"You want me to put my head in this sack?"

"Now."

"You think I'm a stupid frog boy," McLendon said bitterly as he slipped it on.

Instead of answering him, Schiller pushed a CD of Handel's Concerti Grossi into the car's player and turned up the volume. Johnny McLendon continued to mumble complaints then gave up as Schiller refused to respond.

The farm was north of Alpharetta. Like the apartment on the Buford Highway, he had been careful to keep its existence a secret from the members of the cadre. The apartment was a day-to-day refuge. The farm was for going to earth. Also, since he had driven to the apartment when his brain was slammed with drugs and hadn't been able to check to see if he was being followed, he had to consider the apartment blown.

The place actually wasn't much of a farm, more a gentleman's rustic retreat with a few farm buildings for atmosphere, sitting on a twenty acre tract waiting for the developer's bulldozers.

Isolated by a large stand of hardwoods, the compound consisted of small outbuildings, a drive-in barn with stalls for four horses, and the main house. Built at the turn of the century, it was a two-story white frame building with a large open room with a stone fireplace at its center which opened to a second floor gallery with six bedrooms.

McLendon had been reasonably quiet during the drive, although every ten minutes or so his frustration would erupt with incoherent protests that he wasn't a stupid frog boy.

Schiller had driven down progressively smaller paved roads without any reaction from McLendon, but when they hit the concrete drive he began wailing.

"Where are we? What's happening?" He started to sit up.

"Stay down, Johnny."

"Call me Spike," McLendon whimpered.

"It will just be a few more minutes, Spike. Then we'll be safe and can talk."

"Safe . . ." McLendon said it like a prayer.

They drove through the woods beyond the curious eyes of the outside world and stopped in front the barn.

"Can I get up now?"

"No. I tell you when. It will just be a few more minutes."

He opened the barn door, drove the car inside, then closed the door after them. It was midday, but the barn was closed tight enough that it was plunged into a late evening dusk. Schiller liked the feel. Instead of using the building's overheads, he reached back into the car and turned the headlights on bright.

"Leave the pillowcase on your head, but get out of the car." Schiller opened the back driver's side door.

"Okay."

McLendon climbed onto the back seat on his hands and knees and wobbled as he stepped to the ground. Schiller guided him about ten feet in from the car.

"Kneel down."

"You want me to kneel?"

"That's just to make it easy on me," Schiller said. "I'm going to ask you some questions. If I like your answers, you can put the bag back over your head, and I'll drive you back to town."

"And what if you don't like my answers?"

"Then it will be my patriotic duty to blow your brains out."

He held the gun in front of McLendon's hooded face, quickly pulled the pillowcase off and dropped in on the ground in front of him. McLendon blinked his eyes from the headlights of the Mercedes, then focused on the pistol barrel a few inches in front of his eyes. He screamed.

Schiller put his palm on McLendon's forehead and slowly pushed it back and as his mouth involuntarily dropped open Schiller slipped the barrel of the gun into the opening.

"The presence of death clears some men's minds. Do you find that to be the case?"

"Moe." Johnny shook his head to indicate no.

"I was afraid of that. You're going to have to work at it, Spike. Listen closely to what I say and think about it."

Schiller removed the gun.

"Our cadre has been penetrated by the enemies of freedom," Schiller said. "I have to sort out the patriots and the traitors."

"They didn't penetrate me."

"And yet they managed to steal your money twice."

McLendon started to speak but didn't say anything.

"And now we have brave men trapped in the field about to lose their lives at the hands of foreign terrorists because you lost their money, Johnny. American women and little children clutching stuffed toys will be blown to bits by terrorist bombs, all because of you.

"The President will announce at a press conference, 'This could all have been avoided if only that stupid frog boy, Johnny McLendon, hadn't lost the money.'"

"I'm not a stupid frog boy," McLendon pleaded.

"No, Johnny, you're not. I agree. You're most definitely

not. Which makes it all that much sadder that you will be remembered as one through all of human history. Students will see Johnny McLendon in their history books as the traitorous frog boy who blew up children."

"Why me?"

"They will need someone to blame."

"You mean those uptight diplomats?" McLendon asked.

"Yes, Johnny. They and their friends who went to those exclusive prep schools, the schools your father couldn't buy your way into because they thought you were a stupid frog boy. They will all laugh at you.

"I don't even need to shoot you to see you destroyed. I can turn you over to authorities. Here is a stupid frog boy who has engaged in the felonious distribution of campaign finances, who assaulted a high ranking member of the Panamanian security service."

"You mean the room clerk?"

"Yes."

"But you said he might be a spy."

"He was a spy. One of ours. I couldn't blow his cover," Schiller said.

"Good God, what have I done?"

"What, indeed. When you destroyed Commander Carlos, you also destroyed some of our best intelligence assets in the region." Schiller wasn't sure how much further he should push this obviously silly bullshit.

"Then there's the little problem of your conspiring to finance a major narcotics operation . . ."

"But you said that was sanctioned."

"Sanctioned, yes. But you allowed it to escalate into the loss of operatives in the field and the killing of innocent civilians at home. It's a case of deniability, Johnny. The government must protect itself, and like a good soldier you must shoulder all of the blame even though it means you will be regarded for all time as a mentally challenged clown and forced to live for the remainder of your natural life in the bowels of a damp federal mental institution as the sexual servant to a psychotic, hairy, toothless, one-eyed giant whose body is covered with pimples and tattoos."

"What can I do?"

"What can you do? It's simple, Johnny. You can stop this weak-kneed sniveling and stand up like a man. You can join the company of patriots. You can stop feeling sorry for yourself and feel sorry for your country."

McLendon stood up quickly and roared, "I am a patriot!"

"That's the spirit," Schiller yelled, and slipped the gun back in its holster.

"America is coming back and I'm coming with it!"

"Go Spike."

"Just tell me what I need to do."

"Nothing to it," Schiller said. "Get that six million as soon as possible. Don't tell anyone about it. Don't discuss it with anyone but me. Give it to me directly."

"Is that all?" McLendon asked. "I thought you wanted me to do something hard."

Breaking In Is Hard To Do

PEANUT DROVE THE van to Maggie Donald's house and parked in plain view across the street. Ray laid back in the Voodoo Cadillac with Ginger, watched him drop a couple of orange traffic cones and begin digging a hole in the right of way between the curb and the sidewalk.

"He said he'd dig a hole if she was still inside," Ray said.

"The way he's wailing away with that mattock he could have it pretty deep if she decides to hang out for a while."

Ray chuckled.

"I'm going to climb in the back," Ginger said.

Ray was expecting her to get out of the car, but instead she crawled over the seat, wiggling her very shapely legs and ass as she slipped past him.

"I enjoyed that," Ray said.

"I'll start doing it all the time," she said.

She lay back letting the skirt ride up past her stocking tops.

"That too," Ray said.

"I was just thinking that as much as we both admire this vehicle, we've never made love in it."

"Oh baby, we can fix that on the way home . . ."

"I thought you might say that."

"You scared?" Ray asked.

"Yes."

"I thought you might be working on something good to think about."

"You're a smart guy, Ray."

"I don't want to scare you anymore, but there's something we need to talk about."

"Okay."

"If she leaves, you're going to do the B&E."

"Right."

"If there's a hand-off, we're going to the Jesse James mode. Guns in the street and all that."

"What do you want me to do?"

"You'll be the wheel. There's a Kevlar vest under the front seat. Slip it on, then put me in close."

"Anything else?"

"You might need to block their car."

"I can do that."

"Good."

The cell phone rang.

"What you doing up there? Playing with yourself?"

"Now that's an idea."

"I've been leaning on my shovel and scratching my head. She's left without any bags or anything."

"You ready to break and enter?" Ray asked Ginger.

Dirty Work

GINGER CARRIED A small nylon duffel bag over her shoulder. Ray had dropped her off in front of the house and she made a big show of waving goodbye. She glanced at Peanut and smiled. He had been digging his little heart out. The hole was waist deep.

Maggie Donald's townhouse was the end unit. She walked purposely around the side to the back yard. Ray had told her, "First thing, make sure your plan can work." There was a cut through from the rear of the lot to the next block. She could leave by that path, as they thought, so that was okay.

She walked across the cement patio, past a round redwood table with an umbrella stuck in the middle and four chairs clustered around it. It didn't look like it got much use. It was the sort of thing you would buy and imagine all your friends sitting around, until you remembered you didn't have any friends.

Ginger had gone through this when she got her apartment. She had bought plates, silverware, glasses, napkins, a tablecloth, the whole bit so she could have a nice dinner party, then she realized her so-called friends mostly liked to do drugs, break shit and dish out lousy fucks.

For some reason, the picnic table made her feel bad about what she was about to do. Stealing from some tight-ass corporation was one thing, but maybe this woman shared the same broken dreams that she had.

She thought about something Ray had told her. "The difference between an amateur and a professional criminal," he had said, "is that the amateur always does things because he wants to, the professional does things sometimes because he has to. You got to put your feelings aside and sort them out later."

She could see Ray's point. Right now the object was to steal the money.

She retrieved the automatic lock-pick from the duffel bag. It was about the size of a rechargeable electric screwdriver. It could open most locks in a few seconds, but it left obvious scratches so it wasn't very useful if you wanted to hide your break-in, but in this case it didn't matter.

She pushed it in the dead bolt, pressed the on button and listened to it chatter for a few seconds, then turned the cylinder. She repeated the process for the slip lock and was inside.

She slipped on latex examination gloves, and went to the front door. This was another thing she had learned from Ray. Take a minute to make sure you got plenty of ways out if something fucks up. The front door wouldn't be a problem if someone came in the back. There was also an upstairs window she could use which was right above the small roof that covered the back door.

There weren't many places to hide a silver suitcase downstairs. She quickly checked the coat closet and the pantry. The living room was sort of pathetic. No suitcase but lots of uncomfortable-looking formal furniture and generic prints. It was so sterile, there wasn't anything personal here. It was like she had bought her life at a store.

This lady has some serious problems. She thought she should lend her Ray for a couple days. That would probably help her relax. It sure had worked for Ginger.

She pulled her phone out of her bag and dialed Ray.

"I'm going out the back after I pick up the package."

"I'm set up," he said.

She hung up and made her way upstairs.

If I was going to hide a silver suitcase full of money, Ginger thought, I'd probably put it in the guest room under the bed.

At the landing, the master bedroom was easy to spot. Its door was open, and it was the only room that showed any signs of human habitation. It looked like this was one depressed girl, spending all her time in the bedroom while the rest of the place looked like a haunted house.

The closed door was a give away. She pushed it open, revealing a small bedroom filled with so many ruffles on the bed, the drapes, the waste basket, and even the tops of the bedside table and the chest, that Ginger felt dizzy and a little disoriented. It was like looking at a day-glow hippie poster after smoking a banana-sized reefer.

Get me out of here, Ginger thought. She dropped on her knees, and sure enough there was a silver aluminum suitcase under the bed. She pulled it out and picked the lock.

"Oh God," she said, "Please let the money still be here."

She opened the top and saw that the case was packed with neat bundles of currency.

She quickly transferred the money to the duffel bag, then called Ray again.

"I'm on my way," she said.

"You'll see me," Ray said.

This is Art

GINGER GOT IN the car and threw the bag in the back seat.

"I'm hot, baby," she said.

"I'll turn up the air." Ray adjusted the climate control on the dash.

"Not that kind of hot. You need to drive someplace where I can get in the back seat and take my clothes off."

"How about back to the garage."

"Howell Mill's about the closest place I can think of, too. Drive fast," she said.

"You got it, baby."

Ray had pulled the car inside the garage and was closing the overhead door. Ginger leaned over to the driver's side and pressed the button to lower all the windows.

"Ray, darling, stay over there a minute and don't look. I'm going to set up a little performance art piece. I want it to be a surprise."

"Okay, baby."

She crawled over the seat to the back, opened the duffel bag of money and began taking the money packets out, breaking the wrappers and spreading them around on the seat until she had it covered with money. She slipped out of her clothes, laid back, allowing one leg to drop casually off the seat, the back of one hand resting on the forehead and the other at her side.

"You can come look now," she said.

Ray grinned as he walked toward the car and bent over, resting his weight on his elbows as he looked in the back seat.

"Don't tell me you got nothing to say."

"You left me speechless," Ray said. His grin got bigger.

"What do you think?"

"That's about the most amazing thing I've ever seen. You're brilliant, baby. Best art I ever looked at."

"I thought you might like it."

"You got a name for it?" he asked.

"Mmm . . . How about, 'Money and Pussy Make the World Go Round.'"

"That's a very important observation on life," Ray said.

"What are you thinking?" Ginger asked.

"How lucky I am that my gorgeous girlfriend has such an unusual and interesting mind."

"I love it when you say things like that."

"I'm lucky to have you."

"Me too, Ray Baby, I'm lucky to have you. Now, are you going to join me back here?" She held out her arms.

"I think I'll do that."

"You know, Ray, I really think it's love that makes the world go round."

"I don't know if love makes it go round, but it sure keeps it from falling apart."

He opened the car door and slipped in beside her.

"This is fun," Ginger said.

Elevator Music

THE SWAT TEAM wasn't in the lobby of the Ritz, nor were there emergency psychiatric personnel with capture nets hiding behind potted plants and furniture. This meant it was likely the cadre had been elsewhere before their minds were melted by the slow-acting hallucinogen Schiller had put in the coffee.

The elevator was empty when Schiller stepped in, but just before the door closed a woman with a broad-brimmed hat pulled low on her face slipped through the doors.

"I've been trying to get in touch with you, Bill."

He hadn't recognized Maggie. He was impressed. Catching him by surprise like that had been a smooth move.

"I got your messages, but I had to settle McLendon down. He was losing his mind."

"I understand," she said. "When Johnny told me Plank was coming to pick up the money, I stole it. I put it in the trunk of my car until I could leave. It's at my house now."

He watched Maggie's face carefully, as he tried to judge if he was showing how he actually felt – like he had taken an emotional punch to the gut and was about to bend over and throw up. Her expression didn't change, so he must not be losing his touch.

"That was quick-thinking on your part," Schiller said. "I guessed what you had done and had someone remove the money from your house so you wouldn't have to worry about Plank coming back for it."

"That was very thoughtful," she said. "But who is there left you can trust?"

"I have another channel."

"Who?"

He decided to tell her. "I've co-opted the hillbillies."

"No . . . how on earth did you do that?"

"The usual combination of bribes and threats."

"You're brilliant," she said.

"One improvises," he said. "But I'm afraid this development means events are out of control. Stick close to McLendon. Don't go to the Foundation under any circumstances."

"We'll hide out in his apartment," she said. She hit the button to stop the elevator at the next floor.

For the first time, Schiller noticed that the elevator music was a particularly horrible symphonic version of the Rolling Stones song, "I Can't Get No Satisfaction."

The Attack of the Mutants

SCHILLER SAT AT the writing desk in his room at the Ritz trying to put his aching mind back together.

The news from Maggie had been too horrible to be true. When he had heard the money was gone, in spite of the general bewilderment that had gripped the others, it was obvious to him that Maggie had taken it. He hadn't known how, but it was the only possibility that had made any sense.

He had asked Ray to steal it out of desperation. As the operation continued to disintegrate, the only real power he had anymore was the power of the purse. For the time being Plank, Oakes and their pals could only sneak around behind his back. If they ever got their hands on enough money to operate completely on their own, they would become a serious threat.

He realized the odds of ever recovering the money from Ray and his friends were non-existent. But he couldn't steal the money himself. He had to take care of Johnny McLendon and the big prize. The important thing was that no money fall into Plank's hands.

He hadn't imagined for a moment that she had stolen the money to protect it for the two of them. That he had thrown the money away like that made him sick, but he suspected the real reason he felt so awful was that he realized too late that he could trust Maggie.

He hated to admit how lonely he had been since his wife left him. He didn't want to feel like that anymore.

So far, the only person to make money from his plan was Ray, and he had made seven-hundred-thousand dollars worth, and he imagined he was waiting for more.

He was startled by a gentle rap on the door. He opened the pencil drawer of the desk and took out the small automatic, chambered a round, switched off the safety and put the gun back, but left the drawer open.

"Come in."

Plank limped in the room. His right arm was in a makeshift sling, his left eye was closed with an ugly swollen bruise that spread over half his face, and the opposite side of his head was covered with a blood-soaked rag.

He imagined Plank was here to see if he was still alive, but he also could be wondering if casting his lot with Oakes had been a good idea.

"My God, man. What happened to you?"

"It was a disaster."

"Have some coffee. I just brewed a pot. It will help you pull yourself together. No let me do it. You're in no shape."

Schiller filled a ceramic mug from the insulated carafe and handed it to Plank who sipped it appreciatively.

"I'm afraid we've lost the cadre, Sir," Plank said.

"What? Explain please."

"Well, Sir, we went on an operation this morning, and it didn't go well."

"I had guessed that already," Schiller said.

"We had a lead on the location of the hillbillies. A mailbox and fax shop north of town."

"That doesn't sound very sinister," Oakes said.

"We didn't think so either, but when we got there we were attacked by . . . I don't know how to describe them. They were Latino giants with beards and overalls and thick southern accents. They were like some experiment gone wrong. They were mutants.

"They thought we were space aliens who had kidnapped their mother and done sexual experiments on her. She was shrieking and turning in circles and yelling orders to them.

"For some reason, the men began hallucinating. They were yelling strange things that didn't make any sense. The mutants got madder. They thought we were speaking space alien. It was terrible. They tried ripping our arms off. I managed to get away."

"What happened to the others?"

"I found an observation point and eventually saw the police come and arrest them. The Fire Department EMTs were there too. The men were hurt pretty bad. There must have been a lot of damage to their shoulders and hips. The mutants were really trying to rip our limbs off. They had a smokehouse going and they were pouring bar-b-cue sauce over us. God . . . I think they were going to eat us. I think the mutants were cannibals."

"The cadre was hallucinating, you say?" Oakes asked.

"Yes, Sir."

"The same thing happened to me, Plank. Someone poisoned me with some of the Company's drugs, a slow-acting hallucinogenic. I thought the Buford Highway was filled with rabbits. I wonder who could have done it?"

"I can't imagine, Sir" Plank said.

"You aren't hallucinating, are you Plank?"

"No, Sir."

"I wonder if Bart Oakes is hallucinating?" Schiller asked.

"I wouldn't know, Sir."

"No you wouldn't, would you?"

"No, Sir."

"Where did you get the information about the location of the hillbillies?" Schiller asked.

"From Oakes."

"I see. So on Oakes's say-so, you went on an operation and lost the cadre."

"Yes, Sir."

"And you were the only one who wasn't hallucinating."

"Yes, Sir."

"And you abandoned your comrades in the field."

"I didn't have any choice." Plank dropped the stoic, dispassionate tone of the report, and for the first time pled his case.

"You were the only one who wasn't poisoned. The other

men could barely function. They were incapacitated and being tortured by lunatics who you suspect were mutant cannibals. You left them to be smoked and eaten."

"It wasn't my fault." Plank's pleading had turned to a whine.

"Then whose fault was it?"

Plank was silent.

"You can't answer because you know damned well what's happened. You and Oakes have gone out on your own. You've sold out the cadre."

Plank laughed. "Coming from you that's a bit much."

"Explain."

"I'm not stupid," Plank said. "You think I am, but I know you're off the reservation. You're the one who's on his own. Oakes is still loyal to the Company."

"Poor Plank. I understand your need to believe. You have made a religion of what Wilfred Owen called 'the old lie.' *Dulce et decorum est pro patria mori*. You need to believe in bugles and flags and the martyr's death."

"There's nothing wrong with believing in a cause," Plank said.

"Of course not. Not at all, but what you've failed to understand is that at the heart of every cause there are always men who are on their own and working for themselves."

Plank worked his jaw but didn't speak.

"Nothing to say to that? It's a little more complicated than medals and silly patriotic speeches, isn't it? You had a chance to enter the elite where the only allegiance is to the other players of the game, and what did you do?

"You switched your allegiance to a pathetic self-important fool. Dunbarton Oakes is a failure at his chosen profession, his wife humiliated him by sleeping with his students before running off with the carnival, and his supposed martyrdom for the Agency, the study on the efficacy of the strategic hamlet program, was so transparently stupid that its publication permanently set back the war effort.

"Bart Oakes was never in the Agency loop, and now he's so far out of it he doesn't know they canned his ass ten months ago. Is this the evidence that you aren't stupid?" Schiller asked.

"I don't see it that way," Plank said.

"You don't see it at all. If you had stuck with me, you would have made a nice sum of money and gotten a good recommendation to continue this line of work, both for the Company and for friends of the Company. As it is, you're through. I suggest you take what money you have and open a bait shop."

"I don't think you have that much power."

"What you think is no longer important." He took the automatic from the drawer and rested it on the desk, his hand still loosely wrapped around the grip. "As a courtesy, I'll give you till the end of the week until I put out the burn letter on you and Bart."

"Fine." He said it with enough sarcasm that Schiller knew he was afraid it was true.

"Be sure you take some painkillers from the medical kit on the way out. It looks like you will need them."

"Yes. Thank you."

"Don't thank me," Schiller said. "If I ever see you again, I'm going to kill you."

"Then we know how we stand."

"I'm not convinced you have any grasp of where you stand," Schiller said. "But I will give you a little hint. Get to where you need to be very soon. I just dosed your coffee."

Schiller sat at his desk and hummed the overture from *The Magic Flute*. He was in a better mood now. Throwing away the money had been a setback, but why cry over spilt anything. It was done. Time to forget the fuck-up and move on. He needed to fix his gaze on the real challenge, separating Johnny McLendon from his money.

Everything he'd told Plank had been bullshit. Noise designed to confuse his mind. At least that part of the operation was proceeding as planned.

My Shoes Have Alligators

BART OAKES WISHED he hadn't given the security man time off. As he got out of his car he heard a muffled screaming from the upper floors of the FFA office. He wondered if he should even go inside.

Unfortunately, there wasn't anyone else to go and see what the problem was, and he didn't need to have the police pay him a visit when he needed anonymity more than anything else.

As he put his ear against the front door, he heard the voice and it sounded more like a frightened hysterical child than anyone dangerous. He opened the door a crack and realized it was Plank whining and crying.

It was creepy. The voice so familiar yet out of character. Like hearing your parents having sex when you were a small child, the primal animal moaning from within the bedroom, hinting at a chaos of fears and hungers.

In the foyer a scrawled note rested on the Persian carpet. Plank had heard him come in and was loudly chanting a sing song string of senseless words. Oakes picked up the note. It said:

"Schiller thinks he scared me off. We're in the clear. Watch McLendon but don't get seen. The cadre got their arms ripped off by mutant cannibals, and I got dosed with the God juice. Going upstairs to dance with the carrots. I think my shoes have alligators."

If Oakes understood the note, it meant Plank was under the influence of a drug, rather than losing his mind, and that was good news. Something strange had happened to the cadre. Who knew what that was?

He didn't have a clear idea about how to watch someone without being seen, but all he really had to do was hold out until Plank recovered. If he couldn't do it well, at least he could do it.

He thought he'd better check on Plank, so he followed the

mumbling to a small office on the second floor kept mainly for visitors who needed a place to work quietly.

Plank was on the floor near the outside wall surrounded by a pool of urine, his right wrist handcuffed to the radiator. He stopped the incantation and looked at Oakes.

"Just because I'm wearing a dress doesn't mean I'm queer," he said.

"You aren't wearing a dress," Oakes said.

Plank looked down his body, until his attention was finally fixed on his shoes, then he began screaming.

Oakes went back downstairs to Maggie's desk. In the lower right drawer she kept shipping supplies. He pushed its contents around until he found a roll of tough, two-inch strapping tape. As he pushed her chair aside, he thought about the many times he had seen her shapely ass sit in it, and he became half erect.

If this entire enterprise came to naught, at least he had fucked her, and it had been the best sex he ever had. Too bad, but it wasn't likely it would happen again. Of course, if he was the only one left with the money, she might be interested. Unless she decided to stick with the cretinous money bags, McLendon.

As it stood, the Foundation was a thing of the past along with Maggie. He had nothing to lose.

He unrolled some tape from the roll.

"I hate to do this, but you can't stop the yelling can you?"

"Please don't make me wear women's clothes," Plank begged.

He was having a bizarre gender crisis under the influence of the drugs.

"I'm going to have to tape your mouth shut. All this noise is going to attract the police."

As Oakes began to wrap the tape around Plank's head he saw that he wanted to say something and he paused a moment.

"Yes?"

"You better wrap my ass too," Plank said. "I don't want them to mess with that either."

Secret Agent Man

MCLENDON BOUNCED AROUND the living room like a monkey during a full moon. He was nervous. Caged up like this he was losing his edge. He needed a mission.

Maggie had tried to help him by fucking him to the point of exhaustion, but in the end it hadn't worked, and it was her that was curled on the bed, looking like an angelic Scarlett O'Hara while she slept.

Schiller wanted him to stay locked up like a zombie in the zoo because he didn't think he could pull his weight on the street. But Schiller didn't understand the changes Maggie had helped him make from millionaire to mad dog. Now Spike was running loose and ready to take a big bite out of the world's ass.

Fuck staying at home, he was going on a training mission. He went to his bedroom and got a sock from a drawer, then got a fresh bar of soap from the bathroom closet. It was time to hit the streets of blackjack city.

The street was empty. He hadn't ever been out here alone this late at night. He wondered if it was safe, then hoped it wasn't. He needed the edge that can only come with facing another human being in armed combat.

He looked for a likely location and crossed the street to a mid-rise office building. Nobody was sleeping in the doorway, but it was warm tonight. Why should they?

Maybe he would have better luck in a more out of the way place, maybe around the back of the building by the dumpster.

On a grass rectangle behind the building he saw a lump that could be a sleeping human being. He walked quietly toward it and saw it was a man. A black man with grizzled gray and white hair asleep on top of a bedroll, wearing nothing but black boots and dirty white jockey shorts.

The man stirred, then leapt to his feet.

"What the fuck you want?"

"I'm here to clean up America," McLendon said.

"Yeah, then get yourself a fuckin' broom and leave me alone."

"It's you I'm going to clean up."

"I take my own showers, pervert."

"You're the pervert. Look at the way you're dressed," McLendon shrieked.

"At least, I don't look like a fucking freak." He looked at McLendon carefully. "Man, you look like a damn frog."

"Shit. Shit. You shit."

McLendon swung the soap blackjack as hard as he could. The man stepped back effortlessly and McLendon almost fell over as he missed.

He swung again, and the man stepped back one more time as the blackjack streaked past his face.

This time McLendon heard an ominous click from the man's right hand. He hadn't noticed the knife.

"Let's see your wallet and your watch, asshole."

"I don't understand," McLendon said.

"I believe that. Just give me the damn wallet and watch."

"But this is an expensive watch."

"Good."

"I don't want to give it to you."

"In that case, I'm going to cut you from your dick to your throat."

"You'd do that?"

"No shit."

McLendon turned to run, but the man caught him from behind by the back of his collar. He jerked so hard that the top buttons on McLendon's shirt popped and McLendon fell back against the man.

The first thing McLendon noticed was the man's stench. It made him gag. Then he felt the knife against his throat.

"Just relax."

It was Schiller's voice.

"I'm relaxed," McLendon said.

"Not you, him," Schiller said.

"Who the fuck are you?" the semi-naked man asked.

"I'm the man with a gun at your head."

"Okay."

"Lower the knife."

"No problem, boss."

"Now step back."

The man stepped back and dropped the knife at his side.

"Good job, Commando Jim," Schiller said.

"What the fuck you saying?" the man asked.

"Johnny, this is Commando Jim. He's part of a specially trained undercover cadre."

"I didn't know," McLendon said.

"No, of course you didn't. How much have you got in your wallet, Johnny?"

McLendon took the wallet from his pocket and cracked it open.

"Looks like about nine hundred dollars," he said.

"We have a tradition in our business. Whenever another secret agent gets the better of you, you give them the contents of your wallet."

"Okay. I see, I guess."

"Give him the money, Johnny."

Johnny handed him the money. The man snatched it and stuffed it in the waistband of his underpants.

"I'm going to keep the watch, okay?"

"Sure, Johnny."

"I'll do this Commando Jim shit again, if you want."

"No, I think you'd better get back to headquarters," Schiller said.

"Yeah, man, whatever the fuck you say. I'm going to headquarters. Sure thing."

"I didn't know," Johnny said. "I was getting stale. I needed a mission."

"Johnny, sometimes a spy has to lay low. I know it's boring, but it's boring for our enemies too. Eventually, they lose their edge. They get sloppy. That's when we strike."

"I'm losing my edge, too," McLendon grumbled.

"You need to get your edge indoors. I'll have Maggie give you some training exercises."

"That's a good idea."

"She can give you some experience with coercive interrogation."

"Sounds pretty neat. What is it?"

"Questioning enhanced with torture."

"That would be a good idea. I could torture her."

"That wasn't what I had in mind," Schiller said. "As long as you are operating in the open like this, we have to prepare for the possibility that you could be captured."

"But I've got my suicide pill."

"You may not be able to get to it in time."

"Jesus, you mean she's going to torture me?"

"I'm afraid so, Spike."

"You're sure this is necessary?"

"It's for the good of the country . . . patriots have suffered more for their country, you know."

"I'm a good soldier," McLendon mumbled. He didn't understand it, but he figured if Schiller thought it was for the best he could go through with it.

Bad Scared

OAKES HAD SCOOTED down in his car seat when he saw
McLendon come from the front of his apartment building, cross
the street and walk down the alley. He had a million reasons not
to follow him on foot, but he knew, really, there was only one.
He was afraid.

God, he wished Plank was here instead of handcuffed to a
radiator shrieking rants of a bizarre gender identity crisis. Who
would have figured Plank for that?

Oakes wanted to cry. He wanted his old life back. When he
had thought he was capable of doing this, he had been wrong.

The only thing that frightened him worse than following
Johnny McLendon down that alley was the thought of eating
dog food while wearing moth-eaten suits in some subsidized
elder hell-hole near a mosquito-infested swamp in central
Alabama surrounded by braying women who watched daytime
talk television.

He fought back tears as he opened the door. The dome light
came on.

"Jesus," he hissed and turned it off, then opened the door
again, closing it gently . . . latching it by leaning his weight
against it.

He walked down the opposite side of the building than the
one McLendon had, then climbed up a kudzu bank to a parking
lot he thought might be a good place to observe the back of the
building.

He couldn't believe what he saw: McLendon and an old black
man wearing nothing but his underpants. They scuffled, then
the man held a knife at Johnny's throat.

Oakes felt helpless. Six million dollars down the drain or not,
he couldn't think of a thing he could do. If he shouted, the man

would probably kill McLendon, then come after him. He hated being such a coward when the situation called for action.

He had barely seen the movement from the shadows. He saw the gun and the arm first, then Schiller's face.

Schiller looked more tired than anything else. Almost as if situations like this were so common for him he didn't even bother to wake up.

Oakes was scared so badly he could barely move. His limbs had locked. He stood in one place and swayed and fought to keep his balance. Finally, he bent over and dropped to his knees.

What he was really about to do was finally clear to him. He wasn't stealing the money from Johnny McLendon. He was stealing it from Bill Schiller and, as far as Dunbarton Oakes was concerned, Schiller was probably the scariest son of a bitch alive.

His only ally was currently handcuffed to a radiator, pissing his pants and yelling maniacal incantations like Antonin Artaud in a Paris asylum.

He couldn't hold his tears back anymore. He felt like going back to the Foundation and handcuffing himself to a radiator.

There wasn't anything more he could do here. As soon as he could walk, he needed to go back and check on Plank.

It was a long time before he could move.

Shock Treatment

SHE FORCED HERSELF awake. There were voices in the living room. She recognized Schiller's.

There was a gentle knock on the bedroom door. She pulled the covers over her.

"Yes?"

"Maggie, it's Bill Schiller. Can I come in?"

She sat up holding the sheet in front of her.

"Yes, come in."

He pushed the door open slowly, stood in the doorway, took a small step forward, then stopped.

She was embarrassed to be seen in McLendon's bed, and she thought he understood that.

"I'm afraid Spike has been a naughty boy."

McLendon edged past Schiller, walked across the room and sat beside her on the bed. She wished he hadn't. Having Schiller here had killed the self-induced illusion that made sleeping with Johnny possible.

"What has Spike done?" she asked.

"I went on a training mission," Johnny said.

"Oh no."

"And almost got his throat cut in the process," Schiller added.

"I didn't know he was a special commando. He looked like a wino."

"Commando Jim is a master of disguise," Schiller said.

"Schiller says you need to torture me," McLendon said.

"Now that's an idea," Maggie agreed.

"We call it coerced interrogation. Johnny needs to learn how to handle it. It's part of trade craft."

"I need some training exercises," McLendon agreed.

"When should we start?" Maggie asked.

"As soon as possible. I saw some cane-bottom chairs in the dining room. Cut the seat out of one with arms. You can tape him to the chair and start with water and whips tonight. Tomorrow I'll bring you an electrical device you can attach to his testicles."

"Oh no . . ." McLendon moaned.

"Don't worry Johnny. At its lowest setting it doesn't leave burn marks and it's likely you won't pass out or have seizures."

"I'm a good soldier . . . I'm a good soldier . . ." McLendon mumbled over and over.

"I won't make it too bad," Maggie said.

She was afraid Schiller was serious until she saw him wink.

Planking Plank

EXHAUSTION WAS ABRADING the edges of his intelligence. He wanted to pop a pill to give himself another ten hours, but the price would be too high. Eventually he would be a mental zombie, and when he finally came down he would sleep for days.

Schiller would have to get through the rest of the night the old fashioned way. He had fought off sleep often enough. Every year it got harder.

He had one last chore. He would do it quickly then get the sleep he so badly needed.

He glided past the Foundation for Freedom in the Americas. There was the dull glow of a light in the back of the third floor.

Plank's car was in a parking lot across the street, Bart's in the driveway in front of the building. There was no sign of activity.

Schiller parked on a side street and retrieved the bomb hidden beneath his folded raincoat in his back seat. As forgeries went, it was a masterpiece. The ATF should pick up the signature right away and wonder why a Lebanese terrorist was blowing up cars in Atlanta.

Until flags went up when they checked Plank's finger prints, and they theorized in disgust that some CIA funny business had spilled onto the streets of America, and they would be forced to become part of the cover up.

He didn't see anyone when he walked up the street to Plank's car. The strong magnets in the package clicked as they made contact with the frame under the driver's seat.

Tomorrow he would stake out the car and kill Plank with one push of the button on the remote control.

He nodded off once as he drove down Peachtree, checked into the downtown Ritz and fell asleep fully dressed on top of the bedspread.

Two Swords To Go, Please

"I FOUND ME a shitass," Peanut said.

"That was quick."

"He wasn't that hard to find."

Ray was talking to him on the phone, lying on the motel bed. Ginger had pulled her chair next to him with her ankles crossed next to his shoulders. She was reading a *W*, naked.

"How's he doing?"

"He limping, but the leg is on the mend. He about shit when he saw me."

"I bet."

"I flashed some money. Told him that since you had seen him work, you had to have him in this new secret organization. Said you had a sinister plan for world domination and so forth."

"He went for it?" Ray asked.

"Right away. I swear this guy would lose a game of checkers to a turnip."

"You brought him back to town with you?" Ray asked.

"Yup. We got us a little love nest down on Stewart Avenue. A motel. It's got some ladies that work out of it."

"Let's set something up for late this afternoon over at the garage."

"What you going to do?"

"Since you told him we had a secret organization that's going to dominate the world, how 'bout making him a Knight of the New World Order?"

"That should work."

Ray hung up the phone.

"Who was that, baby?" Ginger asked.

"Peanut found the Shitass. They're back in town."

"What's the plan?"

She leaned forward, and Ray looked at her breasts.

"We're going to make him a Knight of the New World Order."

"Ooh, Ray baby. That sounds like fun. We're going to have a ceremony?"

"That's right, sweet thing."

"Can I get the costumes? Can I? Can I?"

"Of course."

"I'll call one of my friends who works at Junkman's Daughter. What do you think . . . some swords, capes, funny hats?"

"Sounds good."

"Are you looking at my tits?"

"Damn right."

She climbed on the bed, quickly straddled him, leaned forward, and began moving her shoulders back and forth, brushing her breasts against his face.

"How about this view?"

"I like the way you do that," Ray said.

"I got some good ideas for ceremonies, too."

"I bet you do."

Fireworks

SCHILLER WOKE TO the six-thirty call. Barely three hours' sleep hadn't helped much but he managed to pull himself into a ragged imitation of consciousness with two cups of hot coffee from the coffee maker in the room.

He looked like a damned derelict. His suit was badly wrinkled, and he could smell himself. No time to pick up clothes at the safe house or even shower. He had to get an early kick so he could kill Plank.

Later he could buy new clothes at a men's shop on Peachtree, take a long hot bath and sleep through the clock.

When he was young, thoughts like this held out a promise that kept him going all night. Now it made him more tired.

He left the hotel through the parking deck and walked to Peachtree where he caught a bus and rode a few blocks south of the Foundation. Plank's car was still in the parking lot, so he found a cafe, sat near the front window, and ordered coffee and a cheese Danish.

The proprietor was cleaning off a table near him.

"Is there any place where I can get a newspaper?" Schiller asked.

"I got one in the back. Just a minute."

He stepped into a small office and came back fumbling with a paper he was trying to refold.

"Don't bother, I'll just be tearing it apart again."

"Sure you don't mind?"

"No, not at all."

He handed the paper to Schiller who opened it to the front page.

"Looks like the President is selling the country to the Chinese," the man said.

Plank's car pulled out from the parking lot followed immediately by Bart Oakes. Good . . . a two for one, he would kill Plank and terrorize Oakes with the same bomb.

There was a lull in traffic so the block was empty except for the two cars, no school buses, no children clutching teddy bears in their small arms, no hapless families squandering their yearly holidays sniffing pollution.

"Is there anything left in the country that hasn't been sold to somebody?" Schiller asked as he pressed the remote control.

"Ain't that the truth," the man laughed, and then the sound of the bomb reached him. It was a muffled "woomf."

Ah, the beauty of a controlled blast, Schiller thought.

"What was that?" the man asked.

"Oh my God . . . a car's gas tank . . . I think it exploded." Schiller stumbled over his words for effect. The man leaned forward to look through the window up the street.

"Oh my God . . . a car's gas tank," he repeated. "I better call emergency. I better call them," he said, but he still stood there.

"Yes, please go call. Go!"

"Yes. Yes." He ran back toward the office knocking over a table. "Oh my God."

The car was burning. Oakes's car was stopped in the street, and he cautiously climbed out.

"Oh shit."

To Schiller's surprise and disgust, the door to Plank's car opened slowly, and Plank rolled onto the street. His right jacket sleeve was on fire. Bart took off his sports coat and tried to beat it out, but only succeeded in fanning the flames.

Plank was rolling on the ground and screaming. When he managed to get the fire out he stood and Schiller saw his left arm dangling limply at his side.

He was temporarily disoriented. Oakes led him to his car, and once he had him tucked in the passenger seat, ran to his side and drove off.

No curious witnesses, no sirens . . . Schiller put seven dollars on the table and left.

"I'm going to see if they need any help," he yelled, but the man didn't answer.

He walked to Courtland and caught a bus back downtown.

Jesus, what's wrong with me? I can't even blow someone up anymore. It was a simple enough job. What didn't work? He was so tired he could barely stay awake to think straight.

For the first time he began to consider the horrible possibility that the Agency had known what it was doing when it let him go.

He knew he was past his prime, but was it possible he had unknowingly joined the ranks of the incompetent buffoons he had elbowed aside as an ambitious young recruit? Men who looked at him knowingly as too green to be trusted, but fucked up everything they touched.

Only they never knew it. They were protected by the safe delusions of people foolish enough to believe that life was a game with rules, rules they knew and understood from the wrong lessons of a long life.

Had he turned into this without even knowing it?

He had to get a grip on himself. If he kept thinking like this, he would turn into an old croaker. He had to get some sleep. Everything would seem better tomorrow. With a good night's sleep, a good meal, a warm bath and new clothes he would put things back together.

He was in Atlanta where, after all, tomorrow is another day.

Rise Sir Shitass

AT FIRST, GINGER had wanted to go overboard with giant orange turbans, purple velvet robes and lime-green silk harem pants, but she decided that in spite of Ray and Peanut's assurances that the Shitass Ronnie Gordon was stupider than your average fungus, there surely was a limit as to what he would believe.

As a result, she decided to go for something conservative yet dramatic, and dress everyone like stage magicians – tails, top hats, opera capes . . . with herself, of course, dressed like the magician's assistant.

Three old Knights of Columbus dress swords rounded out the ensembles. She decided that as the only girl present she should have a bouquet of flowers.

A courier delivered their outfits to Peanut and the Shitass, while she and Ray arrived at the garage early, armed with props and four bolts of blue velvet cloth and staple guns.

After an hour they had one end of the garage converted to a good imitation of the throne room of the Queen of the Hookers, which was the feeling she had been looking for.

She was attending to finishing touches when she heard voices outside the garage.

"When do I get me one of them fucking swords? Huh?"

"As soon as you get made a knight. Then you get one of these swords like this here.

"May we come in, oh Master of the New World Order?" Peanut asked.

"You may enter when the Master is ready," Ginger yelled.

Ray sat on the throne and Ginger walked to the door and opened it.

"The Master of the New World Order will see you now."

She had gotten Peanut's size almost right. The pants were a

bit high water, but everything else fit well. The Shitass's suit was several sizes too small.

Maybe this was for the best, she thought. He probably associated dressing up and formal occasions with being uncomfortable. The collar looked like it was about to strangle him, meaning the blood to his brain was being cut off and he'd be even stupider than usual.

"And what Worthy do you bring me to be made a Knight?"

Ray was cute, and he was playing it just right. She wanted to take him in her mouth and eat him up. In fact, tonight she would do just that.

"I bring the Worthy Shitass Ronnie Gordon," Peanut said.

"Step forward and kneel Worthy Shitass, and answer the questions of a Knight of the New World Order."

Ginger took the Shitass by the shoulder and he limped as she led him in front of Ray's chair and helped him kneel.

"Do you swear to accept money from the New World Order?" Ray asked.

"Oh yes," Gordon said.

"Do you promise to use it to buy fancy cars and attract fancy women?"

"Wouldn't do nothing else!"

"Do you promise to inform all that you meet that you are a Knight of the New World Order and to exalt in your importance."

"I'll do that, too."

"Then the time has come for the blood initiation."

"You say blood?"

"Hold out your thumb."

"My thumb?"

Ray took it in his hand and quickly pulled a straight razor from his pocket. He cut a deep slice in Gordon's thumb.

"Jesus, you cut me."

"That was the idea. Now hold it to your forehead."

It was bleeding freely.

"That's good. Now rub it on your face."

Gordon began smearing it around on his forehead and cheeks.

"You may not wash it for a week so all shall know you as a newly-made Knight of the New World Order. And now the time has come."

Ginger handed Ray a sword with a flourish and he pulled it theatrically from his scabbard, then touched it to Gordon's shoulders.

"I dub thee Sir Shitass, Knight. Rise Sir Shitass."

He stood and without thinking rubbed blood on the front of his shirt.

"Each new Knight must have his first quest."

Ginger leaned behind the throne and picked up a silver tray piled high with twenty-dollar bills and carried it to Gordon. She smiled like a game show hostess.

"This tray contains ten thousand dollars. Your quest is to spend it all in one night at the Clermont Lounge. Do you know where that is?"

"Sure, that's the titty bar in the basement of the hotel on Ponce."

"Correct. You have other money as well? Is that true?"

"That's right, Cap," Sir Shitass said. "Peanut gave me some."

"Very well. You will be contacted in one week and given your first weekly pay of fifty thousand dollars. The only condition is that you must have spent all of the money you currently posses. Understood?"

"Boy, do I . . ."

"Go forth and spend, Sir Shitass," Ray said.

"Peanut, you going with me?"

"I'm afraid you must go on your first quest alone."

"But I don't got a car."

"Walk to a pay phone and call a cab," Peanut suggested.

"I don't mean to seem ungrateful," Gordon said. "It's going to be great being a Knight like this and getting all sorts of pussy."

They waited until they were sure he was gone before they started laughing.

"You made us a hell of an Oswald," Peanut said admiringly. "A week from now everyone in town will be talking about the crazy fuck who is covered with blood and spending money like wild, the cops will have found the guns and paper, and he'll be too broke to run."

"I wondered if I was going to feel sorry for him," Ginger said.

"Did you?" Ray asked.

She laughed.

Red Mist

THE NEWSPAPER HADN'T really called to Ray and said, "Read me or else." He had picked it up without thinking as they walked from breakfast at the Majestic on Ponce.

"We really going back to the store?" Ginger asked.

"Seems like a good place to run things for a while. It's close to the action, it's got a phone, and we can stay out of the weather."

They walked to the Voodoo Cadillac, which was parked in front of the Plaza Theater, and Ray opened the door for her then let himself in and handed her the newspaper. She flipped it open casually, glanced at the front page and drew a breath.

"Fuck a duck . . ."

"Huh?"

"They got a picture . . . Oh man, I can't believe this, they got a picture . . . somebody blew up a car on Peachtree, and they got a picture of it in front of that Foundation the Shitass liked to drive to."

"Now that's a coincidence."

"You're being pretty cool about it," she said.

"Gangsters are supposed to be cool."

"I bet this was your damn dope addict Federal man. That guy is crazy. Running down rabbits and asking you to kill his friends. He's a fucking maniac."

"How many were killed?"

She skimmed the story.

"It says here that there wasn't anybody in the car when the authorities got there. No witnesses are coming forward. Jesus, Ray, that crazy fucker is taking the bodies with him and doing something with them. I bet he's eating them or using them in a ritual."

"Don't jump to conclusions," he said. "There could be a simple explanation."

"Yeah, I'd like to hear that one."

"I guess we better make Peanut start the car from now on."

"I don't see how you can joke about it. Just a bright light and poof, you're a red mist ruining everyone's new outfits."

Ray looked at her, and she started laughing.

Ginger had her own key to the shop, and so she let Ray in but stopped by the door. When he came after her, she put her arms on his shoulders and stood on her tiptoes and kissed him. He took her in his arms and returned the kiss, then brushed his lips against her neck just the way she liked it.

"This is just about the most romantic thing possible," she said. "I can't tell you the number of times I stood here and wished you would do that." She felt the hunger for him again that she had known when she thought she could never have him.

"Same for me," Ray said.

His cell phone rang in his coat pocket so he answered it.

"This is Schiller."

"Looks like you made the paper," Ray said cheerfully.

Seeing the irritation on her face, he could tell Ginger knew who he was talking to. God, she was so beautiful it almost hurt.

"Things happen." Schiller didn't bother to pretend he didn't know what Ray was talking about.

Peanut walked in the shop. Ginger recovered the newspaper and showed the bombing story to Peanut. He didn't look to be enjoying this development.

"How's that working out? A guy could get real pissed, you blowing up his car and everything."

"It's nothing for you to worry about."

"I usually decide what I need to worry about," Ray said. "Right now I'm thinking how much I like my ride."

"We don't have a problem."

"If you say so . . ."

"I do say so. I need a little help with a part of the operation that's falling apart. You have to go to Panama."

"What's going on?"

"The briefing papers will be there when you arrive. I need you to leave this afternoon."

"Okay. I don't want to travel down there as myself. Let me check on what ID I've got available. I'll get back to you. Give me your number."

"Okay."

"And don't blow up the fucking airplane."

"We don't have a problem."

"Whatever it is he's up to, it's going down soon," Ray said.

"How can you tell?"

"He's trying to get me out of town, wants me to go to Panama today. We need to work fast. You know anybody with a picture ID who wants to go to Panama?"

"Most the guys I know would think that sounded pretty weird," Peanut said.

"They've got no sense of adventure," Ginger said. "I know a guy that likes to travel a lot. He's a drummer, but his band just fell apart. You know Lawrence, don't you Peanut?"

"Yeah, sure . . . he'd be perfect."

"Make sure he's awake and ready to roll. Will he show up?"

"Sure."

"Can he take care of himself?"

"Sure baby. He's a real bonehead."

"Tell him to get his ass over here quick. And ask him the full name on his picture ID."

Ginger made a phone call, then said. "He's on his way over. The name on his ID is Lawrence Spagnetti."

"We need to work out how we're going to do this. If Schiller wants to take me to the airport, we'll have to work out a switch. My bet is that he will let me take myself and just check that I arrived at the destination. You can do that now that they got all this security stuff."

He took the phone from Ginger and called Schiller.

"I got the most convenient ID card," he said.

"Is it good?"

"The best."

"What's the name?"

"Lawrence Spagnetti."

"You don't look Italian."

"We're from the north."

"Good enough. I'll call in the reservation. You just show your ID at the Delta counter."

"Got you."

"There will be a packet waiting for you down there. Just ask at the ticket counter."

"Okay."

"Don't be put off by the hotel. It's a brothel."

"Sounds interesting."

"We use it as a safe house."

"Sound's like a good place to hide."

"You can get yourself out to the airport?"

"Sure. I'll leave my car on the long term deck . . . don't get any ideas."

Schiller chuckled. "You aren't going to let me forget about that, are you?"

"Nope."

"Well, good luck. I know you got plenty of walking-around money."

"Right."

"We'll settle up when you get back."

"That'd be fine."

"Help me think through this," Ray said.

"You don't need any help, darling. You think real good," Ginger said.

"Just listen then, and tell me if this makes sense. He wants me out of town, so he sends me to Panama. This means he's about to do something. We don't know what," Ray said.

"No, but I bet it's in a silver suitcase."

"I like them silver suitcases," Peanut said.

"So it's possible he's about to move another silver suitcase full of money," Ray said.

"That makes sense . . . but how do we find out where it is?"

"About all we can do is watch and wait. We're spread pretty thin, so I guess we need to be careful about where we do it. My guess is that Schiller . . ."

"You mean the dope addict spy," Ginger said.

"Right. I bet he's going to be hard to find. I doubt we are going to pick up anyone at the Foundation so here's my top picks. We got that McLendon fellow, he seems to be the money-bags of the outfit, and the woman we stole the second suitcase from. Ginger darling, why don't you phone McLendon and see if he's at the office?"

Ginger retrieved the business directory, looked up McLendon's number then dialed the old black phone.

"Hello. Mr. McLendon's office please." She mugged to Peanut and Ray. "Hello, yes. This is Matilda Butz-Spankington, and I'm a reporter with the *Industrial Machinery and Livestock Gazette*. I need to confirm a few facts. Could I speak to Mr. McLendon please?

"Oh, is that so? Next week? No, I have plenty of time. I'll call back . . ." She hung up the phone and picked up the residential directory and thumbed through it.

"They said he's out of the office till next week. We got a bunch of McLendons in here. There's a B. J. in midtown."

"I bet there is," Peanut said.

"Here we got a Johnny in midtown too. I'll give it a try."
She dialed again.

"Hello, Mr. McLendon? Yes. Are you the Johnny McLendon who is CEO of the McLendon Company, Timber, Textiles,

Manufacturing? You are? How nice for you. Well, I'm Matilda Butz-Spankington, a reporter for the *Industrial Machinery and Livestock Gazette*. That's right. I need to ask you a question. Okay, here it is: Would you consider using ESP, divination, the reading of bull livers or any other occult practices if you thought it could give your corporation the competitive edge? Well thank you very much . . . yes, Sir."

She cradled the telephone.

"Assuming he hasn't moved and kept the same phone, now we know where McLendon is," she said.

"That was damned smart," Peanut said.

"I want to know the answer to your question. Would he use the occult?"

"He said he already does. Some lady who uses cards," she said.

"You're kidding . . ."

"No.

"Damn, you learn something every day. I always thought these business guys had scientists telling them what to do."

"Funny world, ain't it," Peanut said.

"Let's get started. Ginger, you take the woman's place. You can probably blend in better over there, and Peanut can camp out at McLendon's place.

"We are going to be pretty spread out, so as soon as we get something definite, we get on the phone and converge. This make sense?"

"Sure man," Peanut said.

"I'm going to drift by the Foundation, get some supplies and see if I can get us a nearby hotel room."

"This address is near the Fox Theater. The woman's place isn't far from there," Ginger said.

"I'll get a room in the hotel across the street from the Fox. We need to be very careful, keep in touch, and cover each other. Y'all ready?"

"I was born ready," Peanut said.

Smoking

SCHILLER LIT A cigarette, the first one in twenty years. His whole life had gone to shit, so why not?

He was exhaling through his nostrils, parked in midtown not far from McLendon's apartment, watching a half-dozen school girls wearing blue plaid school uniforms play tag.

They were having fun, but it seemed sad. His son had played like that with his friends. His wife had certainly played as innocently with hers. He remembered as a kid walking down the street, glove in hand, to his friend Jimmy Godfrey's house, looking for an after school game of catch.

Jimmy had gone on to Wall Street. Had put together a good career but developed a fondness for the bottle. Eventually, he was caught with his hand in the till and was sent to the same federal prison as all those jazz musicians.

What happened to us, Schiller wondered? Were we all infected by some horrible virus?

"Hello, Dad."

He looked in the back seat. Nobody was there, of course. He hadn't really heard it. He had just imagined his son's voice, and it had seemed real.

Shit, he was losing his mind.

He had to forget this for now. These thoughts were only the after-tremors of a mind that had been soaked with a hallucinogenic drug. They didn't mean a damned thing.

His son was dead and he wasn't talking to anyone.

Here was what was important. Plank was injured and out of the picture. Bart Oakes had never been in the picture. Ray would be on his way to Panama in a matter of hours. However awful this ordeal had been, it was almost over. He could retire in comfort without waiting each month for the Agency's pathetic handout.

He was losing his touch, all right. He hadn't noticed the man walk up beside him and was startled when he heard the tapping on the window. The man looked like a citizen but was angry.

Schiller rolled down the window.

"Yes?" he asked.

"What are you doing here?" The man trembled.

"What on earth do you mean?"

"You've been sitting here for a long time."

"Correct. I've been smoking a cigarette before going to a meeting. The streets are free aren't they?"

"Don't get smart with me, buddy. I've been watching you look at these little girls. How would you like it if I called the police and got you arrested?"

"What?" He couldn't understand the man's point . . . Jesus, he thought he was a child molester. This was too much. His life was going to shit, and he was being mistaken for a child molester.

His hand was closing around his pistol as he tried to subdue his rage.

"Stand back from the car, please." He spoke in his command tone. The man was bewildered but stepped back from the car obediently. Schiller opened the door, slid out and stood next to him.

"Act friendly and very casual and look at what I am about to show you."

"What are you doing?" The man was frightened.

Schiller opened his jacket and took a Federal ID out of his inside pocket, making sure the man saw the pistol at the same time.

"Do you recognize this as official Federal identification?"

"Yes . . . yes."

"You are interfering with a sensitive surveillance. Do you understand?"

"Yes, Sir."

"Now wave and act friendly as you leave."

The man walked backwards waving like a moron, then turned and walked briskly away.

"Great to have met you." Schiller waved.

Shit, you couldn't even smoke these days without some geek being a good citizen all over you. What was this damn country coming too?

He got back in the car, lit another cigarette, and drove off. You could never tell. Maybe the geek would call the police after all.

The cigarette tasted okay, but what he really needed was some reefer.

Waiting Game

GINGER PARKED HER old orange Toyota up the street from the townhouse she had broken into. She hadn't sat there very long before she realized she looked stupid sitting in the car pretending to be interested in her finger nails.

She pulled the copy of *Princess Naughty* from her purse, got out of the car and walked across the grass yard in front of an old frame apartment building. The view was good so she sat under a tree with her back against its trunk.

She opened the book and pretended to glance at it. It really was almost as stupid as Ray had claimed, but it was entertaining in a strange way, too. She was more than half way through the book, and Princess Naughty had all the men of the pueblo mowing her lawn, trimming her plants and painting her eaves, just for a few glances down her blouse and a suggestive roll of her eyes.

She wondered if the unnamed author, X, was really a woman. Whoever it was had a firm grasp of how easy men could be.

There was some heavy mystery in the air about whether she was going to give it up to this guy named Pedro, but Ginger couldn't see why since Pedro tended her garden for free just for the opportunity to look up her dress when she stood on her balcony.

One of the things about Ray was that he had always been kind but had never been easy. She hadn't really had a clue about how he felt until that day in her apartment, and then she found out he had been sweet and noble because of Peanut but had loved her all along.

A tiny old man, bent with a cane, was walking down the sidewalk. He stopped to make conversation.

"Nice day there, young lady," he said.

"Yes Sir, it is."

"What you reading? Is that one of those romance books?"

"No Sir. It's a porno."

"A porno, huh?" He chuckled. "You want to do the wild thing with an old man?"

"You're a very bad boy," she said. She had to admit, it was sort of an entertaining idea. Sort of like a public service.

"You got that right."

"I'd like to help you out, but I got a boyfriend."

"Nice to think about anyway. Well, maybe next time," the man said.

"Never can tell."

She waved, and he continued shuffling down the street. She hoped she could be that unruly when she was his age.

Nothing happened for more than an hour, no more propositions, no conversations of any kind, the only company was a squirrel that eyed her cautiously while it gathered nuts.

Then a woman walked casually from the townhouse, stood on the porch while she fumbled for her keys and locked the door.

Ginger walked to her car without acting like it was a big deal, and recognized the woman as she walked across the street to an old Volvo.

They both started their cars. After following her for a few minutes as she wound through the maze of little midtown byways, she realized they were going toward McLendon's apartment.

She steered with one hand and dialed the mobile phone with the thumb of the other.

"What's up?" Peanut asked, only he drawled it more like "wazzup?"

"I'm following the woman. Looks like we're heading toward you."

"I'll call Ray and sit tight."

Movement

THE VOLVO DROVE into the parking deck of the high rise. Ginger had wondered what sort of apartment some rich guy would live in and now she could picture it − lots of expensive furniture, big windows and big views . . . assholes standing around drinking martinis and making fun of the people who worked for them.

"Did you see her?" she asked on the phone.

"Uh huh. You see me?"

"Yes."

"Come on down. The van is better for watching from. The two of us will blend in better."

"Sure thing, Peanut."

She wasn't sure if she should lock her car since it would make it slower to get into, but decide to. Just because she was down here ripping someone off, didn't mean some other jerk wouldn't come along and steal her poor car. Silver suitcases or not, it was paid for.

As she opened the door of the van and slid into the cab she realized she felt nervous, and it wasn't because of what they were doing. It was because of Peanut. It wasn't that long ago that they were rubbing naked over each other and being alone with him felt awkward.

"Nice outfit," he said. That didn't help.

"Thanks."

"You look like a lady with a lot on her mind."

He could still read her.

"I've been worrying about you. Just because we aren't going together doesn't mean I can't worry. All these drugs and shit . . . It isn't good."

"Yeah, I know." He was sad. "I ever tell you about the time my old man took a bath that lasted three days."

"No. You never mentioned it."

"When he finally got out, it was something awful. His skin was wrinkled up and he was so stiff he could hardly walk. Me and my momma helped him to the bed. He was naked as a jaybird and soaking wet when he laid down. Wouldn't let us towel him off. I didn't think it was that odd at the time. It was just the way things were."

"I'm sorry. My family had it's weird shit, but it wasn't nothing like that," she said. "It must have been very hard."

"I don't know," Peanut said. "It just was."

He glanced at a Mercedes that was cruising slowly down the street.

"Nice car. He's looking for something."

"Looking for love," she suggested.

"That would be a few blocks over." He shook his head. "Anyway, back to what we were saying, things have been getting weird. It wasn't just running into the Shitass again. Things have been going funny in my head. It's like I'm becoming my father."

"Peanut that would never happen. Don't think like that."

"Anyway, that's the reason I broke up with you. It wasn't that I didn't care anymore. I just couldn't make my mind work right. It was like I just wanted to sit in the bath tub."

"Peanut . . ."

"Shit, he's turning around at the end of the street and coming back."

"Don't look too hard."

"I won't. Can you see him?"

The car was barely rolling up the block, then it turned smoothly into the apartment building's garage.

"Bingo," she said. "Should we call Ray?"

"Just hold on. When I told him you were coming over he said he was taking care of business and not to bother to call him unless we needed back-up, and I don't think we're at that point yet."

"No. We ought to wait for something more."

"We oughta just shoot the breeze and see what happens."

"Sure."

"Like I was saying. I'm getting mental. I'm just sitting around and thinking crazy stuff. Once I get my share of the money, I think I might use it to go to the mental hospital."

"Peanut, don't be crazy . . ." She wished she hadn't said that but he didn't seem to notice. "There's nothing wrong with you that cleaning up won't fix."

"You think so?"

"For sure. I think you lost track of how much you were putting in your body. It was a lot. I think maybe you should go to one of those meetings like some of my friends go to."

"My name is Peanut, and I'm an alcoholic. You mean that type of thing? Think that would help?"

"Sure can't hurt."

Company

As MAGGIE OPENED the door, Schiller heard Johnny McLendon holding forth as if he were addressing a group.

"Who's here?"

"Nobody. He's nervous."

"Schiller, Schiller . . ." McLendon repeated.

"I'm here, Johnny."

"Schiller, come in here. Schiller, Schiller . . ."

McLendon was pacing in the middle of the living room.

"You have any drugs?" Schiller asked?

"Sure, I've got just about anything. What do you want?"

"I meant for you. We need to calm you down."

"He's been taking Valium with scotch. It hasn't slowed him down," Maggie said.

"I'm real nervous," Johnny explained. "You need to take the money so I can get calm again."

"We'll get to that. But first there's a little wrinkle . . ."

"There's always something. Some thing or other . . ."

Schiller wanted to slap the silly frog-face dipshit.

"It's hard work being a patriot."

"I know it's hard," Johnny said. "It's too hard. I'm so sick of this shit, I'd join the damn Communist Party if it still existed."

"They'd take away your money, Spike," Maggie said.

"I don't care. I only want to be left alone."

Schiller thought that Maggie may have hit upon a way to get his attention.

"Spike," Schiller said in a loud firm voice.

"Huh?"

"It's time for an operation."

"An operation?" His eyes focused and sparkled.

"Yes. Let me show you."

He led Maggie and Johnny to the balcony.

"If you look at the street in front of the building, you'll see a light-green van."

McLendon bent over the railing.

"Stand back a minute, Johnny. You don't want to give the enemies of America the chance to shoot you."

"Oh, right. I should have thought."

"There's a couple in the van," Schiller said. "I think they are part of the Shitass's Satanic Hillbilly Army."

In truth, Schiller didn't know who they were.

"Oh, my God! You want me to cover you when you leave the building with the money?"

"No Johnny, you're going to carry the money yourself."

"Me? Why me?"

"Very simple. It's because they won't rob you."

"Why not?"

"Because you can go to the police. A six-million-dollar robbery is going to attract more attention than they want. I can't go to the police, Johnny. Once the money leaves your hand, it's cloak and dagger, and nobody can talk about it."

"It makes sense, Spike," Maggie said.

It did make a certain amount of sense, Schiller supposed. But his real reason for saying it was that if anybody got his ass shot off for the money, he wanted it to be Johnny and not him.

"Then what are we waiting for?" McLendon asked.

"First, we need a plan," Schiller reminded him.

Going Down

THEY WERE WORKING on the blueprint for a comprehensive mental health recovery by the time Peanut saw the Mercedes pull out of the parking garage and make a left turn onto the street.

"Heads up. The Mercedes is rolling."

"Should I call Ray?"

"Not yet . . . fuck a duck there's the Volvo. Call him now. I think it's coming down."

She pressed the speed dial. Ray picked up after six rings.

"Yes."

"It's happening," she said.

"I'm rolling."

"Stay on the phone."

The Volvo turned left and headed toward them fast.

"They made us. She's got a man with her. I got to do a huey."

The Volvo shot past. Peanut pulled out but the road wasn't wide enough to make in one turn, so he backed up then raced after the car.

"They turned on Juniper heading south."

"I'm a ways off but I'll head in that direction and try to intercept."

"They're moving out." Ginger said. "Look for a late-model black Mercedes."

"Schiller."

"I guess so."

The Volvo turned east onto a small side street.

"They're turning."

Peanut goosed the accelerator, and they caught up to the street and turned.

"Oh shit. They got the street blocked."

The Volvo was completely blocking the road. On the other side, McLendon was tossing two silver suitcases in the back seat of the Mercedes.

Peanut screamed, "They got us blocked. I don't think ramming them will do no good."

The woman had a revolver on the dashboard.

"She's packing. What the fuck are we going to do? Are we going to go Jesse James?"

She heard Ray yelling, "No, no, no," in the telephone."

"Ray says no."

"No shit. We'd get our ass shot off."

McLendon slammed the door of the Mercedes and it streaked off.

"There getting away. We blew it."

A car behind them was honking and the driver was yelling hysterically.

"Tell me what's happening," Ray said.

"The Mercedes took off."

"Okay, don't worry. I'll try to pick him up on this side."

The woman picked up the pistol and pointed it at them as the man jumped back in the car with her.

"He does look like a frog," Ginger said.

"She's going to shoot us," Peanut yelled.

The woman squeezed off a round, but it wasn't at them. She heard a man's voice beside them yell, "Ahhh!"

"She's shooting at somebody else," Peanut said.

"We got a regular convention," Ginger said. "That woman just shot at some other guy."

"Get the fuck out of there," Ray said.

"I'm getting the fuck outta here," Peanut said.

"That seems to be the idea," Ginger said.

The woman shot again. Peanut put the van in reverse, floored it, ran into the car behind them, put the van in drive and turned around.

Two men stood beside a plain Jane rental car that belched steam from a caved-in grill.

"Jesus, look at that man," Peanut said.

One of the two was screaming wildly, clutching a bleeding shoulder. His face was a mass of bruises and burn marks, his scalp and eyebrows were burnt off and his wounded arm had already been wrapped in a cast.

"That guy's a mess."

"Doesn't seem like he's had much luck lately," Ginger agreed.

"In this neighborhood that gunshot is going to draw cops."

Peanut floored it till they got back to Juniper, then turned cautiously and merged into the traffic. The Volvo straightened out and headed in the opposite direction.

"What's going on?" Ray asked.

"We're back on Juniper."

"Good. I'm looking for the Mercedes. Why don't you head back to the apartment and see if you can pick up McLendon again."

"Okay, sweetie."

Oops

PEANUT PARKED THE van in front of the apartment building.

"I don't think there's any reason to hide," he said.

"No, I guess not, but I'm wondering if they'll drop the dime on us and get the cops to run us off."

"Could be, but my bet is that they're feeling cop shy."

"You're probably right."

She looked out her side window and saw the two men from the shoot-out walking toward her. The awful-looking one was dripping blood and pointing a pistol at her head. It had a squat silencer like the ones she had seen at the garage.

"Peanut, honey, don't do nothing crazy. There's a man with a gun pointed at my head."

"Shit." He looked past her and saw them. They closed the distance quickly. The man with the bruised and burnt face looked horrible.

"Don't get any ideas," he said.

"I don't have any ideas," Peanut said. He kept his hands on the steering wheel.

"Do anything stupid and first thing, I'm going to blow your girlfriend's brains all over your shirt. Then I'm going to kill you. Got it?"

Ginger felt her whole body go tight and realized she wasn't breathing.

"I got it," Peanut said.

"Now, when I tell you, I want you to hand your piece to the lady, butt first. Real slow so I can see it. Then I want her to hand it to me same way. Understand?"

"Yes."

"Then do it."

Peanut edged the gun toward her slowly. She was frozen. She couldn't make herself take it.

"Go ahead, Ginger."

"I'm scared," she said, but she took it and handed it gently to the man.

"It's good that you're scared," the man said. "That's going to make it easier for you. You'll be good and willing."

"You touch her, I'll kill you," Peanut snapped.

"Don't think I don't know that," he said. Then he shot Peanut twice in the chest.

Peanut jerked and grunted then went limp. Ginger started to scream and the man slapped her across the face with the gun.

"Shut up," he said.

"Okay, okay. You killed him."

"Damn right I did. And here's what you've got to realize. I'd kill you too if you weren't such a juicy-looking thing, but I'm going to keep you alive for the party. What you got to understand is the better the party, the better the chance I'm going to set your pretty ass out on the roadside once I get tired of you. You going to throw me a party or what?" he asked.

She wanted to spit in his face but instead she said, "I'll throw you the best party you ever had, cowboy."

"You hear that Bart?"

"Yes. I'm looking forward to that."

The voice came from behind her and she realized that the other man had opened the back door and was in the van.

"Slide back there to my friend Bart, so he can fix you up."

"Okay."

She crawled to the back. Bart looked like he had started out respectable enough, but his hair was tousled, he had amphetamine eyes, and he had the sickly sweet smell of someone at the butt end of a speed run.

"Put your hands behind you so I can put on the cuffs."

She complied, and he clipped the handcuffs on. The situation was going to shit.

The other man was walking around the front of the van. He looked through the windshield and smiled, then opened the driver's door and roughly pushed Peanut into the cargo area.

She was definitely going to kill this asshole, the first chance she got.

"We got a hot one here," Bart said.

"You can have her first, if you want. But we've got things to do now. Pull this sack of shit back there and cover him up with one of those blankets."

"Sure thing, Plank."

He began tugging at Peanut until he had him fully in the cargo area, then he threw an oily rug over him.

"Come up here and sit so you can see what's going on. You can wait an hour for the other stuff."

"Sure, Plank."

"I'm going to go upstairs and get the idiot and the whore," Plank said. "The keys are in the ignition. If anyone looks curious, you can circle the block and pick us up. Should take five minutes."

Ginger was quiet until the one called Plank was gone.

"Bart," she said.

"Yes."

"I'm not going to be able to move later if I can't get into a comfortable position."

"Go ahead."

"Thank you."

Her skirt had manage to ride up, so she scooted backwards pulling it back down as she moved against the side of the van. The she pulled her legs back beneath her.

As far as she could tell, the man named Plank was in charge, although he seemed in much worse shape than Bart. It wasn't only his injuries. He had the scary feeling of a man out of control. Like he was being pulled in two directions and was going to tear in half and really lose his shit, guns blazing.

She suspected he was sharing Bart's Doraville marching pow-
der as well as handfuls of kick ass pain pills. She was beginning
to suspect that he might be the body that wasn't found in the
bombed car outside of the Foundation.

On the minus side, she was handcuffed and being held by two
assholes who were crazy on drugs and were probably about to
rape and murder her. That wasn't very good.

She did have a few things going for her though. From the
sound of it, she had an hour before the real shit happened. The
two of them were cosmically fucked up, and the soon-to-be-
dead Plank – if she could manage it – had been so gripped by
madness that he hadn't had Bart frisk her so they had missed her
little derringer still tucked in the side of her stocking.

When the time was right she would try to pass the cuffed
hands around her hips and legs, get the gun and kill both of them.
Until then she had to play along, no matter how awful it was.

Two things would make it easier. One was she knew Ray
would find her. The other was that when Bart had thrown the
rug over him, she had seen Peanut breathing.

Surprise

MAGGIE WAS WIPING her face with a cold washcloth wondering how she could get in touch with Bill Schiller, or if he would disappear without calling her. She hoped it hadn't been stupid to trust him.

"Maggie, could you come out here? I have a surprise," Johnny yelled.

"Sure," she shouted back. She imagined it was another stupid dog trick. She walked to the living room and felt her knees buckle as she saw Plank with a pistol pointed at her.

He looked even more grotesque up close than he had when she had shot him. His face was bloated, bruised and burnt, and he was dripping blood from the shoulder of his injured arm.

"I let him in. I thought it might be Schiller," Johnny explained.

Her days of being too depressed to act were suddenly looking better.

"Hello, darling. Let me show you my special friend."

He struggled to reach a back pants pocket with his wounded arm and produced a pair of pliers.

"You shall tell the truth, and I shall set you free," Plank said. "You don't mind if I take your whore apart with these pliers do you?"

"I wish you wouldn't," McLendon said.

Maggie felt her stomach churn and fought the urge to vomit.

"I'll do anything you want," she said.

"Don't think I don't know that. That's later. Now I want to know where Schiller is."

She shook her head, pleading.

"I don't know. I'm telling the truth."

"That's what I'm about to find out."

"I really don't know . . ."

"Don't tell him. No matter what he does, don't tell him," McLendon screamed.

"So you do know," Plank said.

"No."

"Don't tell him."

"Don't worry. You'll get your turn to be brave. After I finish with her, I'm going to do you next."

"Me?" McLendon was shocked.

"Yeah. What did you think?"

"I thought you were only going to take her apart with the pliers."

Plank laughed and drool collected in the corners of his mouth.

"No, I'm doing both of you."

"You don't have to do that. I can tell you where Schiller is. It's a farm north of town. He took me out there with a bag on my head, but I saw it anyway. I recognized the barn. I used to go there with my father when I was a kid. My father and his friends would hunt and make fun of me."

"You can find it?"

"Sure."

Plank pointed the gun at Maggie.

"Did she make you wear women's clothes?" he asked.

What was this shit, she wondered. He asked her that when he broke into her house.

"No, she made me dress like a dog and have sex with her."

"I knew it," Plank said.

Six Is a Crowd

LUCKILY, BART STAYED in the front seat, but he did discuss some disgusting scenarios he had planned for her. About all she could do was repeat a dozen different versions of "That sounds like fun" without much conviction. He didn't seem to notice or care.

Jesus, Bart was worse than any of the pervos that came in the store. Of course, none of them had handcuffed her. She probably would have found out more about them than she wanted to know if they had.

"Here they come," he said to no one in particular.

"We've got company?" she asked.

"Yes, Maggie and Johnny McLendon. Johnny is an idiot zillionaire and Maggie used to be my secretary and lover." He said it like he was proud of it, but could hardly believe it himself.

Ginger wanted to say, wasn't she the lucky girl, but made herself keep quiet.

The door opened and Plank looked in, then shoved an attractive woman ten years or more older than Ginger in the back.

"Get in Johnny," he said. "Climb up front."

McLendon climbed in, stood up and walked in crouch.

"He knows where we can find Schiller," Plank said. "He's seen the light. He's going to help us."

"She made me have sex with her so she could get my secrets," McLendon said.

"They'll do that," Plank said.

"Why don't you drive, Johnny? I'm feeling a bit thin," Oakes said.

"Sure."

He stepped on Peanut as climbed in the driver's seat.

"Don't step on my friend," Ginger said.

"Jesus, there's a dead person under that blanket."

"That's what happens to people who fuck with us," Bart said.

What a bunch of shit, Ginger thought. When Ray gets here, they're going find out what happens to people who fuck with him.

Plank got in the van and pulled the door shut after him.

"Put your hands behind you," he said to Maggie. He cuffed her, then pushed her next to Ginger.

"I like the way you got this one fixed up." He reached over and fondled Ginger's breast, then ripped the front of Maggie's blouse open. She wasn't wearing a bra.

"Look at this. We've got quite a show going," Plank said.

Maggie looked at Ginger and was frightened. Her face said both here we are two women in a bad place together and if it gets bad I hope they take you first.

"Okay, Johnny, let's go."

"Okay, Bart. What should I do?"

"You know the place?"

"Yes."

"Then drive us out there."

"Okay, but how do I do that?"

"What do you mean? You follow the roads that take us there and then we're there."

"I know that. But I don't know how to make the van go."

"It's like a car, Johnny."

"I don't know cars either."

"Jesus, you don't know how to drive?"

"No. But I can learn."

"Why didn't you tell us?" Bart said.

"I was afraid you might shoot me."

"We wouldn't do that. We need you, Johnny. Slide over here."

"I told Plank."

"That's right. He told me but I forgot." He struggled with a pants pocket and produced a pill bottle. "Damned child-proof caps." He pulled the top off with his teeth and slid three pills that looked like Lortabs in his mouth. He gagged as he swallowed them.

Bart was in the driver's seat, and he started the van. Ginger was afraid the cavalry had been a little slow showing up and she was on her own.

Plank looked at both Ginger and Maggie and was amused.

"Eenie, meenie, meinie, mo . . . we got a long ride out there, and I'm wondering which one of you lovely ladies is going to give me my first blow job."

Oh man, it looked like the shit was going to start sooner than later. She thought it over, then forced herself to speak.

"I'll do it first. That's something I'm real good at, if I do say so myself."

"You hear that? We got a willing volunteer," he said.

Bart and McLendon were mumbling to each other, she caught something about north of Alpharetta.

"Glad to hear it," Bart said.

"Oowee, you are a sweet thing," Plank said.

"The only thing is, if you cuff me in front, I can show you my magic fingers." And use my magic trigger finger to blow your shit away.

"That's okay, baby. No reason to do that. I suspect you can do it real good with your hands just the way they are."

Well, that had been the downside of the plan. "I'm sure I can," Ginger said.

"I do hate to disappoint you baby, but Maggie and me are the ones that have the grudge match. I think I'm going to have to let her go first."

He was slurring his words slightly. She was beginning to doubt that he could do anything of a sexual nature, and that actually scared her worse than thinking he could.

"That would be okay," Ginger said.

"Come on over here, Maggie baby. You and I have got a date."

"Sure Plank. I've been looking forward to it." She had picked up on Ginger's willingness to humor them. Good thing. Ginger was hoping she wasn't the hysterical type.

"That's okay. You can stay there."

He was nodding off. This might be her chance. If he dozed for a minute, she was sure she could work her hands in front of her and get the derringer.

"Need to get my medicine." He wiggled around trying to get in his pants pocket. "Doing the hoochie-coo. Here we go. Rocket fuel. Blast off." He threw a white pill in his mouth.

It didn't look like he would be going to sleep.

"Well, girls, now that we're all here let me let you in on a little secret. Some men wear dresses. Did you know that? Huh?" He was acting like they were the best of friends. Like he was one of the girls.

"Seems like I heard about that," Ginger said.

"You did? Is this something you women talk about?" He was nasty again.

Ginger and Maggie looked at each other and shook their heads.

"You don't talk about it? You don't talk about it and laugh?"

"No, we don't laugh. I know that some men like to wear women's clothes. That's all," Ginger said.

"I'm not talking about the ones that like it. I'm talking about the ones who are forced to do it."

"I'm not familiar with that."

"It's true. Some women force their sons to wear women's clothes."

"I'm sorry," Ginger.

"That's why they need to be punished."

What a bag of shit. Here she was – tooling down the road,

handcuffed and kidnapped by a drug-crazed killer who was mortally pissed at his mother. As situations went, it sucked very large.

She was trying hard not to be frightened but it wasn't working too well.

Where the hell was Ray?

Losing Ginger

Ray SIZED THE situation up quickly, and it wasn't good. As he looked down the street, he saw Ginger's old orange Toyota, and it was empty. A man who looked like a walking corpse was pushing a woman in the back of the van. Through the open door he thought he caught a glimpse of Ginger.

He followed them on a twisting erratic journey that could only have been navigated by an idiot. The thought of losing Ginger twisted his gut with rage until his emotions were gone and he felt nothing, and he began to pray to whatever cruel god ruled the monsters of the night, to the god who crushed compassion, who burned cities and filled fields with rotting corpses.

And the god answered his prayers and he became a crazy cracker death machine.

The Crazy Cracker Death Machine

THE REST OF the trip turned to bipolar hell. They drove for forty-five minutes or an hour, from near dusk to night, as Plank went through eight cycles of bubbling rage which deflated to a depression so cool it was worse.

Ginger had got an awful earful of his plans for her and Maggie, who seemed tagged as his special demon and doomed for the worst of it.

She listened to the van sounds as the pavement degraded with each turn onto progressively smaller roads, and she began sinking into a paralyzing despair. When they turned onto the dirt track, she forced back tears.

"Kill the lights," Plank said.

"He says it's at the end of the driveway," Bart said.

"How far?" Plank asked.

"Two hundred feet," McLendon said. "Just follow the ruts."

Plank let himself out of the back of the van silently. It was pitch black so he couldn't see a damned thing.

In spite of the fact that his mind was fried, he seemed to be functioning well. Ginger suspected that he was one of those people who could go on after ingesting amazing amounts of drugs.

"Give me five minutes, then come on up," Plank said.

Bart waved the gun toward them. "Don't get any ideas," he said. Then to Ginger, "Are you getting ready for Uncle Bart, luscious?"

"Sure, Uncle Bart."

"I'm getting ready for those magic fingers of yours."

"Ooo . . . me too. You'll never forget them. I promise."

He prattled on and the green lights of the dash outlined the side of his face. She knew he was looking at her, but couldn't tell how much he could see. Her one chance at the gun had to work, because it was looking like her only chance to live.

She saw him look at his watch, and as he flicked on the van's headlights she saw the road was covered with a canopy of the limbs of old oaks.

Ginger started to move then stopped quickly.

"Watch them, Johnny."

McLendon switched on the dome light and gave them the evil eye. "I won't let them get away with anything."

"You shit," Maggie hissed.

"You made me have sex with you. You made me act like a dog," McLendon said.

"No kidding? Like a dog?" Bart was amused.

"It's not funny . . . you going to let me hold the gun so I can shoot them if they move?"

"Not yet, Johnny."

"Here we are."

"You get out, Johnny. Just stand there."

Johnny opened his door and slid out and Bart climbed in the back of the van. He kneeled in front of Ginger and took her breasts in his hands.

It looked like the show was getting started. There wasn't much she could do about it other than go along and wait for her chance.

She knew that in a moment he would have her clothes off and would find the gun. She would have to deal with that. She hoped he didn't get mad so she could fuck him into some happy dick oblivion where she could save herself.

"You're making me so hot," he said.

"Me too. Do you think we could find a bed?"

He pulled back. "Good idea. We should do it right."

"That's right," Ginger said. "We need to give it the respect it deserves."

Maggie was rolling her eyes and mouthing the words "pencil

dick." God, she was so grateful for that. She needed help, even if it was just a joke.

Bart led them both into the house. Plank was standing inside the door.

"Hello, Maggie darling. Recognize these?" He held a pair of pliers in front of him.

Ginger couldn't help it. She let out an ear-piercing scream. She tried to get away, but Bart had a firm grip on her arm.

"Jesus Christ," Plank yelled.

Bart held his hand over Ginger's mouth as she twisted.

"Calm down. Are you going to calm down? I'm not going to let him come near you with those things. Do you understand?"

She nodded, and he released her, and she strained up on her tiptoes and met his mouth with hers and hungrily scoured his mouth with her tongue and pushed her breasts toward him and made herself sigh when he took them.

She was totally shit terrified and knew she would do anything Bart asked and even things he had probably never imagined, as long as he would keep her away from Plank.

She pulled her head back and said, "Let's go upstairs and fuck."

"Good idea."

He turned her toward the room and she saw on its far side an older man in a blue linen blazer sitting at a trestle table. His arms were behind him and she imagined they were cuffed or tied.

He looked at Maggie and said, "I'm sorry."

Maggie started crying and he looked stricken like he was really sad about it.

Ginger realized this was probably the drug addict Federal man, and he was different than she had imagined, very civilized and, as he looked at Maggie, he seemed very kind.

Ginger was starting to feel glad that Ray wasn't here to be made to watch what was going to be done to her.

The place looked ancient. The inside walls were dark wood

paneling and there was a large fireplace in the center of the room which reached to a thirty-foot ceiling. In front of the hearth sat the two silver suitcases. An open gallery on the second floor held rows of doors which she imagined led to bedrooms and baths.

She felt sorry for Maggie and wanted to help her, but at the same time wanted to get out of that room as soon as possible.

She was edging Bart toward the stairs to the gallery, almost pulling him by the arm he held her with.

"Aren't you the hot one?" he said.

"Very hot."

The terror had receded enough that she had a plan. When she was upstairs she would offer to blow him and ask him to cuff her hands in front. She would say it would be sexier if she took her own clothes off, and once she had him in a state of suspended bliss, she would get the gun and give him quite a different bang than he had imagined. Then she would get Bart's revolver and kill Plank.

"Just wait two minutes and then you can take her upstairs and fuck all night."

"What for?" Bart asked.

"We need to get organized. Figure out how we're going to handle everything. Go over there and sit."

He waved the gun at Ginger and Maggie. Bart walked Ginger over to the table, pulled a chair out for her and helped her into it, like he was her date at the cotillion. He stood behind her and caressed her breasts with one hand and held his pistol with the other. Her nipples were getting hard from the night chill.

Maggie stumbled into a chair next to Schiller. It was touching. Ginger could see they were sweet on each other even if they didn't know it.

Johnny McLendon was wandering around the room and started to sit at the table, until it seemed to occur to him that the sitters were the losing team and he joined the standers.

"We got us a little group here, don't we?" Plank howled like a wolf.

"Good God, man. Pull yourself together," Schiller said.

"I don't have to pay attention to you anymore."

"You can't imagine I haven't put out the burn order on you two?"

"You aren't with the Agency any more," Bart sneered.

"True, but they still take my phone calls."

"I don't believe you."

"How do you think I was going to stage my escape? I was going to get them looking for you," Schiller said.

"So fucking what. Two can play at that game," Plank screamed.

"What's that supposed to mean?" Schiller asked.

"Shut the fuck up or I'm going to kill you."

"Do I look like I give a shit?" Schiller said.

"You want me to kill you, don't you? That way you won't have to watch what I do to her."

Maggie had quit crying and was staring directly in front of herself getting ready for what was going to happen.

"We need to get organized," Plank said.

"You're too fucked-up to get organized," Schiller said. "You want to torment us awhile and then kill Bart and take all the money."

"I don't like this," McLendon moaned.

Bart went stiff but he pretended nonchalance. He left his hand on Ginger's breast, but she felt the one with the gun brush behind her back.

"Don't try it, Plank," Bart said.

"That's bullshit and you know it. He's just causing dissension in the ranks. I'd never do that."

Johnny McLendon looked toward the door and started screaming.

Ginger looked up and saw Ray standing just inside the front door looking so cool she could hardly stand it.

"What the fuck do you want?" Plank asked.

Ray stood there quietly.

"You dumb shit. You just come walking in here like that," Plank yelled.

"We're going to fuck you up," Bart yelled.

Johnny picked it up and started yelling, "We're going to fuck you up," over and over again.

It was so smooth, totally unexpected, nonchalant but fast. Ray pulled a pistol out of his waistband and shot Plank in the head. The noise was unbelievably loud, and there was red shit flying through the air, and Plank's knees buckled, and he collapsed on himself, and his arm flopped like a discarded towel.

It's going down, Ginger thought, and threw herself under the table and began working her arms under her butt.

"I can't be captured," McLendon screamed. He popped a pill in his mouth, swallowed it and looked confused. "Nothing's happening," he said. Then his head tilted sideways, his eyes drooped and he fell on the floor.

Bart was looking frantically from Johnny to Ray to Ginger, who had worked her hands free and pulled out the derringer.

His eyes bulged as pop, pop, pop, pop . . . she emptied it into his chest.

"You . . . uh . . . you shot me." He dropped the gun and fell backwards. Ginger was struggling to get up. She felt Ray's hand on her, helping her.

She stood over Bart, and he looked up at her.

"You shot me," he repeated. He seemed at a loss as to why.

"You're goddamn right I shot you, you piece of shit." She spat in his face then stepped over his arm and kicked his head twice. "You asshole."

"Let me get your cuffs unlocked, baby," Ray said.

"That guy you shot in the head has got them in his pocket," Schiller said.

"Give me your gun, Ray baby. That piece of shit molested me. I'm going to kill him."

"Please don't," Bart said.

Maggie spoke with a voice like ice and Ginger, Ray and Schiller looked at her.

"Let me kill him," she said.

"I want to do it," Ginger said.

"I have more reason than you," Maggie said.

"Jesus," Ray said. "First time I ever saw two women arguing over who got to kill some man."

"That's because you never hung out in a beauty parlor, honey," Ginger said.

Booty Time

RAY DUG INTO Plank's pocket and found the handcuff key. He unlocked Ginger's wrists and she moved her hands and arms to get the circulation going, then rubbed her wrists.

Ray didn't say anything. He figured she'd just as soon not think about it right now. He gave her the key, and she released Maggie.

"You doing okay?" Ginger asked her.

"Yes. I'm alive."

Ray nudged McLendon with his foot, then rolled him over so he was face up.

"He's breathing," Ray said.

"I told him it was a suicide pill, but actually it will knock him out for a couple hours. He'll wake up feeling hung-over and confused," Schiller said.

Ginger was standing behind Schiller with the handcuff key, looking to Ray to see if he was ready in case Schiller tried something stupid.

"Go ahead," Ray said.

She patted him down for weapons then uncuffed him.

"Put your hands on the table so I can see them."

"Certainly."

"I want to get out of here, Ray." Ginger said

"Sure thing, baby."

"There is a matter we need to discuss," Schiller said.

"Talk fast. My friend out there is still alive. I need to get him to the hospital."

"Thank God," Ginger said.

"I'm giving you a simple choice. Kill me or give me half the money. If you take it all and don't kill me, I'll make your life miserable. I have the means to do it."

"Bill, don't. You don't need the money," Maggie said.

"True, I don't need it, but I want it."

Ray shook his head, simply amazed by Schiller's guts.

"How's the money divided?"

"Three million in each case."

"That much?"

"It's pocket change to that dipshit on the floor. All this was over pocket change," Schiller said.

"I'd guess you're in luck, mister. I already exceeded my quota for murders. I'd be just as happy not to do another. Pick one," he said to Ginger. "We'll go halves."

"But you already have seven hundred thousand," Schiller said.

"Don't press your luck. I'm not feeling all that damn easy to get along with tonight," Ray said.

"Good point . . . I'll take your friend to the hospital. I think I can dampen the curiosity of the authorities."

"Thanks."

"Let's get out of here, darling. I'm about to go crazy in this place," Ginger said.

Schiller looked at Maggie. "I think retirement could be very lonely alone. Care to join me?"

She didn't answer, so Ginger prodded her.

"You get him to stay off the dope, and he might shape up to be a pretty good guy. A girl's got to look out for herself."

"I was thinking along those lines, too," Maggie said.

"One last thing," Ray put the gun on the table. "If either of you still has the heart for it, use this gun. Don't leave any prints on it. We're working on a patsy."

"I just want to go," Ginger said. She picked up a silver suitcase, then turned and looked at Ray.

"You're a real gangster, darling," she said.

"You too baby, you're a real gangster."

Maggie picked up the gun, wrapping the grip with her skirt. She walked around the table and stood astride Bart Oakes.

"Please don't do this," he cried.

As they walked through the door they heard Maggie say, "Bart, you were a lousy lay . . ." then the gunshot.

Retired

EXCEPT FOR THE horrible last act, the plan had unfolded as Schiller had hoped. Losing half the money had been a tough break, but finding Maggie had more than made up for it. He wished he'd met her twenty years ago, but they would have been different people and probably wouldn't have had much to say to each other.

It was about time she got back from her walk. He went to the deck and saw her walking up the beach.

He had imagined someplace warmer, but she loved it here and he was settling in. Tonight, he would build a fire and they would watch the logs burn and feel comfortable together.

She looked up, saw him and waved. He waved back.

Retirement was cozy, all right, and it was agreeing with him, but if he ever got bored, he figured he could look up Ray Justus and see how much trouble they could get in.

Maggie on the Beach

THE GUSTS FROM shore were blowing the whitecaps so they collapsed on themselves – a sure sign the season was finally changing.

She looked down the empty beach and saw that Bill had come out on the deck in anticipation of her return from the walk.

He waved, and she waved back with the hand that wasn't holding her canvass shoes.

She had wondered if being a killer would scar her in some way, but mostly she didn't think about it very much.

Bill had said he thought it made their relationship stronger because it meant she could understand what he had done for a living.

He said that the ability to be honest with someone he loved made him feel twenty years younger. He certainly was acting like it.

She no longer thought much about Vivian Leigh. She was just Maggie. It was time to go easy on everyone: Bill, herself, the whole world.

Life can be hard, and survivors can't always afford the luxury of judgments.

Spike Redux

THE WHOLE ADVENTURE had cost him better than twelve million, but so what?

His first move had been a big mistake. He had awoken between the corpses and not even noticed his red lipstick clown face. In a panic, he had called the law, then realizing he himself could be a suspect, had run through the woods, slept in an abandoned shed filled with spiders, then made his way back to town at first light.

The chauffeur, Gordon, had been arrested. Questions of his own involvement were eventually resolved with the presentation of golf weekends with exotic dancers to the appropriate civil authorities.

No amount of golf or exotic dance could prevent the prosecution of Gordon, however a multi-million dollar defense had secured his acquittal.

The general public had considered his willingness to finance it a quixotic loyalty, but the fact was that the man knew too much. As a result, McLendon had been forced to hire him back as chauffeur at an exorbitant rate, put up with his bizarre stage magician's costume, cape and sword and his bull-headed insistence at being called Sir Shitass. He had even had to pay a congressman to fuck a goat.

It had all been worth it, though. Now that he knew who he was. Twelve million was nothing to find out who you really were. Now he knew his inner Spike.

He was the wild pit bull of Atlanta's night-time streets – Spike the Dog of Justice, the Hound of Hell, on a one-man campaign to clean up the human refuse of the inner city.

It was almost three in the morning, and he had followed the

man for four blocks before he saw him walk casually into the alley between the two old buildings.

He pulled the ski mask down over his face and pulled the homemade blackjack from his pocket. It was time to clean up America.

His ski mask was half covering his eyes. He couldn't see worth a shit in the dark and stumbled into the man peeing against the side of the building. He was much bigger than he had looked at a distance.

He turned toward McLendon, his member still out.

"What you want, you dumb motherfucker?" he asked.

McLendon panicked, pulled his wallet from his pants and threw it at the man.

"What the fuck?"

"There's fifteen-hundred dollars in there. Take it, it's yours."

"Okay, but what do I have to do?"

"Just don't hurt me," Johnny said.

The man grabbed McLendon's wrist in a grip he knew he could never escape from.

"I understand, man. Don't worry. I had me a white punk in Reidsville. I was real gentle."

"Oh God," Johnny moaned in sheer liquid bowel terror. "That's not what I want."

"I understand that game," the man said. "You're going to pretend you don't want it."

"But I don't want it."

"I understand, man. You want me to force you. So you can pretend you don't like it. I'll give you every dollars worth. You'll want to come back and see the big python again."

Johnny tried to break away but couldn't. He didn't like the way this operation was going.

"It's time for you to go back to headquarters," he yelled.

"Hey man, we'll slip it into your headquarters in one minute, but first I'm going to do your hindquarters."

Ginger Justus

W HEN GINGER HAD called back to Atlanta to tell her friends that she was married, one of them had asked, "Are you going to keep your name?"

"I don't know," Ginger said. "I know it isn't politically correct, but I sort of like the sound of Ginger Justus."

"It does roll off the lips," her friend had said. "I think you ought to use it. You can do anything you want."

She loved Ray so much, and he had to be the sweetest man alive. When he had walked into the room that night, he had proved to Ginger that he was the sort of guy who would die for someone he cared about. There weren't many men like that.

For his part, Ray thought Ginger was the reason he was still alive. Ray was certain Oakes would have shot him if she hadn't made her move with the kinky sex gun she had tucked in her underwear.

"We're a great team," Ray had said, and he was right, they were.

She was living her dream, all right. She wasn't Ginger Loudermilk anymore, the girl with hair the color of a wharf rat who made shitty grades, who people laughed at in class and was doomed to marry a shit kicker and live in a baby-piss soaked trailer house or go to women's prison or the insane asylum.

Hell no. She was Ginger Justus, gangster girl deluxe with oodles of money, a sexy husband who treated her like a goddess and a life that was filled with fun.

Forget the high school heroes. From now on, she was the star of her own fucking movie, and they weren't even in the cast.

Destiny's Highway

RAY FELT REAL bad about the way things turned out for Peanut. He had survived the shooting, but he was never quite the same again.

When he was in surgery under anesthetic, he said an angel of the Lord spoke to him and told him to go forth and preach the Gospel.

So now he was out on the revival circuit, saving souls and healing the sick. Ray hadn't heard any word yet as to whether Peanut had raised up any dead people. Though, he had been as close to dying as a man can be without actually doing it, so maybe he had raised himself up.

Peanut hadn't even wanted his share of the money.

"I don't see how I can do the Lord's work with money I stole, even if it was from assholes. I guess I'm not supposed to talk like that anymore either," Peanut had said.

"As long as it makes him happy," was Ray's philosophy, but he didn't think much of it himself.

Ray had to admit that the night when he thought he had lost Ginger for good had changed him too. He had finally understood what was really important to him.

Now, he mainly wanted to drive down the highway to happy destiny with Princess Naughty in the Voodoo Cadillac, and if that's your plan, you got to keep a few simple things in front of you all the time.

Things like finding a woman you can love, one who is a good fit, and not being afraid to buy a smooth ride just because it carries a curse of death.

The other thing, and this is important, is that you got to be careful not to believe any voices you hear when you're under anesthetic.